ICE
FALL

Michael Edelson

Acknowledgements

Thanks to all of my test readers for your feedback: Jillian Torres, Hillary Dickinson, Rebecca Glass and several others I can't remember (I wrote this book in 2008). Thanks to Ilya Iseman for help with various aspects of title and setting.

Special thanks to Michael Ahrens, my very own apocalypse expert, who made sure I was on the right track with fans of the genre.

Special thanks to Jake Norwood, who has a way of fixing the things that are wrong with my stories by pointing them out in an honest, brutal and unapologetic way. It's exactly what I need.

Special thanks to Betsy Winslow and Rosie Emerson for combing the manuscript for errors. If you find any typos, it's their fault!

Finally, a very special thanks to Dr. Jerry Goldstein, PhD., who not only helped with the science (with the caveat that the liberties I took to fit his suggestions into my plot are not his fault) but more importantly made me aware of the dangers of vilifying science itself. Science is neither good nor evil, nor can it ever be either. Science is a tool, the greatest tool the human mind has ever devised, and ultimately, what we do with that tool will be a reflection of our nature, for good, or ill.

Table of Contents

And there is a Catskill eagle in some souls that can alike dive down into the blackest gorges, and soar out of them again and become invisible in the sunny spaces. And even if he for ever flies within the gorge, that gorge is in the mountains; so that even in his lowest swoop the mountain eagle is still higher than other birds upon the plain, even though they soar.

— Herman Melville

Prologue – Reaper

...for there is no folly of the beast of the earth which is not
infinitely outdone by the madness of men.
— Herman Melville

Mark felt the rumble a few seconds before he noticed it. It was like a subway train passing by underfoot, filtered out by a mind long accustomed to a cacophony of urban noises. He became aware of it partly because it was gradually building in intensity, and partly because it was out of place on the twelfth floor of the NYMEX building. It would take a hell of a train to reach that high. His first reaction was to press F3 to save his work, his second was to laugh at his folly. Finally, a proper worker drone, thinking of the Exchange before himself.

"Mark!" someone shouted. It was Nancy, the tech writer, her dark hair silhouetted against the twinkling lights of the office Christmas tree. Her knuckles glared white as she gripped his cubicle wall. "What the hell is that?" She was trying to put on a brave face, but he could see the sparkle of moisture on her pretty auburn eyes.

"I don't know." He was on his feet, moving around the cubicle to join her as they merged with a throng of curious coworkers headed towards the closest window. They were near a row of offices that robbed them of a decent view and had to turn towards the receptionists' area where a window ran along the entire wall.

"I'm scared. Nine eleven..."

"Don't worry," Mark said, giving her a pat on the shoulder. "They're probably just moving something big down one of the nearby streets. Some rich asshole's mega yacht or something." He would have loved to do more, to hold her and comfort her, but a sexual harassment suit and dismissal were a more immediate danger than whatever was causing the rumbling.

They heard a scream somewhere up ahead and suddenly the crowd they were following was moving in the opposite direction, towards the elevator and stairways. The first few faces that passed were confused and annoyed, but then came the ashen ones, and suddenly Mark was afraid. More screams joined the first until the pounding of his heart subdued all other sounds. He felt a hand on his and turned to see Nancy holding onto him as tightly as she had gripped his cubicle. Mark had never been much for crowds and so he pressed onwards. When he rounded the bend past the corner office he saw the window.

The Hudson River, the Jersey City skyline. Nothing out of the ordinary. What had caused the screams? He heard Nancy's sharp intake of breath and felt her grip tighten until he almost screamed out and yanked away. Instead of looking at her, his gaze swept sideways towards the bay. He saw it, just past the Statue of Liberty.

At first, he did not believe his eyes. It looked more like something out of a big budget Michael Bay movie than something that belonged in the real world, but he was looking at a window, not a theater screen. It was real, even though he couldn't understand how it could be.

He felt Nancy's hand pulling on his own. "Come on!" she shouted frantically. "We have to go!"

"No," he said, strangely calm. "There's no point." Everything he knew about reality screamed that what he was looking at could not exist, and yet, there it was. Nancy tugged a few more times, then stopped. She did not let go. Mark watched it get closer. In seconds it engulfed the statue. In seconds more it would sweep over NYMEX and then the rest of Manhattan. His whole life, studying, working his ass off, no love life to speak of, all for nothing. And it didn't matter. Once death was certain, it was surprisingly easy to accept.

"I'm scared," Nancy said once again.

"I am too."

No longer fearing sexual harassment charges, he pulled her towards him and held her tightly. She put her head against his shoulder and closed her eyes. Her hair smelled like lavender.

He watched death sweep towards them. It was strangely beautiful. He wondered how they would die, and whether it would hurt. Only a few more seconds, and he would have his answers.

Chapter 1 – Isolation

Cold in the earth, and the deep snow piled above thee,
Far, far removed, cold in the dreary grave.
Have I forgot, my Only Love, to love thee,
Severed at last by Time's all-wearing wave?
-Emily Brontë

The rubber ball bounced off the corner of the windowsill and hit the top of the curio cabinet, knocking down a little crystal frog. The figurine broke into several pieces that scattered under the couch and dining table. Only the green head remained in sight, one clear eye staring above the swirl of orange glass that passed for a mouth. The ball continued into the kitchen, where it rolled to a stop near a stack of empty bottles.

Peter stared at the frog's head, not sure how to feel. It had been Jennifer's, one of the few things she bought to decorate their vacation home. The divorce judgment and notice of forced sale were in the kindling pile he used to light the wood stove, but he always skipped over them, wanting a reminder of the pain she had caused. It was hard to hate someone who was most likely dead, but he was determined to try.

He got a dustpan and broom from the closet and swept up the fragments, then carefully picked them out of the incidental dirt and placed them on the dining table next to his rifle. It was a tangible reminder of his old life, and he needed as much of that as he could get, even if it included her. There were several types of glue and epoxy in the utility room, he was sure he could find something that would hold the thing together. It was a project, something to work on, to occupy his mind.

"Playtime's over," he said. He took his clipboard off of the wall and sat down on the nearest couch. He didn't need to itemize his tasks, but keeping track of work had become a chore in itself, and that had value. Keep busy, keep the mind active and avoid thinking about the snow—or the fact the he no longer made any attempt to stop talking to himself.

"*Clean and lubricate rifle,*" he said, reading the first item on the list. "I did that yesterday." He wondered why he hadn't checked it off. Grabbing a pen, he put a mark next to the entry.

"*Rotate magazines.*" That he hadn't done for a while. He had never been sure if it was better to leave them loaded or to periodically swap them out for fresh ones. Perhaps that was something they taught in the last two weeks of SQT and thus he would never know. But he knew what was better for *him*, and that involved doing something. "I'll do that tomorrow." He read down the list, skipping over boring things like inventorying food and clearing snow.

"*Kill yourself.*" He crossed that one out. "Real funny, asshole."

"*Chop wood.*" He looked at the small pile of logs next to the wood stove. They would last a couple of days if he stretched them out. Why had he buried it at the bottom of the list? Was that seeming oversight perhaps related to the previous item? Setting down the clipboard, he turned to the window and looked through the frosted glass. The snow was falling harder now, pushed to a steep angle by a steadily strengthening wind. Craning his neck to see above the trees, he caught a glimpse of dark clouds rolling in from the north. He closed his eyes and sighed deeply.

"I guess I'd better get to it." He sometimes felt like a soldier, fighting an endless battle against a relentless horde of tiny white invaders. He was constantly clearing paths around the house so he could get to the shed, the woodpile and the propane tanks. No matter how hard he worked, more always fell, covering his tracks as though consciously trying to wash away any trace of his existence. If Peter believed in god, he would have imagined that the creator was starting over, erasing his canvas by painting a layer of white so thick that nothing would show through.

He made his way to the coat closet and took out his green parka, still damp from the last time he had been outside two days before. He stared at it for a moment, then put it back and closed the door.

"Maybe later," he said. In the house, he could pretend that things were normal, at least sometimes. If he didn't look outside, or notice the slight sag in the roof over the extension where the contractors had taken liberties with the building codes, he would never know that the world was being buried. That he was being buried. Buried alive.

Feeling the sudden onset of panic, he grabbed one of his flashlights and rushed down to the ground level basement and into the utility room, the only part of the house without windows. Slamming the door shut behind him, he rested his elbows against the laundry machine, held his head in his hands and stared down at the pan of unused cat litter his ex-wife had never bothered to put away.

Cat litter, a laundry machine, a dryer, some tools, a water heater, pipes. Perfectly normal things, and not a hint of snow anywhere. It was like a museum of the old world, unmolested except for the hand pump next to the pressure tank.

The books were the most important items in the room. He had stacked them on the high shelves where the now useless power tools had been. They were not the modern genre fiction that he read for general escapism—those he kept upstairs—but classics from the courses he taught. He had resented teaching literature at first—his degree was in writing, but creative writing classes were for tenured professors. Over time, the near futility of trying to foster appreciation for these timeless works of art among dull minded students began to rub off on him. Jennifer used to buy him expensive leather-bound editions as holiday gifts, assuming that he would want them because of his job. Eventually, through no merit of her own, she became right.

The windowless utility room was the perfect place to escape from his reality by projecting it into fiction. He found inspiration in the words of Herman Melville while fighting his own great white terror, and sailed a hauntingly familiar snowscape with Mary Shelly's tragic anti-hero. He also found solace in the works of the classical poets, thanks in part to an old professor who had asked Peter to cover some of his poetry classes due to failing health. And while he started out hating it, his appreciation had grown until he found himself reading and sometimes even reciting them on his own.

When he felt like killing himself, he read Thomas's *Do not go gentle into that good night*. It helped, but he wasn't sure for how much longer. In *Purgatorio*, Dante encountered 'un'anima sola soletta,' a soul all alone. This soul was singled out for its unusual isolation. Damnation, purgation and eternal salvation were portrayed as collective experiences in the Commedia, meant to be shared with others. Even the damned were, for the most part, spared the hell that Peter was forced to endure.

He decided to stay in the utility room for a while until the panic left him, and took a book down from its shelf. *Robinson Crusoe.* It had seemed at first like an ironic way to escape his misery, but Crusoe had coped with isolation a lot better than Peter, and there was comfort in his optimism. Peter only wished he had a parrot and a goat to call friend, or even a cat to use the lonely litter box. He found the bookmarked page and started reading.

A while turned into the better part of an hour. There was no hurry, he could stay as long as he wanted, but knowing that he would eventually need to get the firewood soured the experience. He decided he would do what he had to do, then come back and spend the evening. Maybe he would start *The Heart of Darkness* again. Perhaps he would even take one of the books upstairs, out of this shrine to the old world, and read it on the couch.

The thought of returning gave him the strength he needed, and he went back upstairs and donned the parka without hesitation. He took his pistol from the holster on his hip and put it in one of the coat's outer pockets. He used to take the rifle, but he just didn't have the energy anymore. He doubted there was anyone left alive out there to bother him, and if there were, the snow was impassable.

Once dressed in coat and boots, he braced himself, opened the door and stepped outside. The wind hit his exposed face instantly, chilling his cheeks and the tip of his nose. He zipped up his hood so that only a small opening remained. The deck was covered by a couple of feet of snow, with the usual drifts on the windward side reaching almost to his waist. This was less than he expected, which was either a meaningless coincidence or a very good sign. He hadn't started counting the days until a couple of weeks after the quake, but as far as he could tell it was April. Spring was long overdue.

The first of the quakes, the big one, had been the first sign that something had happened. It had been fairly mild. There was no damage to the house or anything in it, except for some decorative beer steins that fell off of their shelves. His first thought was that earthquakes didn't happen in upstate New York. He almost didn't believe it, thought perhaps he had imagined it, or that it was something else, like an airplane crash somewhere close to the house. Then the lights went out.

He remembered standing in front of the television, staring stupidly at the blank screen while the generator raced noisily outside. Had it in fact been an earthquake? Had it knocked down some power lines? If so, why wasn't his satellite receiver getting a signal? It couldn't have been a coincidence that the snow came shortly after the first quake. More tremors followed, weaker, less intense, but the snow never stopped. He was fortunate that his log cabin was situated where it was, saved by some fluke of elevation or wind patterns from being completely buried like the houses all around it. Or was he? Considering his circumstances, perhaps they were the lucky ones.

He kicked the snow in front of him as he walked around the side of the house. Up by the pond, the snow was barely a few feet deep despite the fact that he had never cleared it, yet only the tops of the tallest trees were visible down by the road. It was possible to move around out there with the right equipment, but one wrong step and he would disappear forever.

By the time he got as close as he could to the shed, there was a layer of frost inside his hood that had partially melted and seeped down to his chin. He got his axe and walked over to the woodpile. The snow here was a bit deeper, almost three feet. He knew he should probably clear it before the storm, but he just didn't have the strength.

"I'll get to it tomorrow," he lied. In the past he had let it pile up until it was almost as tall as he was, then gone out with the shovel and pushed himself until his muscles cramped up and he could barely stand. Those nights, in the grip of exhaustion, were some of the only times he could sleep peacefully. Usually it wasn't until dark, when he lay alone on his bed listening to the wind beat against the windows, that the pain found him. Loneliness was longing, and it was the longing that would kill him, long before the food ran out, or the firewood.

After digging through the snow and finding a suitable log, he placed it on the nearby stump and chose his position carefully as he hefted the axe. If he were going to die, he would decide how and when. He had no desire to bleed out slowly, freezing to death while the endless flow of white filth erased him from the world. Lifting the axe over his shoulder, he arched his back and let it drop, allowing the heavy steel blade to do its job. It bit into the wood with a satisfying crack, splitting it neatly. He picked up the two halves and tossed them aside before reaching for another log. As he did so, he looked down the hill and saw someone walking towards him. Not one hundred yards away, and he hadn't seen or heard a thing.

Chapter 2 – Salvation

Whose woods these are I think I know.
His house is in the village, though;
He will not see me stopping here
To watch his woods fill up with snow.
- Robert Frost

He stood, frozen, mesmerized by the approaching figure's lumbering gait. The snow was at least ten feet deep where it walked.

"It's finally happened," Peter whispered. "I've lost my god damned mind." He closed his eyes, shook his head, then opened them. It was still there, moving slower than before. Its gait was absurdly methodical, like that of a goose-stepping soldier parading across Red Square—an odd way for a hallucination to walk. There was something strange about its feet, though Peter couldn't quite make it out through the barrage of snowflakes.

He tried to dispel the apparition, first by closing his eyes again, then by counting, but it persisted despite his efforts. As it came closer, Peter was able to glean more detail and the reason for the odd gait became apparent. There were objects strapped to its feet that reminded him of oddly shaped tennis rackets. No, not tennis rackets—snowshoes.

Suddenly, Peter's eyes widened and he tensed. This was no hallucination. Someone was coming towards his house. He stared, unable to act. Months alone with the snow, believing, *knowing,* that there was nothing out there, that there could be nothing out there, and now this?

It wasn't until he heard the crunching of the snow under its feet—*his* feet—that he was able to break free of his paralysis. Slowly, carefully, he set the axe down, turned and started towards the house, taking great pains to move casually despite the awful pounding in his chest. There was no need to alert the intruder to the fact that he had been spotted.

Peter shoved his way through the snow towards the stairs leading to his deck and front door. As soon as he turned the corner, he bolted into the house. Slamming the door shut behind him, he pulled off his mittens and went straight for the rifle. In his haste, he knocked some pieces of the crystal frog off of the table. Weapon in hand, he moved to the window.

Nothing. Where there had been a man, there was only empty snow. A strong gust swept a tidal wave of powder across an otherwise lifeless landscape. Peter stared, his body shaking as the adrenaline slowly left his system.

"Son of a bitch!" he swore, lowering the carbine. So it was true. He *was* losing his mind after all.

"The utility room," he said, nodding. That was where he kept all of his gun cleaning supplies. Yes, that seemed like a good plan. That was why he had gone for his rifle, not because he saw a phantom, but because he needed to clean it. It was really, really dirty. The clipboard loomed oppressively in his periphery, reminding him that the weapon was in fact spotless, but he ignored it.

Just as he was about to set the carbine down on the table, an impulse made him turn back to the window. There was something out there, something about the snow that wasn't quite right, though he couldn't see clearly through the frosted panes.

Frowning, he went back out onto the deck, carrying the rifle casually in one hand. As he strained to see through the snow, his eyes wandered over the white washed hell that had once been his summer getaway. He could almost see Jennifer's Mercedes pulling up the driveway, slowly making its way around the uphill bend. Just past that last turn up to the house, two stately willows had draped their weeping foliage over a walking path around the back side of the pond. There used to be a swing there, tied to the limb of an old tree. He and his wife would sit and talk until she complained of mosquitoes or whatever rural nuisance-de-jour occurred to her that particular night. One of the willows, the taller one, was now a white mound above the frosted surface, barely taller than Peter, or so it appeared from his vantage point. Sometimes, on a windy day, the gusts tore enough of the snow from its limbs for some of its bare branches to show through. The smaller willow was gone.

He was about to turn back towards the door when he saw it—a disturbance in the smooth while shell just past the edge of the driveway where the snow was shallow enough to echo the contours of the land beneath. Tracks.

Peter followed them with his eyes as far as he could. The tracks turned towards the tree line parallel to the driveway, beyond which a capillary pattern of black branches obscured them.

"Okay," he said, hefting the carbine. "This is good. It means I'm not crazy." It also meant that there was an actual intruder, and that he was now hiding, aware of having been spotted. More importantly, it meant that Peter was a great big target, standing still on his deck just asking to be shot.

For a moment, he hesitated. Would being shot really be so bad? It would mean he wouldn't have to worry anymore, not about shoveling the snow, not about the house collapsing and burying him alive. He could just let go...

Long dormant training took over, and he crouched, bolting towards the stairs. He headed straight for the mound of snow in the shape of his Jeep and took cover, using the vague outline to determine the location of the engine block. He waited, risking an occasional glance towards the direction of the tracks. Several minutes passed, but there was no sign of movement.

He knew he should be cautious and wait. It wasn't likely that the intruder had been able to move very far without being noticed. He was probably hiding in the snow, waiting for the opportunity to get a clear shot. It was only a few degrees below freezing, and Peter was dressed warmly and was well rested despite the mild exertion of chopping wood. He could stay out for quite a while without major discomfort. The intruder, on the other hand, would have been out for a long time. He would be cold and, Peter had to assume, exhausted. The trespasser would be the one to crack, to make the first move, and then Peter would be the one with the clear shot.

At least that was the idea, but like most exercises in logic, it had little bearing on reality. After a few minutes, Peter began to wonder if he had in fact seen the disturbance in the snow at all. Perhaps it was part of the hallucination, a lingering aftereffect that his subconscious had conjured to torment him.

"Screw it," he mumbled, and stood up. He moved slowly around the corner of the Jeep mound, watching for movement in the direction of the tracks. With each step, the visible area increased, but he was still protected by the mound from the part he couldn't see. It was called "slicing the pie," and allowed him to stay behind cover while clearing an ever larger area beyond the corner. Of course much of the mound was only snow and wouldn't stop a bullet, but people were not likely to shoot at something they couldn't see.

During BUDs, one of Peter's instructors told a story about a lawyer who was confronted by a pistol wielding former client. The lawyer panicked and unfolded his newspaper, holding it before him like a shield. Rather than shoot through the paper, the attacker kept trying to get around it and get a clear shot. The lawyer had been able to hold the man at bay until police arrived with nothing more than the illusion of cover.

Once the area of the tracks was completely in sight, he waited, watching, rifle at the ready. The wind had died down, leaving almost absolute calm. Peter shuddered, taking an involuntary step back. He usually avoided going outside on still days. The silence hung over the world like the mist that clung to an old cemetery, a reminder that there was nothing but death beyond the confines of his property. But was there?

That last thought was more than Peter could handle—he *had* to know. Leaving the safety of the Jeep, he advanced on the area of the disturbance, moving as fast as he could in the deepening snow. When he turned the bend in the driveway, the going became very difficult. This was past the area he normally cleared, and though the wind had moved much of the buildup closer to the trees, there was still enough left to bury him waist deep. If he went much farther down the driveway, it would become chest deep, then neck deep, and then so deep he would never come out.

He considered going back for a shovel, but thought better of it. He didn't have much more to go, and it would take more effort to walk back and get it than it would to push through the last few meters to the area of the tracks. As he struggled forward, he saw a patch of green just over the lip of the disturbance. He stopped and brought his weapon to bear, but there was no movement. As he advanced, more of the intruder became visible, enough to see that the man had collapsed face down and lay still. After brushing away the dividing wall of powder, he was up to his thighs in the snow with the man lying on its surface before him as though it were a white hospital bed.

Peter poked him with the rifle's muzzle, but there was no movement. He poked again, with enough force to hurt, but the man lay still. He was small, perhaps a teenager, though a hooded green parka concealed all features. Holding his rifle with one hand, he grabbed the man's collar and, in one smooth motion, turned him over and pulled the hood off of his face.

His eyes widened and he inhaled sharply. It was neither a man nor a child, but a girl, a young woman. Her nose was a deep shade of red, as were her full lips. If it were not for her disheveled state, he would have questioned his sanity yet again.

Peter stared, frozen, unsure of what to do, until his right arm began to tremble under the weight of his rifle. He raised the muzzle into the air to ease the burden, then put his left hand over the girl's mouth and nose. A slight warmth tickled the palm of his hand. She was alive.

Peter slung his rifle and grabbed her by the hood of her coat, dragging her behind him. When he made it to the cleared area, he picked her up and slung her over his shoulder. As he carried her into the house, he felt something crunch under his boot and looked down at the floor. It was the green frog's head that he had knocked off of the table earlier, crushed into dust.

Chapter 3 – Anticipation

I died for beauty, but was scarce
Adjusted in the tomb,
When one who died for truth was lain
In an adjoining room.
- Emily Dickinson

He set her limp body on the couch, his heart pounding, mind racing, full of questions. He thought back to the first time he and Jen had come to the cabin almost five years before. The local phone company hadn't yet come out to install their phone line, which also meant no internet. It had been three days before they finally showed up, and one more before everything was working. Peter had felt so isolated without the web, as though he were cut off from reality, lost on some savage frontier. If only he had known then what terrible isolation was in store for him.

When that blessed Google screen with its rainbow colors finally popped up on his laptop, his connection to the world had been restored, and with it came a hunger, a need to know what he had missed in the seemingly endless interval of its absence. This girl, with her blue jeans, red cheeks and yellow hair—she was his Google. She *had* to know, *had* to fill in the dark chasms of missing time that had so tormented him in his isolated impotence. But there was more to her sudden presence than that.

He found himself staring at her face. Her skin was blotchy from the cold, her eyes closed and hair frizzy with static. But despite all that, she was one of the most beautiful sights he had ever seen. A face. Two eyes, a nose, a mouth, cheeks, a chin, a forehead. A pattern that his mind immediately recognized and latched onto. It had been months since he had seen a face other than his own, and he was mesmerized.

After what had to have been a minute or more, he forced his eyes to let go of her face and pulled off his parka, laying it over his rifle, hiding it.

"Let's get you warmed up." He walked over to the couch and

unzipped the girl's coat, then turned her on her side to get it off. Underneath, she wore a dirty maroon sweatshirt with the letters "MIT" printed on the front. Was it hers? That school only accepted the best and brightest, unlike where he had worked. Not that there hadn't been many brilliant students, but dealing with the imbeciles had been taxing. It would be good if she were of the former variety.

Peter continued pulling off her coat. Dark blue showed through the holes in her ragged jeans, probably thermal leggings. Her mittens fell away as he pulled the sleeves off, revealing red fingers laced with patches of white.

"Shit," he said, staring at the discolored skin. Did she have frostbite? He reached out to touch her hand, and it was shockingly cold. Walking over to the sink, he grabbed a pot and filled it with water. The hand pump he had rigged to pressurize his water tank was working well, though the pressure died down to a trickle by the time he filled the pot half way. It would have to be enough, at least for now.

He set the pot down on the wood stove to heat it. The room started getting warmer almost as soon as he opened the vent to increase the burn rate. The wood stove had been a concession made for a house that didn't warrant an expensive stone fireplace, something Jennifer had been quick to point out. She had wanted one of the fancier log homes on a private lake, with ornate river-stone hearths and homeowners association rules. If they wanted rules, Peter had pointed out, they could have stayed in New York City. Fortunately, she relented. If she had not, that lovely stone hearth would have long since burned through his firewood, leaving him a frozen corpse.

He realized that the girl's feet would be no better off than her hands and fetched four bowls from the kitchen and filled them with warm water from the pot. He sat her upright, tilting her head back to rest on the couch cushion, then tugged off her snow shoes and boots. He was about to position the bowls when he noticed something metallic tucked into her waist band. He tugged at her sweatshirt and exposed part of the checkered wooden grip of a handgun.

He blinked, staring at the weapon in surprise, then allowed his eyes to drift up to her face, incongruously innocent. He pulled the sweatshirt and thermal undershirt higher and saw the upper half of a 1911, absurdly large pressed into her slender waist. Its hammer was cocked, and the pistol left an almost perfect impression in her skin once he pulled it out of her jeans. His eyes lingered on her bare waist, smooth and well defined, specked with tiny hairs briefly highlighted by a rogue beam of sunlight. His fascination wasn't sexual—it was someone else's body. Someone other than him. A miracle.

He held up the weapon and examined it, his lips pursed and brows crinkled. The pistol was cocked and the thumb safety was off. That was a particularly dangerous way to carry it. It was a modern version of Browning's venerable design and had a firing pin block, but inside her pants, with her jeans or her skin pressing against the grip safety, something could have easily snagged the trigger. Had she realized that and decided to chance it, or was she merely ignorant of the danger? The answer would tell him a lot about why she carried it.

After removing the magazine, he saw that there were only two rounds left. He checked the chamber, finding a cartridge there as well. Three rounds, out of a total of eight or nine. She had most likely used this weapon. The realization made Peter pause. Whom— or what— had she shot?

He put her 1911 away in his bedroom closet, then got his own pistol and tucked it into the holster on his belt. Seeing the gun had reminded him that despite her youth and pretty face, she could be a serious threat, and he had been a fool not to take precautions. She could have been feigning unconsciousness.

After patting her down for more weapons and finding none, he positioned the bowls next to her hands and feet. She was still unconscious and didn't flinch as he lowered her extremities into the warm water.

It took a while, but color eventually returned to her skin and she began to move, twisting and turning. She tipped over one of the bowls, soaking the couch, and Peter decided she'd had enough. Fetching a blanket and pillow from one of the spare bedrooms, he lowered her into a lying position and covered her.

"Well," he said, looking her over. "You don't have frostbite, whoever the hell you are."

He debated leaving her alone until she woke, but that pistol had made him uneasy. Better to remain vigilant.

He retrieved his rifle and sat on a nearby love seat with the weapon across his lap. Time passed slowly at first, but then his mind began to wander and fighting sleep distracted him enough to let it pass more quickly. His excitement, however, remained. Sometime soon she would wake, and he would have his answers, and he would no longer be alone. He suddenly felt self conscious and tried not to look at his reflection in the window just above her head. The face in the glass was that of a frightened man hiding in a locked utility room with a pan of old cat litter, trying not to think about a cry for help on a clipboard, or a rifle with a chambered round for only one purpose.

Chapter 4 – Frustration

I never felt at Home—Below—
And in the Handsome Skies
I shall not feel at Home—I know—
I don't like Paradise—
- Emily Dickinson

"Are you going to need that?"

The voice startled him. He turned to look at her, lifting his rifle instinctively. She was sitting up, propped on one elbow, regarding him warily. It took him a moment to understand what she was talking about.

"You tell me," he said, lowering the weapon slightly.

"Depends what you want from me," she said defensively. Her face in repose had been lovely enough, but animation transformed it. Her pouty lips, prominent nose and cheeks framed expressive eyes that were hard to look away from. For a moment he forgot what he had been waiting for, wanting only to look at her. A human face, a beautiful face, alive in his living room. Until she had regained consciousness, she had been an idea, a possibility not yet manifested. Now that she had woken up, she was something much more exciting, and far more frightening.

He remembered her question and frowned. "What do you think I want from you?" Was she playing stupid? What else could someone want, but to *know*?

She flinched as though struck, then turned away. "Then you just might." Her hands moved under the blanket and he instantly realized what she was doing.

"Looking for your gun?" he asked. "I took it." And good thing he had, apparently.

She glared at him, but then her face turned expressionless. "Then I can't stop you."

He frowned, confused. "Why would you want to stop me?"

Her eyes widened, and she made a sound, almost like laughter. Then he realized what she was talking about.

"No," he explained quickly. "That's not it. That's not what I meant." His face burned with embarrassment. She thought he was going to rape her.

"What then?" she demanded. "I don't understand."

"Answers," he said quickly, eager to get past this blunder. "I want answers. I want to know what's going on out there. I've been stuck here, in this cabin, ever since the first quake. What the hell happened to the world? What caused it? Who did it? How can you think I want anything else?"

She narrowed her eyes at him, but seemed to relax a little.

"Oh," she said. "I thought…" She hesitated. "Never mind. What do you want to know?"

Was she kidding? "I want to know what happened!" he demanded. "What the fuck else would I want to know?"

"I don't know what happened," she said, turning away. "If that's why you pulled me out of the snow, I'm afraid you'll be disappointed."

He frowned, starting to get angry. His internet was working again, but he couldn't seem to get web pages to load. "You were out there," he said flatly. "You have to know more than I do."

She shrugged. "I might, but since I don't know what you know, I can't really say."

He started to say something angry and demanding but stopped himself and took a deep breath.

"Okay," he said. "How about I ask you some questions? Can you handle that, or are you too tired?"

She shrugged. "Sure. I owe you that much." He wasn't sure what she meant, but then he remembered that he had saved her life. If he had left her out there, she would already be dead.

"Okay, so let's start with something simple. What's your name?"

"Penny," she said.

"Is that short for Penelope?"

She nodded.

"I'm Peter," he said. "Peter Anderson." He waited for her to give him her last name, but she just looked at him. She certainly wasn't making this easy.

"Okay," he said finally. "Just Penny. Where were you? When

it started? When the first quake hit?" As annoying as she was proving to be, he couldn't help looking at her. The green speckles in her brown eyes caught the morning light, lending accent to a face that still had his mind reeling in its attempt to acclimate to the presence of another human being.

"I was with some friends," she said, looking in his direction, but past him. "We tried to wait it out, but ran out of food." For the briefest of moments, he thought he saw a hint of moisture in her eyes, but she blinked it away.

At least now they were getting somewhere—that was the first bit of information she had volunteered.

"So you went out looking?" he asked.

She nodded. He waited for her to say something else, but apparently she was done volunteering, at least for the moment.

"So where are they? Your friends."

"We got separated." More moisture, more blinking.

"Are they still out there?" he asked, suddenly nervous. "Should we go look for them? They could be hurt…" The last thing he wanted was to go out into the snow. He wasn't even sure that he could, but if she asked, he would feel obligated. He couldn't just leave people out there to die if they were somewhere close, somewhere he might be able to get to.

"No," she said, shaking her head quickly. "They're dead."

He raised an eyebrow. "You just said you got separated." He was grateful despite his suspicion and felt terrible about it—what kind of bastard would be glad that people were dead? Still, what was a little guilt compared to going out there, into the frozen emptiness?

She glared at him again. "Yeah we did get separated. When they died."

He sighed. This wasn't what he had pictured when he dreamt of finding people and having someone to talk to. Not only was she annoying, but a part of him was starting to resent her presence, as bizarre a reaction as that was for someone who had been alone as long as he had.

"How did they die?" he asked, continuing to push her. This was his house, his wood stove, his fire. She was alive because of him, and she owed him, just as she had said.

"They were killed," she said tersely. "Look, I don't want to talk about it, okay? It's rough out there, all the snow, nothing to eat."

"I understand, but…"

"No, you don't understand!" she snapped. "You've been locked away in your winter chalet." Her eyes swept the house from the vaulted ceiling to the log walls. "You're not emaciated, so you've got food. Not everyone out there does, and—" She stopped, her eyes tearing up. "I just want something eat, a place to rest for a while. I'll trade for it. Please."

He wanted to press her further. There were people out there, survivors. It was better—and worse—than he had imagined. But it wouldn't do to push her, or she might freeze up. He had waited this long, he could wait a bit more.

"Trade?" he asked. "What do you have?" As he considered it, he realized how alien the concept of trading for food and shelter was. If this had been just a bad snow storm, it would have been simple politeness to put her up for the night, or longer, until it cleared. But now, with no end in sight, he wasn't sure what was proper. She seemed to expect to have to trade for her life—just how bad were things out there?

"My gun," she said. "You can have it." He wanted to say he already had it, but that wasn't really true. He wasn't a thief, and he had taken it from her because he didn't want her to shoot him, not because he wanted it for himself.

"That won't do me much good," he said. "I already have more guns than I need."

She narrowed her eyes. "Fine, then what do you want?"

"First, I want answers, and I don't give a shit if it hurts your feelings, you're going to tell me everything that's happened to you." She opened her mouth to protest, but he held up his hand to silence her. "Not right now. Eat, rest, then."

She considered a moment, then said, "Fine. What else?"

"This is not exactly the idyllic winter hideaway you think it is. The only reason I'm not buried under the snow is because I work hard, every day." That was a small lie, it was actually every few days—he liked to stall as much as possible. Perhaps with her helping, he could stall a bit longer.

"I can help," she said, and seemed to relax, sitting more upright. "I'm weak, you know, from not eating, but if you feed me, let me recoup a bit, I can work. What do you need, like snow shoveling?" Her tone was different now, less hostile.

"Yeah, that, and more. I'm running low on firewood, for instance."

"Okay, I can do that too."

He frowned at her, suddenly feeling agitated. This was all a bit too sudden. She was getting too comfortable with the idea of staying here, in his house, eating his food. He was the one who had prepared, he was the one who had a closet full of food and guns and bullets. What right did she have to benefit from his foresight?

"What's wrong?" she asked, reacting to the expression he had adopted to manifest his sudden self loathing.

"Nothing," he said quickly, shaking his head. "Nothing at all." He had been alone for far too long. "I'll go get you an MRE."

"MRE?" she asked. "Meal, Ready to Eat," he explained. "Military rations." He got up and went down to the storage closet, taking his rifle with him.

"You're a survivalist?" she asked when he came back. He handed her a small package wrapped in brown plastic.

"Steak and mash," he said. "And no, not quite a survivalist. It was just a hobby." He hesitated, trying to stop his mouth from moving, but he found he had little control. "I'm not quite a lot of things." He didn't want to tell her that it had been more than a hobby, that preparing for the apocalypse was a way to cope with the realization that his life was completely devoid of purpose and that only wiping the slate clean could give him a chance at relevance. If he had known what to expect, he would have prepared a sweet tasting poison instead.

She cocked one eyebrow at him, still holding the closed ration pack, then shrugged and tore it open, laying its contents on the coffee table. "This is what you've been living on?"

"No," he said. "These are a luxury. I have other food. Mostly vacuum packed rice and beans, but also some frozen stuff." He motioned at the window. "Easy to keep, these days. I have some cans too, but not many left."

"Thank you," she said as she tore into the package containing the beef patty. He went to get her two cups of water, one to drink and one to rehydrate the meat, but when he came back she was tearing into the dry chunk with her teeth. She took the water, but gave the meat only a cursory dunking that did little to soften it as she fumbled with the mashed potato pouch.

He sat there for a moment, watching her eat. She stuffed bits of meat and potatoes in her mouth as fast as her still clumsy fingers would allow, pausing every third or fourth bite to drink. She chewed noisily, seemingly oblivious to his presence.

"It's been a while, huh?" he said.

She looked up at him, suddenly conscious of what she was doing, and her eyes widened. Setting down what was left of the beef patty, she chewed what was in her mouth while fumbling with a napkin.

"Sorry," she said once her mouth was clear. "I haven't eaten in days."

"Please," he said, motioning for her to continue. "Don't mind me."

"Thanks," she said, her tone softening just a bit. "And I'm sorry to be so difficult, but you have no idea what it's like out there. Most people starved or froze to death a long time ago. Those that didn't went from house to house, looking…" She stopped talking, and her eyes turned misty again. She looked down at her food and scooped up some potatoes with the supplied plastic fork.

"You don't have to tell me now. It can wait." Whatever she was hiding, it was dark. He could tell that much.

She finished her meal in silence, then put all the empty packets and wrappers into the brown plastic shell. She had eaten everything except the salt and pepper.

"So we have a deal?" she asked, somewhat timidly. "I help you work, you let me stay and feed me?"

"Yeah," he said. "But don't forget the part where you tell me everything you know."

"Sure. So then…can I sleep? I mean do you have a room I could use? Or maybe this couch?" She looked uncertain, even a bit afraid. A stark change from the attitude she had manifested before.

"I have a few spare bedrooms," he said. "I'll go get one ready."

Taking his rifle with him, he went down the stairs to the first floor and into the guestroom. He dusted off her bed, but there wasn't much else to do. The room had been empty for a long time. He found some of Jennifer's clothes in the walk-in closet and dumped a pile of them on the pillow. When he walked out, she was standing in the hallway. He jumped, startled, reaching for his carbine, but she was unarmed.

"That's twice," he said, breathing deeply to relax himself.

"Twice what?"

"That you've snuck up on me. You seem to have a gift for it."

"Sorry."

"It's ready. Bathroom is right across the hall. It's okay to flush, but don't do it every time, save it. I'll show you how to use the water pump later."

"Thank you," she said, then went into her room and closed the door behind her. He heard the lock click.

"Not a bad idea," he muttered to himself, feeling tired.

That night, lying in bed behind a locked door, he couldn't relax enough to sleep. His thoughts alternated between delight at no longer being alone and the way she had reached for her pistol when she'd first woken up. He was only certain of one thing. She was dangerous. Though in what way, he couldn't know.

Chapter 5 – Fellowship

She walks in beauty, like the night
Of cloudless climes and starry skies;
And all that's best of dark and bright
Meet in her aspect and her eyes
- George Gordon Byron

Peter sat on the couch, waiting, feeling uncertain. He'd had a routine, a way of doing things, mostly the same things every day. Wake up, wash up, check the clipboard, do some chores, read, and so on. If he started to do something and she woke and interrupted him, how was he supposed to react? A part of him wanted to send her away. Give her a pack full of supplies, some ammo for her gun and bid her farewell. That part scared him. *For sudden joys, like griefs, confound at first.* He had come across those words in a particularly annoying poem by Robert Wild, but they hadn't meant anything to him until he read *Robinson Crusoe*, where Defoe had used them to describe Crusoe's feelings after being washed up on the beach, having narrowly escaped death in the turbulent sea. True to the ancient words, Peter was confounded in his sudden joy.

When he heard the stairs creak, his heart raced and he braced himself.

"Morning," she said as she came into view. She wore a familiar t-shirt and shorts from the bundle of clothes he had left for her. She was clean too, her hair was brushed and the smudges on her face were gone.

"Morning," he said. "Sorry to be so abrupt, but, you've rested, so it's time for our talk."

"Talk?"

"About what you know," he reminded her. "That was part of the deal."

"Oh, okay. Can we do it over breakfast? I'm, uh, still a little starving." Her voice was soft, high pitched but not screechy. Her tone and general demeanor had changed from the first time he'd spoken to her. She sounded more relaxed, more polite in an apologetic way that some uncertain people exhibited. She lacked confidence, but her actions hid it better than her words did.

"Of course. How do formerly frozen carrots sound?"

"Amazing."

Peter grabbed the carrot filled pot from the wood stove and set it down on the coffee table. After fetching plates and forks, he sat down on the couch and motioned for her to join him.

"Thanks," she said, and settled down on the opposite end.

"So," he said. "Did you get any information about what happened? After the quake? TV, maybe radio?" He had relied on his satellite receiver and had never bought an off-air antenna or a radio.

"Sort of," she said, scooping some carrots onto her plate. "For a little while, maybe five minutes. Local broadcasts and stuff. But there was nothing but speculation, then it all went dead." She attacked the meal with enthusiasm, though not as ferociously as the night before.

"Did you try calling anyone? I tried calling my parents in Brooklyn, but all I got was a busy signal, and then the phones died."

"My folks were in the city too," she said. "They lived around here, but they went down to Manhattan to see the sights. I was supposed to go with them, but…" She exhaled slowly, then turned away momentarily. "Sorry."

"Don't worry," he said. "For all we know, we're just stuck in a freak storm. Climate change and all that, maybe new ice age or something. Maybe people down in the city are just fine, worrying about us." He had told himself that same lie many times, but each passing day made it harder to swallow.

"I wish I could believe that," she said, her words echoing his thoughts, and resumed her meal.

"So were you able to reach them?" he asked, eager to get back on track. "Your folks?"

"All circuits are busy," she mimicked, managing a weak smile. "Then I lost the signal and never got it back."

"Cell phone?"

"Yeah. The land line was dead by the time I got to it."

"So," he said. "There's a big earthquake, then the satellites stop broadcasting, the power goes out and cell phones lose signal. That doesn't sound good."

"No," she agreed.

"And you're telling me you don't have any more idea than I do about what actually happened?" he asked, feeling frustrated. He had hoped to get a lot more out of her.

"No, sorry, I don't. I was almost in the same situation as you, just not as lucky."

"Yeah," he said. "Real lucky. So do you have any theories? Nuclear war, maybe?"

"I doubt that very much," she said.

"Why?"

"It doesn't mesh with the climate models for nuclear winter. And of course there are the seismic waves…the tremors."

"But what about the snow?" he protested. "Doesn't that fit with nuclear winter?"

She shook her head. "It's been snowing almost nonstop since it happened, and that doesn't add up. Nuclear winter is caused by smoke and soot rising into the stratosphere and being circulated by prevailing winds. The stuff cuts off the sun, cooling the earth. The last study I read found that such rapid cooling would significantly weaken the hydrological cycle."

"The what?" he said, taken aback. She looked way too young to be talking the way she was.

She opened her mouth to speak, then stopped. She looked at him as though measuring him, perhaps trying to figure out how much to dumb down what she was going to say.

"Just don't use jargon," he said. "Hydro, water. Rainfall patterns? Evaporation, condensation, precipitation?"

"Yes, that's right. But you forgot evapotranspiration, sublimation…"

"Now you're just being a smartass," he said, smiling despite his irritation.

"Sorry. But the point is, yes, a nuclear winter would mean a weakening of the cycle, by as much as forty, maybe fifty percent. That means a lot less precipitation. So the fact that it's been snowing the whole time…"

"Doesn't add up," he finished. "I see." He was starting to enjoy this conversation. She may not have any information about whatever happened, but her theories were a hell of a lot more informed and better thought out than his own.

"And there's the snow itself," she continued. "It's not radioactive, or we'd both have died a long time ago. Well, maybe not you, since your water comes from underground."

"Makes sense. I considered it, and didn't eat the snow, but I always had it all over me."

"That would have made you sick, if it were radioactive," she said. "But of course none of that is definitive. The climate research is based on computer models, and the experts disagree too much to put much stock into any of it without a lot more data. The thing is, though, the snow started way too soon to be a nuclear winter. I'm not sure of the exact timescale, because it would depend on… why are you staring at me?"

"How do you know all this?" he said, no longer able to hold back his curiosity. "You're what, twenty-five tops?" He realized as soon as he said it that it was his prejudice talking—he had spent too much time among the latest generation of students to have much regard for their intelligence as a group, but there had been many exceptions. There was also the fact that he taught at a city university—not exactly the Ivy League.

"Thereabouts," she said. "I am, or was, a grad student. Climatology isn't my field, but it hasn't been too long since I took all my undergrad sciences, so a lot of it is still fresh."

He remembered her maroon sweatshirt. "That MIT shirt," he said. "That was yours? I mean really yours, not like a gift or something?"

"Yup."

"What were you studying?"

"Physics," she said. "First year of grad school. What about you? What did you do?"

He wanted to hear more about her ideas, but decided it would be best to answer her questions. Perhaps she would open up more if she knew more about him.

"Nothing interesting," he said. "I taught English at Brooklyn College. Adjunct professor."

"You did not!" she said excitedly. He should have realized that she would react that way. Having been a college student, his being a professor would be a pleasant familiarity.

"I did."

"Oh yeah? Quote me a poem then."

"What makes you think I taught poetry?"

"All English professors can quote poetry, Peter." Her transformation was startling. She had been hesitant, withdrawn even, but that was gone now. She was grinning broadly and looking at him with anticipation. Familiarity was a powerful motivator, it seemed.

"Okay," he said. "Um…." He cleared his throat, considered a moment, then said, "Fly envious time, till thou run out thy race. Call on the lazy leaden-stepping hours, whose speed is but the heavy Plummets pace—"

Penny cut in. "And glut thy self with what thy womb devours, which is no more then what is false and vain, and merely mortal dross. So little is our loss. So little is thy gain."

Peter cocked an eyebrow. "You like poetry?" he asked.

"I like submarines."

He stared at her, confused. "I don't—"

"You haven't heard that poem until you've heard it read for the intro to Silent Hunter 4."

He continued to stare, this time blankly.

"For fuck's sake," she said, smiling. "It's a PC game, Peter. Really good introduction video with a reading of that poem set to scenes from WWII naval battles. Very moving." Her smile reached her eyes, which narrowed and glowed with warmth. Was this the cold and hard woman who had confronted him from this very couch the day before?

"Oh. Well, I guess I'll take your word for it."

"So," she said. "An English professor. Then explain this!" She pointed an accusing finger at a pile of paperbacks on the coffee table. "Peter Clines? James SA Corey? *Jim Butcher*? Really, Peter? Wizards?" He couldn't get over how different she had suddenly become. She leaned forward, her eyes fixed on him. She seemed comfortable, relaxed. He thought that there had to be more to it than just the university connection, but he had no way of knowing. She was a blank slate to him, with only surface details starting to coalesce.

He chuckled. "Guilty as charged." He wanted to get back to talking about the disaster, but a part of him was resisting. Their conversation had become so normal that he was starting to take refuge in it. It was becoming his utility room, only much more compelling.

"You prefer those to the classics? I've always wondered if you pretentious bastards read the crap you push on us."

He wasn't sure she wanted a real answer, but having been alone for so long, he couldn't stop himself from speaking. "Yes and no. In terms of being immersed in the story, being transported, modern literature is far superior...in fact the classics are downright clumsy by comparison. Peter Clines or Jim Butcher can pull you into a story so hard that Jane Austen's dress would rip off in their tail wind. It can be argued that it's partly because the language of the classics is a bit too archaic for modern sensibilities, but I don't think that's the case. From Beowulf to the Odyssey to Pride and Prejudice, you see a gradual evolution of storytelling. The stories themselves don't get better, but the telling of them does. The language and structure of the classics are generally a lot more sophisticated, poetic by comparison, but in modern fiction the language has been streamlined to paint a picture in the reader's head and make him hardly aware of the words. But the classics are so full of meaning, full of the big questions. What it means to be human, what it means to make mistakes, to own up to them, or not to. And they got there first, so their portrayal has the ring of original thought missing from modern works. In that respect, the classics transcend ordinary storytelling and immerse us in a journey of exploration, but of our own minds."

As he stopped talking he realized with some embarrassment that he had been lost in his words and was rambling. Penny was staring at him.

"Wow," she said. "I feel like I'm back in the lecture halls of MIT."

He blushed and looked down at his feet. "Sorry."

"So should I call you Doctor Anderson?" she said, pointing at him with a fork. "Or do you prefer Professor."

He was surprised that she had remembered his last name. "Not 'doctor.' I didn't have a PhD."

She cocked an eyebrow. "I thought you needed a terminal degree to be an adjunct."

He nodded. "You do. I have an MFA in writing."

"Ah."

"Yep, almost a professor. Like I said before, I was almost a lot of things."

"Such as?"

"Almost a writer. Tried to get some stuff published...outside of academia I mean. I didn't get the MFA to teach writing, I got it to write. Almost made it." He smiled. "Had some short stories published, almost sold a book but the publisher backed out at the last minute."

"There has to be at least one more," she said. "To qualify as 'a lot of things.'"

He hesitated, not sure that he wanted to tell her. The pain of that particular failure had almost killed him. He finally decided that there was no reason not to.

"I was almost a Seal."

She blinked. "For real? Seal like Navy Seal?"

He nodded, then frowned and looked away, fighting back powerful emotions. "Injured out two weeks shy of finishing SQT...that's Seal Qualification Training, the last thing before being assigned to a team. More than a year of training, down the toilet."

"I noticed you limping a little..." she started, then bit her lower lip.

"My foot started to hurt. A lot. I knew that if I went to the doc, I would probably have been recycled...sent to a later class. That would have sucked, so I worked through the pain. It wasn't a serious injury. That is, unless you're in the middle of Seal training and try to ignore it. Then, as it turns out, you can become a cripple for life. Had I stayed off it for a few months it would have gone back to normal."

"I'm sorry," she said.

He shrugged. "I'm a lot better now. I can run and stuff. I just limp a little."

"Still," she said. "You were a Seal. Or close enough to one, anyway." She looked hard at him, as though taking his measure.

"There couldn't have been too much important stuff in the last two weeks, right?" He noticed her appraisal and wondered why it mattered to her.

He shrugged again. "I suppose I'll never know. I got a medical discharge, then after I got my MFA I applied for a direct commission in public relations. They made me a Lieutenant JG in the reserves. Paperwork though, nothing exciting. No budweiser. No guns."

"Budweiser?"

"That's what we called the Seal insignia. Anchor, eagle, trident, pistol. Looks like the Budweiser logo." He tried to fight off the tightness in his chest. That had been a very dark part of his life—putting on a uniform that was a constant reminder of his failure, and yet not being able to let it go. Before the snow and the isolation, there had been two times in his life when he had put a loaded gun in his mouth. The first was right after his discharge from active duty, on the day his former brothers had graduated from SQT without him while he sat on a couch, alone, with a bottle of whisky. The second was the day before he resigned his reserve commission, no longer able to stand the torment of sitting behind a desk writing about the exploits of others. If he had just told them about his foot, he would have ended up a Seal. His life would have had meaning—and he would have died in whatever disaster had befallen the world. Maybe it would have been better that way.

"You don't look old enough to be an ex-Navy Seal English professor."

He jumped a little at her words as she snapped him out of his brooding. He sensed by her tone that she was trying to cheer him up.

"Thanks," he said. He looked at her, her smiling, youthful face, and realized for the first time since meeting her how much distance there was between them. When Jennifer had announced she was divorcing him, he had reacted badly, frightened by the sudden change in the comfortable life he was accustomed to. By the time he was living on his own, things were very different. Being with Jennifer had left a void in his heart, a hunger born of deprivation. It was as though he were coming out of a long sleep, and all the years with her were part of a bad dream that had steadily faded from memory. He remembered being genuinely surprised that he was in his late thirties. A part of him had expected to be able to pick up his life exactly where he had left off. He felt like a much younger man, perhaps as young as Penny, only he wasn't. Fly envious time indeed. If he believed in the supreme throne, perhaps those words would give him comfort.

They finished their breakfast of thawed frozen carrots, then Peter taught Penny about the house, about how everything worked, and, finally, took her outside with some snow shovels. By the end of the day, they were both exhausted. After eating rice, beans and canned beef, they retired. Peter was asleep almost as soon as his head hit the pillow. It was only the next morning that he realized that he had forgotten to lock his door, or put away his rifle.

Chapter 6 – Deliverance

There's little joy in life for me,
And little terror in the grave;
I've lived the parting hour to see
Of one I would have died to save.
- Charlotte Brontë

She was standing in his bedroom, holding his rifle, muzzle pointed at the floor. Peter sat up quickly, blinking away sleep. At first he panicked, but as his mind regained full consciousness, the fear receded and a bittersweet pain flooded in to replace it. He had trusted her, and she had betrayed him. He had almost found salvation in his desolate new reality—another "almost" to add to his collection. He looked for his pistol, but it wasn't where he'd left it.

"Why?" he said. It was the only thing he could think of. He had offered to share his food with her, maybe the last food there was in the whole world, and in doing so he had cut his own life in half. Maybe that wasn't good enough for her. Maybe she wanted it all, to stretch her life as long as possible and hope for a thaw.

She walked closer, lifted the rifle to her shoulder and pointed it at him. He saw her thumb move on the safety as it clicked into the fire position. He looked into her eyes and nodded. Better to die than to ever be alone again.

"Bang," she said. "You're dead." Then she lowered the rifle, flipped it around, and handed it to him.

"What? Why? What are you doing?" Peter took the weapon, dropped the magazine and cleared it, then put it on the bed next to him. The chamber had been empty.

"You were very careful to hide all the guns from me," she said. "Then you forgot, so I took advantage. I want you to know you can trust me, Peter. Anything bad I wanted to do to you, I could have done right now. I'm sorry if I scared you, but I thought it was important for you to know that."

"That was a hell of a way to make your point," he said angrily.

"Would you have believed—really believed—anything less?"

"I—" he started to speak, then closed his mouth and considered. "Point taken."

"Good," she said. "Then let's get to work."

She left his room and he got dressed, then met her out on the deck. She was already shoveling snow. He joined her, and working outside didn't seem so bad anymore. The day passed quickly, and after they worked and ate dinner, Peter dug out his old Monopoly board game and set it on the kitchen table.

"Are you sure?" Penny said, grinning mischievously. "I don't want you to cry when I school you, Professor."

After she beat him, he demanded a rematch, and as they played, he realized that he had completely let his guard down. She had done exactly what he needed her to do, at exactly the right time. He couldn't shake the feeling that she was hiding something, maybe even something big, but if she were not a danger to him, then it didn't matter. Once he allowed himself to relax, the initial feelings of resentment quickly faded. He no longer felt as though she were intruding on his life and disrupting his routine. Instead, he developed a new routine and included her in it. Her company became as exhilarating as he had hoped it would be.

With Penny working by his side, he had a lot more energy and will than he'd had in a very long time, and he set about finishing projects that he had left stagnant. Over the next few days they cleared the snow around his shed and inventoried its contents, finding a collection of antique knickknacks that had belonged to the previous owners. Some of them would prove very useful, such as a pair of old snow shoes and a sizeable collection of kerosene lanterns.

The snow didn't stop—it hadn't fully stopped since it had started back in December—but Peter was certain that it was letting up. A couple of days after Penny's arrival, there were little more than flurries, mostly slow moving big flakes that seemed to hover in the gentle breeze. A day after that, the flurries became even lighter.

Peter took advantage of the letup and his newfound vigor to get rid of as much of the snow as he could. He dared not approach the mountainous pile that loomed ominously over the far side of the house, but he cleared much of the rest, including his deck. For the first time in months, he could go outside, stand on firm wood and gaze out over the alien landscape that revealed itself before him. The latest flurry was so sparse that it danced on the edge of stopping altogether, and visibility was better than it had been since the snow began. Peter could hardly believe what he saw.

"My god," Penny said, coming to stand next to him.

As far as the eye could see, there was nothing but white. The once stark contrasts between the tallest mountains and deepest valleys was muted, and Peter finally understood why his cabin had been spared. The snow tended to drift down to the lower elevations, and he was almost at the peak of the mountain he lived on.

"It's like an alien planet," she said.

"Yeah, I was just thinking that."

They watched the sun disappear behind the closest mountain, then ate dinner and called it a day, both exhausted and demoralized by the foreboding visage. Nothing could be alive out there. Nothing except a few scattered survivors desperately clinging to life until their supplies ran out. If the snow didn't stop very soon, no one would survive much longer. Perhaps it was already too late.

*   *   *

They went back to work the next day, clearing more of the snow. The flurries seemed to let up more and more as the days passed. The cleared area around the house grew steadily, and Peter discovered another pile of logs that he had completely forgotten. With the lessening snow came slightly higher temperatures, which combined with the new log pile meant that they would be okay for a few more weeks.

Penny proved to be an excellent companion, practical, level headed and strong of will. She never disturbed him when he was reading or otherwise wanted to be alone, but was always willing to talk or to play games such as chess or Monopoly when he was in the mood to do so. He felt a bit guilty that she was catering to his whims—something he was not at all accustomed to—but then again he was giving up a substantial portion of his remaining life to sustain hers.

"Wanna take a break?" he asked, setting his shovel down.

"We've been at this for hours."

She smiled. "Sure. I'm beat."

He went to the house to fetch a couple of MREs and they sat down on the deck steps and ate their lunch.

"Drinking the snow makes things easier," he said. "Thanks for putting some sense into my head."

"My pleasure," she said, then pointed to his rifle, which he had left leaning against the house. "So how'd you get your hands on that?"

"What do you mean? I bought it."

"Isn't that an M4?" she asked. "Military issue?" The fact that she recognized the weapon impressed him.

"Close, but no, it's the civilian version. They call it an 'M-forgery.' Get it? M-four, M-forgery?"

She smiled. "That's clever. What's the difference?"

"The real one is select fire, meaning you can choose semi or fully automatic, this one only does semi…that is, one shot for every pull of the trigger."

"Is that a big difference?"

"Not really. We were taught to use semi-auto for almost everything. A skilled shooter can put more rounds on target in less time with semi. It's only in movies that people shoot rifles on full auto all the time. The barrel gets too hot to touch after just one magazine on auto…a few more and you'll start cooking off rounds. That is, the bullets in the chamber will go off by themselves because of the heat."

"But isn't it still illegal in New York?"

He grinned. "It was. But I'd like to see them do something about it now."

She giggled. "You really know a lot about this stuff." She tilted her head as she looked at him.

He smiled. "Almost a Seal."

"Would you mind," she said, hesitantly. "If we have time later, showing me how to use it? I mean I know how to shoot, but…"

"How about now?" he said. "It's not like the snow is going anywhere."

She nodded, smiling. "Sure! If you don't mind."

"Come," he said. "Let's go up there." He motioned towards the gazebo to the right of the pond. "The wind keeps that area scrubbed for me. Should be a few feet deep at most." They ascended the terraced path up the slight hill, almost falling more than once in the slippery mess.

When they were near the gazebo, Peter reached under the snow and pulled out an empty gasoline jug. It had been red once, but now it was a light pink, bleached by the sun and riddled with bullet holes. It had been so long since he'd seen it.

He twisted his body to chamber a pitch, then flung the jug out as far as he could up the hill. It sank in the snow a bit as it touched down, but most of it was still visible.

"About twenty meters," he said, pleased. "That'll do just fine."

"That doesn't seem very challenging," she said. "When my dad and I would shoot we'd usually do one hundred yards or more."

"I'm not going to show you how to shoot," he explained. "Shooting is easy, anyone can do it. I'm going to show you how to fight."

She raised an eyebrow. "I'm intrigued."

"Here, put these on." He handed her a pair of foam earplugs that he carried in his pocket. "Roll them up, then stick them in your ears. They're a bit stiff from the cold, so give them time to soften up from your body heat."

"Is it loaded?" she asked, taking the weapon.

"Always. Don't put your finger on the trigger until you're ready to fire. There are iron sights, but the red dot is much better. You turn it on like this…" He pointed to the actuator. "That little knob controls the brightness of the dot. Turn it…no, the other way, good. Look in the sight and see if it's bright enough."

"Now it is," she said, after messing with the dial. "It doesn't magnify?"

"No, but that little thing mounted behind it does," he said, reaching out to flip the magnifier in line with the red dot sight. It pivoted on its mount and clicked into position. "You can flip it back when you don't need it."

"Oh cool," she said, looking into the sight. "That's just the neatest thing!" She flipped it back and started fumbling with the sight's brightness knob.

"What are you doing?"

"Making it brighter," she said. "The sun is in my eyes."

"Good, you'll need to…wait, the what?"

"The sun, it's—" She stopped talking and her mouth fell open. They both looked up at the sky.

"Holy shit!" Peter swore, almost unwilling to believe it. Since the snow started, it had varied from full on blizzard to light flurries, but there was always something, and the sky was always overcast. Now the sky was perfectly clear, and a bright golden orb shone overhead.

"A clear sky," she said excitedly. "Could it…"

"Let's hope so," he said, not wanting to jinx it. "It could just be a brief pause." His heart was racing, but to his surprise his emotions were mixed. First Penny's arrival, now this—he wondered what would be next, a television signal and news that nothing serious had happened? That it was all some freak storm and things would go back to normal? The prospect was exciting, but also frightening.

"And that?" she asked, pointing back to the house. "You think that's a brief pause?"

He looked where she pointed and gaped. Drops of water fell from the roof, poking holes in the hard white crust over his deck. As soon as he saw that, he realized he was still sweating in his parka, despite the fact that he was no longer shoveling. It was too warm for the clothes he was wearing.

"My god," he said. "It really is over."

"The only question is," Penny said grimly. "What's next?"

Chapter 7 – Damnation

Had he and I but met
By some old ancient inn,
We should have sat us down to wet
Right many a nipperkin!
But ranged as infantry,
And staring face to face,
I shot at him as he at me,
And killed him in his place.
- Thomas Hardy

They spent the rest of the day in the storage room inventorying Peter's food supply. Now that the sun had come out and there was hope of a spring thaw, he could afford to be a lot more liberal with his rationing. If any deer had survived, then they would come soon, and with the snow gone he could go up into the mountains to hunt. There had been a dairy farmer down the road a bit, and that was going to be worth looking into. Frozen cows would make good eating.

"Pork and rice and barbeque sauce?" she asked, holding up the brown plastic packet. "That's your favorite?" She sat cross legged by a pile of cans, wearing shorts and her MIT sweatshirt, now clean.

"It was, like ten years ago," he said. "It's actually quite good, considering it's god knows how old and kept in a plastic bag."

"What are these?" she asked, holding up what looked like a frozen dinner box. "Meatloaf and mashed potatoes? Aren't you supposed to keep this in a freezer?"

"Not those," he explained. "Those are heater meals, they're essentially canned in plastic bags, like MREs. Shelf stable."

"Heater meals?"

"They come with a chemical heat packet. You fill it with water, the chemicals mix and it gets real hot in about ten minutes."

"Exothermic oxidation," she said, looking at the box with interest.

"What?"

"The heat is generated by the oxidation of iron...essentially rust. The packet contains iron powder and maybe magnesium and some kind of salt or acid. Magnesium reacts with water at room temperature when catalyzed by something else, like hydrochloric acid. That causes the oxidation."

"What are you, some kind of genius?" he teased. Her mind intrigued him. Jennifer had been smart—her position as an investment banker demanded it—but not like Penny. He had always been drawn to women who were his intellectual equal, but Penny was leagues beyond him.

"Nah, chemistry is not my thing. I don't even know how the reaction works. Besides, knowledge and brains aren't the same thing."

"Thanks for trying to not make me feel dumb," he said, laughing. If only he had met someone like her before he had met Jennifer. But even if he could turn back time, he doubted he would have had the wisdom to recognize her for the wonder that she was. Such was the folly of youth, or at least his youth.

"Don't mention it. Can we try one?" she asked eagerly, and he couldn't resist her.

"We can try two. Pick a flavor. I'll take Salisbury Steak."

"Okay!" she agreed, taking a few out of the cardboard box. "Hmm...turkey with stuffing sounds good, but so does teriyaki chicken. Which one do you think is better?"

"Have both," he suggested, smiling. Her eyes lit up.

"Really?"

"Just this once, I guess it's okay. If the snow comes back, we won't be any worse off than we are now, and if it doesn't, well, we can't live on these things forever."

"Thank you," she said. "You're sweet."

"Don't bet on it," he said mischievously. "If we run out of food I'm going to have to eat you."

The look of sudden horror on her face shocked him. He scrambled towards her, reaching out, but she pulled back, terrified.

"Oh my god I was just joking!" he cried. "Please believe me!" Her terror transformed into mirth as she burst out laughing. He stared at her, shaking his head.

"You little shit!" he said, finally breaking down and laughing with her.

"Had you," she said, poking him in the chest.

"I guess you did."

"Guess my ass, I so had you."

They took the dinners out of the boxes and filled the heater bags with water, then set the trays on top. The clear plastic covers started to steam over in a few minutes.

"Wow, that's fast," he said, touching the tray. "I've never tried one of these before."

They peeled the plastic off the trays and started to eat.

"Oh my god," she said. "This is so good. It's like real food."

"Yeah," he agreed, enjoying his steak, if a chemically pre-served ground beef patty could be called a steak.

"Do you hear that?" she asked suddenly, her body stiffening.

He froze, listening. Two decades of shooting had not been kind to his ears. The storage room had a small window facing the driveway. He barely heard crunching snow. Someone was coming up the road.

"Shit!" he cursed, then jumped up and grabbed his rifle. "Stay here!" There was panic in her eyes, but she nodded and didn't move. *More* people? First her, then the snow and now this? He had been afraid when Penny showed up, but this was worse—he had her to think about now.

He ran upstairs, preparing the weapon as he scooped up an old laptop bag filled with loaded magazines. Crouching low as he ran past the windows, he caught a glimpse of three men, rifles slung over their shoulders, plodding along in snow shoes. He cleared the door, not bothering to close it behind him, and sliced the corner.

Seeing that the three men were not holding their weapons, he didn't fire, but lined the dot up with the first one's head.

"Stop!" he yelled, trying to keep himself from shaking. Adren-aline flooded his body, compromising his aim. "What are you do-ing here?" Keeping his distance from the corner gave him protec-tion—they saw less of him than he saw of them.

"Hold on friend," one of them shouted back. "We just want to talk." It was the man in the middle, stockier than the rest with glasses and a brown mustache. They all wore light parkas, unzipped. That meant that they had they had set out after the sun came out. The man who spoke had a full sized AR-15, similar to Peter's carbine but with a longer barrel and stock. The two others had rifles with wooden stocks and long magazines, Mini-14s maybe. Serious firepower.

"Talk," he said, looking around nervously, keeping the dot in his peripheral vision. If these men were anticipating trouble, they wouldn't just approach his house like they had. They'd leave at least one shooter behind, out of sight.

"We're looking for a girl. Young, blond, pretty. We heard she came around this way. Seen her?" The other two, one older with a gray beard and the other tall and lanky with no facial hair, started to look around. One of them spotted the tracks leading up to the gazebo. Two sets of tracks.

"No," he said, though his mind raced as fast as his heart. What did they want with Penny? How the hell did they find her here?

"You're here alone?" the tall man on the right said.

"No, my wife," he lied. "But it's none of your business." There had to be a fourth gunman, he was sure of it. He could pick off these three as easily as ducks in a shooting arcade, but if there was a fourth, and if Peter didn't find him, he would be dead shortly thereafter.

"You're lying," the one with the brown mustache said. "You shouldn't be protecting her."

"I'm fucking lying?" Peter shouted, feeling the blood pumping in his ears. "Fuck you! Who the fuck are you to tell me I'm lying?" He was angry, shouting foolishly, but he couldn't help himself. High on adrenaline, confused, he didn't know what to do. Why the hell did they want Penny?

"Sir," the man said patiently. "Just hear us out, okay? You really want to hear what we have to say." The one with the gray beard leaned over to Brown Mustache, whispering something in his ear. Peter could still taste the teriyaki chicken Penny had shared with him. From being completely alone, to being with her, to this? It was too much.

"I'm not protecting anyone!" he cried. "Just get the hell off my land!" If he were them, where would he put the shooter? The snow may have stopped, but there was just as much of it as there ever was. There was still only one way they could have come up. He scanned the tree line.

"Sir," the man said patiently. "We know she's here." It would be so easy to take them out—one, two, three. Just like that. If he could find the fourth.

A bit of movement, a flash of light...there. Peter saw him. In the trees about seventy yards away, about the first place along the driveway road with a clear view of the house that wasn't too deeply buried in snow. He was too far away to see the man clearly, and there was a lot of glare.

The tall one pointed suddenly and all three looked at the house. Peter risked a glance and saw Penny walking toward the open door. The three men could see her through the windows.

"I told you to stay there!" Peter shouted and she froze, her eyes wide with fear.

"Fuck!" he cursed. "Fuck!" This was all so bizarre. If he didn't figure out what was going on soon, his mind might start overloading. It had happened to him before. He would get dizzy and lose all ability to focus. He couldn't afford that now.

"We need to take her," Brown Mustache said calmly. "And you really want to let us." On hearing his voice, Penny's mouth dropped open and her eyes welled with tears.

"No!" she gasped weakly, then clapped her hands over her mouth. Peter's gaze darted from her to the three men and then to the shooter, not daring to completely take his eyes off any of them.

"They're not going to take you," he said to her. "I won't let them." Instead of relief, she looked even worse. It was strange, the way she was looking at him, as though he were the one who needed sympathy.

"There's something you need to know about her," Brown Mustache continued. "She's a murderer. Her and a bunch of her friends broke into a house, just like yours. Murdered an old couple and were living off their food when we found them. She killed two men getting away."

"What?" Peter demanded, more confused than ever. "You've got to be kidding me. That's the most ridiculous thing I've ever heard!"

"Peter I'm so sorry," Penny said from the doorway. "I wanted to tell you…"

He whirled to stare at her, his mouth open. "What? It's fucking true? What he's saying?"

She started to speak, then stopped, tried again, stopped.

"It's true," the man said. "The couple was in their sixties, they'd lived there all their lives. That stone cold bitch and her friends shot them dead and left their bodies to the snow. She has to pay for what she's done. I don't know what she's told you, but you can't believe any of her lies."

Peter ignored him, still looking at Penny. He spoke slowly, firmly, his eyes boring into her.

"Is. It. True." He knew that she had been hiding something, but this?

She looked away, tears flowing full force down her face. "Peter, I…"

"Is it true?" he yelled.

"It is, and it isn't," she said, shaking her head, still looking away. "It's not easy to explain. It wasn't like they said."

"Sir," Brown Mustache said. "I can see you didn't know about it, and we can't blame you. We don't want any trouble. We're building a community, you're welcome to be a part of it. You don't have to be alone. But she *has* to come with us. We can't tolerate murderers, not if we're going to be able to count on each other to survive."

Peter lowered his weapon. He looked at Penny, standing there in the doorway, shivering. She was a murderer? He remembered how she had reached for her pistol. Would she have killed him too if she'd had the chance?

Only…she'd had the chance. And Peter was still alive.

"Penny. How could you?"

She didn't answer, didn't try to explain. She turned back inside and walked to the coat closet, reached in and pulled out her parka, then slid into her boots.

"I'm very sorry, sir," Brown Mustache continued. "Very sorry it had to come to this. You're very lucky to be alive."

"Am I?" he said softly, not caring if he was heard. He wanted to ask them what they would do to her, wanted to ask if they would leave if he refused to hand her over, but he knew the answers. People were simple creatures, doing what they thought was best regardless of the consequences. He was no different. He knew that he had to turn her over. He would have believed her if she'd denied it, but she hadn't. What they told him was true.

Penny was in the doorway now, standing there, looking at him. He could see the fear in her eyes, but also the pain, and part of that pain seemed to be directed at him.

"Peter," she said softly. "Please, forgive me. I never meant to hurt you." He watched her approach, already looking past him. "I'll leave, and they'll leave you alone. They only want me."

In his mind he saw them taking her, leading her away. Would they stand her against a wall and shoot her? Would she gasp for air through punctured lungs as her blood spread out around her in the crystalline snow like the wings of a broken butterfly? And would she think of him as she died? How he could have saved her?

She started to walk around him. She was leaving, for him. Returning to the hell from which she had narrowly escaped. For him.

"She has to hang for what she's done," Brown Mustache said. She had to hang, and she didn't even slow down. She kept walking towards them. His weapon still lowered, Peter flipped the magnifying scope into position.

"Stop," he said softly. Penny froze. His shaking stopped. What they said she had done, that did not make sense. Everything he knew about her said it could not be so. *I'll leave, and they'll leave you alone. They only want me.*

"What is it?" she asked, confused. He was almost a Seal. Almost would have to do. His racing heart slowed. The thumping in his ears subsided, and he was tranquil.

"Hooya," he whispered, spun around and raised his weapon, pointing it at the fourth man. The magnification was just enough that he saw him clearly, crouching by a tree, his hunting rifle supported by the stub of a branch. He lined up the dot and pulled the trigger.

The blast of the rifle reverberating off of the wall deafened him. Penny jumped, startled. He could see her turning to run to the house, slowly, moving very slowly. The three men fumbled for their weapons, staring in fear and shock. He moved the rifle slightly, pointing the dot at the first man, the tall one.

One. He squeezed the trigger twice and the rifle twitched in his hands, the blast barely audible above the ringing in his ears. The tall one's throat exploded, splattering blood on Brown Mustache's face. Peter moved the reticle to the second.

Two. Gray Beard's head snapped back as a spray of blood painted the snow, the red a stark contrast against the glimmering white shell.

Brown Mustache had his rifle in hand and fired. A log by the roof splintered, sending a cloud of dust to dance on the wind. Peter put the dot on his head.

Three. Brown Mustache screamed, dropping his weapon as he clutched at his face. Blood welled from between his grasping fingers. Peter shot him again, then again, and again, until he stopped moving. He then whirled on the fourth shooter and searched for him in the tree line. He saw him, moving, crawling. He braced the rifle on the rail of his deck, lined up the dot, fired. Aimed again, fired. He could see the red snow beneath the gunman's body. He turned his weapon back to the first three, fired once at Gray Beard and once at the tall one, though both lay still.

He dropped to his knees, exhausted, as the adrenaline left him. Penny was on him in an instant, feeling him, lifting his coat.

"Are you hurt?" she cried through hysterical breaths. "Oh my god are you shot?" She took his rifle, tossed it in the snow, lowered him to his back. She patted at him, looking for blood.

"I'm okay," he said weakly. "I'm fine." She stopped searching and glared at him, then pounded his chest with her fists.

"Why?" she demanded, chocking back sobs. "Why did you do that? Why? You stupid bastard, why did you do that? They only wanted *me*!"

Confused, angry, hurt, he looked up into her eyes.

"I don't know."

She tried to speak, couldn't. She ran into the house and slammed the door shut behind her. As he climbed to his feet, he looked through the window and saw her collapse on the couch, press her head into the cushion and grab the pillows tightly. He saw her shudder, and even through the glass he heard her sobs.

Still confused, still shaking, he picked up the rifle and made his way down to the bodies of the three men. The snow was red at their feet, the blood still spreading slowly. He had an absurd vision of a bowl of fruit punch spilled on a snowy sidewalk. All three were dead, not moving. He didn't dare turn Brown Mustache over to see his face. He had shot him there more than once.

Slowly, with measured steps, he walked as close as he could to the fourth gunman. The man had chosen an excellent vantage point. He could have shot Peter easily, if that were his intention.

Tears welled up in Peter's eyes, but he choked them back. It didn't matter anymore. What they said was true, Penny had not denied it. He had murdered innocent men. He had crossed a line, and there was no going back. He wasn't going to try to rationalize what he had done, wasn't about to acknowledge his growing fear that he would one day face a final judgment. What was done, was done.

Chapter 8 – Contemplation

Once on a time, a Dawn, all red and bright
Leapt on the conquered ramparts of the Night,
And flamed, one brilliant instant, on the world,
Then back into the historic moat was hurled
And Night was King again, for many years.
- Sidney Lanier

When he walked into the house, smelling of smoke and sweat, Penny was sitting on the couch, staring down at the floor. Her nose and cheeks were red like the day he'd met her, though this time it wasn't from the cold. He could see the veins in her bloodshot eyes.

"It's done," he said, hanging up his coat. The sun had started to set an hour ago and the faint sunlight that shone through the window was drowned by the dancing orange glow from the fire. It hadn't taken much gasoline to get it going and it showed no signs of slowing down.

"Can I stay the night?" she asked softly, barely audible. "I'll be gone in the morning, before you wake up."

"No," he said, without looking at her, as he filled the teapot and put it on the stove. "You don't have to go." He wanted to say more, but he was numb. Nothing made sense anymore.

"Don't I?"

"No."

"They'll come back, you know."

"I doubt it," he said, speaking slowly, every word a strain. "They had no radios, no way to communicate. Their snowshoes were mismatched. Looks like they put together whatever they had. Besides, whatever trail they left, it'll be gone by tomorrow, day after at the worst. These people are busy trying to survive, they have more important things to do than devote all their resources to catching you."

"What are you going to do with me?" she asked, still looking down at the floor.

"*Do* with you?" he asked, not sure what she meant.

"You know the truth now."

"Do I?"

"Not all of it." She brushed a lock of hair away from her face, but it fell back into place. The strands caught the light of the flames outside and glowed a pale orange.

"Sometime soon," he said. "Maybe today, maybe not, I'm going to ask you to tell me what you did, and you're going to tell me the truth. Do you understand?" She nodded. "In the mean time, we're going to take precautions. We'll stand watch, be armed at all times. When the snow melts, if it melts, we're going to go see what's really going on out there."

She looked up, her eyes wild. "I'm not going back there," she cried. "You'll have to shoot me too if you think—"

"I didn't mean back *there*," he snapped. "But we can't just stay here and pretend the rest of the world doesn't exist anymore. Things are happening out there."

She nodded, relaxing slightly. "I'm sorry," she said.

"So am I."

They looked at each other in silence for a moment. Her skin, wet from tears or perspiration, glowed with dancing reflections of the fire.

"Go to bed," he said. "I'll see you in the morning."

She got up slowly and disappeared down the stairs. After watching her go, he took a bottle of brandy from one of the kitchen cabinets and started to pour some in a glass, then thought better of it and drank from the bottle. If the snow didn't stop melting, there would be a lot of work to do in the days to come—getting his other weapons set up, getting his jeep ready to go, deciding what he would take and what to do with what he left behind. Tonight, he just wanted to forget everything. As he drank, a small part of him worried that there was a murderer sleeping in his house. For some reason he could not entirely explain, he did not lock his bedroom door.

* * *

In the morning, Penny was gone. So was Brown Mustache's AR-15, one pair of snow shoes and the two spare magazines Peter had found in the man's coat pockets. She had also taken three MREs and a canteen. He stood there for a while, staring at the empty bed in the guest room, engulfed by conflicting emotions. It served him right, he supposed. She had never been his to kill for.

Taking up his rifle, he ran to the shed and grabbed one of the pairs of snowshoes he'd salvaged. It took him a moment to figure out the straps, and longer to learn to walk without tripping over himself. When he made his way outside, he looked for her tracks. The wide prints of her snow shoes were easy to follow. He had a hard time getting started in the uneven ground around his house, but soon he was making good progress over the deep snow.

He tried to move quickly, but the cold air burned his lungs and soon he was panting. Not even the continuous exertion of shoveling had prepared him for this type of movement, and he was tiring. The snow shoes worked his legs in a way he wasn't used to.

During Hell Week, the grueling five and a half day hazing that Seal candidates were subjected to in the first few weeks of Basic Underwater Demolition school, Peter had learned that the human body could handle a lot more than it let its owner believe. Refusing to slow down, he kept going, staring ahead, hoping to spot some sign of her.

Penny had stuck to the very top of the mountain where the snow wasn't nearly as deep. Peter followed her carefully chosen path across lots of what used to be vacation homes and upscale residences. The snow drifts filled in uneven terrain so that everything looked mostly flat, but there were some parts much deeper than others, and there were limits to how much snow he could safely walk over, even with the shoes. The lots ranged from five to twenty acres, sometimes more. There used to be trees and field-stone walls separating some of them, but only the trees showed above the snow, limiting visibility. At one point, the snow was so deep that only the tops of trees obscured his view, though he shied away from that area, as had Penny. If it were not for the snow shoes, most of the terrain would be impassable.

Every now and then his foot would start to sink into the snow. When that happened he stopped, lifted it out carefully, backtracked and chose another route. Penny's tracks showed fewer signs of such backpedalling, but she was a little over half of his weight.

As the sun rose higher in the sky, it became a lot warmer than he'd anticipated, substantially above freezing, and he was starting to sweat inside his parka. He paused a moment to loosen his zipper and drop his hood. His legs stiffened up almost immediately, and he had a very hard time getting back on the trail. As he struggled along, he tried to fight his growing fear. Fear of never finding Penny, or finding her dead, buried in the snow where it collapsed under her feet. Or perhaps dying himself the same way.

"I shouldn't even give a shit," he mumbled to himself. "The bitch lied to me, and she's a damned murderer. I should have given her to those assholes and called it a day." Only he knew that that had never been an option.

He walked for another hour and his ability to exert his will over his tired body started to fade. Penny's tracks were still clearly visible, but the top layer of snow was melting more rapidly than before. She was young and healthy, and she could easily outpace him. He couldn't afford to slow down, not even for a moment. Just as he pressed forward with renewed vigor, he saw her. She was coming back towards him.

He stopped, confused. She saw him too, and pointed her rifle at him. She was about a hundred yards away.

He stood there a moment, not sure what to do, then started walking towards her. If she wanted to shoot him, then it was fitting that he die this way, considering what he had done. She kept the weapon on him, but didn't shoot. When he got closer, she lowered it. He kept going until they were almost face to face.

"Are you going to shoot me?" he asked, breathing heavily, making no move for his own weapon.

She shook her head. "I didn't know who you were. What are you doing out here?"

"I could ask you the same thing."

She shrugged.

"That's all you have to say?"

"I thought you'd be better off without me." She was looking all around her, everywhere but at him.

"What made you change your mind?"

"Who said I changed my mind?"

"You were coming back."

She opened her mouth to say something, then seemed to think better of it. "Maybe I forgot something."

"Cut the shit," he snapped. "I came out here to find you."

"Why?" she demanded, finally looking at him. It was more like a glare.

"I don't know."

"Again with the 'I don't know,'" she said angrily. Why was *she* mad at *him*? It made no sense. Nothing did, and wouldn't, not until he knew the truth.

"Tell me what you did," he said.

"Now?"

"Now."

"Can't we get back to the house first?"

"I need to rest. I'm not twenty something." He looked around for a low spot in the snow and found one by a patch of trees near what used to be someone's driveway. "Come on, let's go over there for a bit."

She followed him down to the low spot, where they took off their snow shoes and sat against a pair of tree trunks, facing each other.

"I need to know, Penny," he told her. "I need to know what you did."

She broke a twig off of a low hanging branch and poked at the snow. He could see her eyes fill with tears.

"Please," he said again. "Tell me."

"You'll hate me," she said hoarsely.

"Maybe, but you'll never know if you don't tell me."

"Maybe it's better that way."

"Penny," he said sternly. "I killed four men. I need to know why."

She nodded. "Okay, I'll tell you." She shivered in her parka and wrapped her arms around herself. He was starting to feel cold as well, so he pulled up his zipper and put the hood back over his head.

"We found this house…"

"No," he cut her off. "I want you to start at the beginning, when all this started." He was afraid that without context he would judge her too harshly, and he didn't want to risk that.

"You mean when the power died?"

"Yes. Take your time, tell me everything."

"We were coming back from a party," she said, staring at nothing in particular.

"We?"

"Zach, John, Sandy, Melissa. Sandy was my cousin, Zach was her boyfriend, the other two were their friends. We stopped for gas when the blackout hit. That was when we felt the first of the tremors, the big one, so we thought maybe that's what it was, you know, that took out the power lines." He was a bit surprised that she had come to the same premature conclusion he had, but perhaps he shouldn't have been. In light of the evidence at the time it was a perfectly reasonable assumption, even for someone as smart as she was.

"We had to walk back home," she continued. "It was cold, but we got there. We waited for days for my mom and dad and Sandy's parents to come back, but they never did. We got through all the food pretty quickly, and the stores we could walk to were stripped bare."

"Were there other people?" he asked. "Did anyone know what had happened?"

She shook her head. "We kept to ourselves, mostly. There were people in the streets with guns, looking for things to shoot. Dogs, cats, anything that moved. There was no food, and the snow wasn't stopping. The plows stopped coming after a few days, not that they could have kept up. There was no way to get anywhere. We just stayed in the house.

"We'd never gone hungry before, not like this, and the guys decided we had to leave, go look for food. There was so much snow, we had a really hard time getting around, but so did everyone else. As soon as we left the village we started looking in the vacation homes, you know, the ones with property…" She stopped, staring at him with obvious discomfort.

"Like mine, you mean," he said softly.

She didn't answer.

"Go on."

"We found some cans in a few of them, stayed in some empty houses for a couple of weeks. The others weren't taking it well, you know, the fact that it wasn't getting better. I was okay, I guess, considering. It's funny how you can adapt to things if they happen slowly enough. At first I was nervous about school, that I'd missed something important, but even then I knew that whatever this was, it wasn't just happening here. I was worried about my mom and dad too, but I figured they were just stuck somewhere like I was. Probably somewhere with more food. Before you say anything, I know that's a fantasy."

"Not necessarily," he lied. The big city was not a good place to be when the power died and didn't come back. He didn't want to know what had happened there. Especially since he needed that fantasy almost as badly as she did.

"We kept going from house to house, all of them empty. Except that one." She stopped, swallowing hard.

"Go on," he said. "That was the house with the old couple?" She nodded.

"They wouldn't let us in, wouldn't share their food. We knew they had some, we could smell it. Sandy and I wanted to leave, go to the next house, but the guys were mad. Zach started to get aggressive, shouting, threatening. The old man tried to lock the door, but Zach forced his way in. We had guns we found in some of the houses, and Zach…he…he shot him."

"So it wasn't you?"

"Not that time."

"Keep going."

"The old woman, she started screaming. Zach yelled at her to shut up, and when she wouldn't, he hit her with the rifle. Sandy and I, we screamed at him to stop, but it wasn't enough. The other two didn't say anything, just stared at him. He hit her lots of times, on the head, until she was dead. We could have done more, should have, but we were so hungry, so cold."

"But you didn't kill them," he said. "You didn't even want to kill them."

"Of course I didn't want to kill them," she said softly as she reached up to tug at an errant strand of blonde hair. "But I'm not so sure I didn't want them to die. I wanted to eat so badly, all they had to do was give us something. I was angry. I could have done more. I know I could have."

"Go on."

"The guys dragged their bodies out while Sandy and I...we cleaned the blood. They had food, a lot of it. A cellar full of pre-serves, wine, cheese...that kind of stuff. We lived there for two months, rationing. That's when they came. Zach told me to answer the door, pretend we lived there. I tried, but they knew. They broke in, they..." she stopped and closed her eyes. "They took us back to the village and put us on trial, if you can call it that. They weren't interested in listening to what we had to say."

"Who is they, exactly?" he asked.

She shrugged. "Just people that got together in the village cen-ter. Mostly idiots from the city, vacationers who got stuck there, and the few locals who didn't go to stay on one of the farms. Uh...no offense."

"None taken."

"The guy in charge was some asshole artist from Manhattan. They all called him 'mayor.' Probably used the whole thing to bol-ster his power base. The old town supervisor wouldn't have stood for it."

"This is our village we're talking about? The one just down the road?"

"Yeah. It was like your place, there was a lot of snow, but it wasn't buried, at least not all of it. Don't ask me how."

"The men I shot, they didn't look familiar, were they..."

"Locals? No. Not the three whose faces I saw. I didn't grow up here, my parents moved when I was seventeen, but I knew every-body. You can't live in a tiny place like that and not see the same faces every day."

Peter exhaled slightly, relieved. For some reason, it was easier knowing that they weren't from the town.

"Tell me about this trial."

She looked away. "I don't want to."

"Penny..."

"I don't want to!" she yelled, turning to glare at him.

"Tell me!" he demanded.

She narrowed her eyes at him and bared her teeth. After a mo-ment, her shoulders slumped.

"They hanged them," she whispered.

"What?"

"They dragged them under a street lamp, one at a time, put a noose around their necks and pulled them up, kicking and screaming, while the whole town watched."

"The boys?" he asked, feeling something hard forming in the pit of his stomach.

"They were first," she said, her voice weak. "One at a time. Then Sandy. She was only seventeen."

"They hanged a teenage girl?" he asked, his voice cold. He didn't understand what he was feeling. There was horror, revulsion, rage, but also something else he couldn't name.

"We were murderers."

"Only one of you was a murderer. The rest of you were just hungry."

"It didn't matter." She sobbed and covered her face with her hands. "She begged them. She begged them to let her go. She told them she hadn't done anything."

"Why didn't they…" he hesitated, finding it hard to say. Would Penny have begged for her life? Would callous hands have placed a rope around her neck and pulled her up, choking, kicking, soiling herself in her agony?

"Hang me too? They were going to, but they only had the three ropes. They wanted to leave the bodies, you know, like examples, so they took us away, me and Mel, told us we would go the next day. There were two of them, the way they looked at us, like we were garbage, but also…one of them said they'd let us go, if we…if we…"

"You don't have to say it."

"Mel told them to go fuck themselves, but I…I didn't want to die…"

"Penny," he said. "You don't have to explain. Not that."

She nodded, tears rolling freely down her face. "She went along, after I told her to. I knew they wouldn't let us go. The things they said while we…I just knew. They were stupid, one of them had a gun in a holster, dangling by his ankles. I took it, shot him, shot the other one. I'd never…never shot…" She faltered, momentarily unable to continue.

"You did what you had to do," he said.

"Maybe." She didn't sound convinced. "I should have shot them again. One of them wasn't dead, he...he shot Melissa, hit her leg. I killed him, but she was dead. There was so much blood..."

"Femoral artery," Peter mumbled. "She bled out. I doubt there was much pain."

Penny nodded, still sobbing. "They'd cleared some of the streets, but when I hit the main road, there was too much snow, mountains of it. I saw a house by the side of the road. There were a pair of snow shoes there, just hanging on the wall. They still had their straps. I just kept going until I couldn't go anymore. The shoes started to come apart eventually, and by the time I got to you...well...I wasn't going to be able to make it much farther."

She sat there in silence for a few minutes, then wiped her eyes and looked up at him.

"That's all there is," she said, waiting for a reply. When he said nothing, she looked away.

"Guess I was right," she said finally.

"About what?" He wasn't sure how he should feel. On one hand, she hadn't killed those old people. On the other hand, she had participated in and profited from a terrible act, and killed two people to get away from justice, however brutal. She was tainted not only by what she had done, but what he'd had to do to save her from the consequences.

"About you being better off without me."

"No," he said, and there was no confusion about that. "I want you to come back with me. I just need..." he hesitated. What did he need? "Time, I guess. To come to terms with things."

"Are you sure?" she asked.

He nodded, then climbed to his feet. "Come on, we should be getting back. Promise me one thing, though." He picked up the shoes and started to strap them on.

"What?"

"If you want to leave again, you'll talk it over with me. No more running away like this, okay?"

She nodded. "I promise."

"And no more lies."

She nodded again. "No more lies."

"Let's go then."

They walked back to the house, setting a slower pace this time. It was just past noon by the time they returned. Just as they were climbing up the steps to the deck, it started snowing. He saw the droplets splatter against the melting snow, then realized that snow didn't come down in droplets.

"Rain?" Penny asked, holding out her hand.

They went inside, where he relit the fire in the wood stove and they ate a small meal while they watched the gradually intensifying rain peck away at the snow.

Chapter 9 – Evasion

There was a time when meadow, grove, and stream,
The earth, and every common sight
To me did seem
Apparelled in celestial light,
The glory and the freshness of a dream.
It is not now as it hath been of yore;—
Turn wheresoe'er I may,
By night or day,
The things which I have seen I now can see no more.
- William Wordsworth

They spent the next several days preparing for the inevitable departure and shoring up the house and its surrounding drainage system to deal with the rain and the runoff. Peter used the propane generator to charge the battery in his jeep, then hitched up his cargo trailer, which he loaded with all of his food, guns and ammunition. He also packed clothing, tools and other supplies, trying to fit as much as he could without overloading it.

His books took up a lot more room than they were worth, but he couldn't leave them behind. Oscar Wilde wrote, *It is what you read when you don't have to that determines what you will be when you can't help it.* Peter didn't know what reading the classics would make him, but he didn't want to be what not reading them would.

It wasn't easy working in the almost constant rain, but the warmer temperatures made up for the inconvenience. Fifty degrees Fahrenheit was absolutely delightful after months of freezing cold and bitter wind. The snow was melting at a very fast rate, but there was so much of it that Peter wasn't sure it would ever entirely go away. The runoff was causing havoc in the valley below, but even up by the house there were problems.

There were two inches of standing water in the outer rooms of the first floor and he was afraid that the shed would be washed away as it lacked a true foundation. He knew he shouldn't care, but

Michael Edelson   61

he couldn't quite get himself to accept that he might never come back, or that his home might not be there if he did. The shed held, but the gazebo collapsed by the third day. The most severe damage was reserved for the lower elevations. Peter had seen flooding there before, but never like this. He didn't recognize the landscape that was emerging from the spring melt.

Penny spent a lot of that time on watch with what Peter called "the big guy," the closest thing he had to a machine gun. It was a full size AR-15 with a long, heavy barrel and an integral bipod. To keep it fed he had four high capacity magazines, twin drums that each held a hundred rounds, giving the weapon the ability to maintain a continuous stream of fire. A free floating rail system gave him a wide range of possible optics and he had three sights set up on high precision mounts that could be interchanged without losing zero. It was an excellent fixed-position firearm. It could lay down suppressive fire, accurately engage targets at long range, and in a pinch, could be picked up and used for close quarters combat. It had cost over four thousand dollars to put together, including the optics, and he hadn't done much with it since to justify the expense. Perhaps that was one of the reasons Jennifer had left him.

He didn't speak to Penny except to exchange basic information or ask for help when he couldn't manage something alone. Mostly they just kept out of each other's way.

On the ninth day the snow was almost gone, revealing the true scope of the devastation. From what he could see from their vantage point, the main road was destroyed, replaced by rocks, gravel and assorted detritus. There were almost as many fallen trees as standing ones, and all of the houses that had been buried by snow were little more than piles of debris. He wondered if leaving was such a good idea after all, but he knew he had little choice. As bad as it was, a four wheel drive vehicle could find a way, if the driver were patient. People would start coming out of their hiding holes soon and they would not be safe here for long.

He could try to keep her hidden. He had no doubt that someone would come looking for her, but they would have no idea what had happened here. Since he had buried what was left of the bodies, there would be nothing to give it away. He also knew that if he did try to hide her, eventually someone would see her with him and report it to whatever passed for the authorities in that infernal community of theirs. Then they would know, or at least suspect, what happened to the men they'd sent to find her.

"It's hard for me to leave," he said as he locked his front door and walked down the bare planks of his deck to the driveway. The rain had stopped, at least for now, and the temperature was somewhere in the sixties. It was the most beautiful day he'd seen in a long time, not a day on which he would have chosen to leave his home forever.

"I'm sorry," she said flatly. "I can go alone, if you want."

He frowned. "Are we on that again? Do you really want to go alone?"

"No."

"Then stop bringing it up. If I wanted you to leave I wouldn't be doing all this." Never alone, never again. Even the thought of it was nearly panic inducing.

"Will this thing even pull out of here?" she said, pointing at the jeep. The flooding had turned much of the area into mud and the vehicle had sunk several inches into the soil. The tires had all been flat, though each inflated without any problems. The weight of the snow had probably warped the stiffened sidewall and broken the seal.

"It's a Rubicon," he said, climbing inside. "It's got locking differentials front and rear, heavy duty axles and a four to one transfer case."

"I don't know what any of that means," she said, going to the passenger's side.

"It means it will pull out of here." The jeep had a little less than a quarter tank of gas, three or four gallons, which would have normally given it a range of about fifty miles, but that was on a paved road.

He cranked the engine, engaged four wheel drive and touched the gas lightly. The jeep effortlessly climbed out of the depressions formed by its tires and continued down the muddy road.

"You're going to have to spot," he said, eyeing the mess that used to be his gravel driveway. "Once we get down to the road." He was an experienced off road driver, but this was new territory for him.

"Spot?" she asked. He probably should have talked to her about it before, but he hadn't wanted to. He needed to punish her for what had happened, but the most he could manage was to ignore her.

"Get out of the jeep and guide me along, tell me where to turn the wheel, that sort of thing. Not all the time, just when shit gets all fucked up."

"How the hell am I supposed to know? I don't know how to drive off road." She was being peevish, but he couldn't blame her. Four wheeling wasn't difficult, it just took nerve, and he was the only one who would need it.

"You'll get the hang of it quickly," he said confidently. "I'll tell you what you need to know as we go."

Going downhill through the mud wasn't hard, but when he got to what was once the end of the driveway, things changed. He whistled.

"So I guess after all that," she said, sounding a bit self righteous. "We walk. You should have at least scouted this far ahead before doing all that work." The road was completely washed away, replaced by rocks and sections of tree trunks that had been broken up in the violent currents of the melting snow. A four foot high bank separated the end of his driveway from the pile of boulders that used to be State Highway 28.

"No, it'll be fine, it just won't be easy to get the trailer up there." It wasn't actually all that bad. There were few places where the rocks weren't packed tightly enough to drive over without scraping bottom. He had been on trails worse than this when he'd taken the jeep off road for fun, but never with a trailer.

"You're kidding, right?"

He ignored her skepticism. "You'll have to get out," he said. "Tell me what the trailer is doing as I go up." She rolled her eyes and got out of the jeep.

"Don't forget this," he said, pushing her rifle towards her. He had given her one of his other carbines, set up identically to his own except with a green stock, pistol grip and rail covers.

"Fine," she said, sighing dramatically. "If anyone tries to kill me while I'm ten feet away from you, I—"

"It's not a joke," he snapped. "There are going to be people out here who want what we have, not to mention ones that might be looking for you."

She glared at him for a long time before picking up the gun.

He reached out to pull the door closed, then put the jeep in gear and approached the rocks. Struggling for visibility, he leaned his head out of the open window to better place his tires where they needed to go. The vehicle went up smoothly, scraping bottom only a little as it rose to the top of the rock pile.

"Okay," he called out to Penny. "What's it doing? Is it tilting?"

She looked at the trailer for a moment. "Turn left a bit, there's a rock sticking out here you should probably avoid." He did as she instructed and the trailer went up smoothly.

"Guess I was wrong," she admitted after climbing back inside. "This jeep is pretty cool." They started rolling slowly forward, heading east, away from the nearby village. The going was tough and physically draining. He was tense, stiff backed and clutched the wheel tightly as he guided the vehicle over rock after rock. He had precious few spare parts and any breakage could be the end of their flight.

Penny wasn't having an easy time of it either. He could see how afraid she was and how she had to keep herself from screaming every time he misjudged a rock and hit bottom or banked the jeep on a large boulder. She was also getting tired of getting in and out every time they came across a particularly difficult section of road.

After almost an hour of driving as slow as he could walk, the rock pile gave way to a pockmarked asphalt road with nothing more than a few cracks and deep potholes to impede their progress.

"I'll be damned," he said. "I thought the whole thing would be washed out."

"That's not how it works," she said. "The water forms channels as it follows the path of least resistance, and only those channels get eaten away. Most of the road will be fine, but we may come across damage a lot worse than what we just went through. There was a lot of water."

He nodded. "I suppose I should have realized that."

She didn't reply. They drove for a while along 28, watching the devastation the snow and runoff had caused. For Peter it was like a trip back in time to an alternate reality, where everything was just as he remembered, only not quite. The big log chalet on the left just a few miles from his home was gone, washed away or crushed by the snow, he couldn't be sure. The little white house with the waterfall in its front yard was gone too, but the big ugly blue converted barn stood unharmed almost level with the road. He gave up trying to figure out why some things were destroyed and others were barely touched. There seemed to be no rhyme or reason to it. He was sure Penny could come up with a logical theory, but it was beyond him.

"Are you going to ignore me from now on?" Penny said suddenly. "Tell me if you are, because I'd just as soon go on by myself if that's the case."

He was about to reply when he spotted a clear patch of muddy ground by the side of the road and pulled over. He realized he could have just stopped the jeep in the middle of the road, but twenty years of driving habits were not easily put away.

"I guess we should talk," he said, staring at the dashboard.

"Yeah," she agreed. "I guess we should. It's kinda hard to avoid each other in a car."

He said nothing for a while, waiting for her to start. What could he say? There was so much going on inside his head he couldn't make sense of it all. There were a few things he felt he understood, but they were his issues and he didn't want to burden her with them.

"You're going to wait for me?" she said, her disappointment obvious. "Fine. I'm tired of this. You've all but ignored me for two weeks now, and I can't take it anymore. I know I deserve it, that's the worst part, but it's too hard. I want to leave. Please give me a gun and some food."

His head whipped around to look at her. "No!" he cried, unable to hide the sudden panic in his voice.

"Why not?" she demanded. "You obviously don't want me around. You say you do, but you don't act that way."

"I want you to stay." It was all he could manage. After all this, just to lose her. But then he had never really had her.

"Give me one good reason."

He looked back at the dashboard.

She opened the door.

"Penny! Don't, please. You don't know what it was like before you came."

"Why? Why the fuck should I stay?" Her voice was strained, and he realized she was crying.

"What do you want from me?" he pleaded. "I'm doing everything I know how to do."

"You can start by telling me why you shot those men. And why you're leaving your home just because it's not safe for *me* to be there."

"I don't understand what the hell you want me to say!"

"Moron!" she cried and grabbed him by the collar, shaking fiercely. "Just open your mouth and tell me why you're doing all this for me but you won't say two words more than necessary! If you hate me, why all this?"

"I…" he started to speak, and she stopped shaking him.

"*What*?"

"It's not you," he said. "It's me. I'm the one I hate."

"I don't understand."

"What you did, it wasn't wrong. None of it. Your friend, Zach, he was a murderer, but not you. Yes, you could have done more, we all could have done more for somebody at some point in our lives, but that doesn't make you evil. You're not the one that killed them. Those bastards from the town, they didn't even bother to ask you…it's a fucking apocalypse, and they barged in because they knew you weren't the owners? And then hanging everyone? A teenage girl? Fuck them, they deserved to be shot." Now he understood what he felt when she had first told him. Righteous fury, and, perhaps, a trace of redemption.

"I never wanted to hurt anyone," she whispered.

"They deserved death," he continued, almost in a growl. "They all do. I don't know what she looked like, your cousin, but I lie awake at night sometimes, seeing her begging for her life, watching them put the rope around her neck. Only it's not her I'm looking at, it's you. I'd shoot those bastards again in a heartbeat, and all the rest of them too."

"Thank you," she said softly. "You can't know how much that means to me. I don't understand, though, what you can't live with if you'd do it all again?"

"Don't you see?" he said. "I didn't know! They said you killed those people, called you a stone cold bitch, and you didn't deny any of it. I killed those men thinking you did just what they said. I'm the murderer, Penny, not you." He felt tears and tried to hold them back, but couldn't. "I'm the murderer" he repeated, barely above a whisper.

"Why?" she asked. "Why did you do it if you believed them?"

"I—wait. What is that?"

"What is it?"

"Listen."

In the distance, he heard the unmistakable sound of an approaching car.

Chapter 10 – Devastation

Some say the world will end in fire, some say in ice.
From what I've tasted of desire, I hold with those who favor
fire.
- Robert Frost

Peter watched the burgundy pickup as it approached. He wanted to glance over at Penny to make sure she was alright, but he didn't dare give away her position. She was hidden behind the road bank, further concealed by the roots of a fallen oak. The sky was gray and there was a light drizzle, but it didn't seem to be picking up, at least not yet.

It was a bizarre feeling, standing out in the open among approaching strangers, brandishing an illegal assault rifle and wielding a self issued license to kill. The guilt over what he had done was momentarily forgotten. By having killed armed men without being held accountable, he had expressed his power, exerted his will over the world. It brought equal parts excitement and caution, for through his books he had known another man who relished the power over life and death. *No one can conceive the variety of feelings which bore me onwards, like a hurricane, in the first enthusiasm of success*, wrote Mary Shelley. *Life and death appeared to me ideal bounds, which I should first break through, and pour a torrent of light into our dark world.* Would he likewise come to regret his elation?

The Dodge pickup rolled up, its bed overflowing with a lumpy cargo covered by a bright blue tarp. It had a two door cab, but three or four people could easily fit inside. He saw only two, and as the truck pulled closer he could make out a gray haired man and a red headed woman, probably in their late fifties or early sixties. They eyed his rifle warily where it hung in front of his chest on a single point tactical sling, but pulled up to him anyway, the window on the woman's side powering down as the truck rolled to a stop. Peter braced himself for the pistol that could come over the edge of that door at any moment.

"Hello," the man inside said.

"Hello," Peter answered, waving at the couple with his left hand. They stared at him briefly, then the man in the truck laughed.

"Damn," he said. "What the hell do you say to a nuclear war survivor? How the hell are you, son?"

Peter smiled, relaxing. "I'm fine, sir. Good to see a friendly face."

"It sure is," the wife said. "We've been alone for months now...but I guess you have too, haven't you dear?"

"Yes," Peter said. "Yes I have. You folks sit it out at home?"

They both nodded. "Wasn't easy," the man said. "All that snow. You seen any others?"

"Not anyone you'd care to meet," Peter said, thinking of the men who had come for Penny.

"Where are our manners?" the woman said suddenly. "I'm Cindy, this is my husband Robert."

"Bob," the man corrected. They seemed so friendly, so jovial, but he knew better. He could see behind the façades to the pain and uncertainty that lurked beneath. They'd lost family, these two, of that he was certain. Children, grandchildren, who knew what else. Months had passed, but did that really matter? He'd been lucky, Jennifer had never wanted children, though he'd never thought of it that way until now.

"Peter," he said. "Pleased to meet you. What about you, have you seen others?"

Bob's face darkened. "Yeah," he said somberly. "We ran into a couple of nice folks from a town west of here. Said they was forming a community, that's where we're going. But..."

"They told us," Cindy interrupted. "About a bunch of gang bangers causing all kinds of trouble."

"Gang bangers?" Peter asked. "Here?"

"That's not what they called them," Bob explained. "Some kind of thugs, maybe skin heads, who the hell knows. We seen 'em. They had some people with them, they was leading them like dogs on leashes. Sonuvabitches took a shot at us, but the road was clear and we got the hell out of there."

"How many were there?" Peter asked, fighting back outrage.

There was no sense being angry about what he couldn't control.

"Five or six, I think," Bob said. "Up by Pine Hill, heading east, like you. You'd best steer clear of them, son, they're bad news."

"I will." He had almost said we, but caught himself in time.

"You sure you wanna head east?" Cindy said. "We could go together, join up with those people."

"No," he said, shaking his head. "Maybe later, but I'm going to scout around a bit, see what's going on. You folks take care. There's a patch of washed out road about five miles up, but you should be okay, your truck has four wheel drive right?"

"Sure does," Bob said. "Not like that monster you've got, but it'll do the job. Take care, hope to see you there soon."

"A pleasure," Cindy called as the truck began to pull away.

Peter smiled and waved, then waited for the truck to drive out of sight. Another minute later, he turned to Penny. "Okay, come out." She scrambled up over the edge of the road and joined him by the jeep.

"You're a regular country Joe," she teased as she brushed some dirt off of her jeans. "You folks take care now, ya hear?"

"Har har," he said, smiling despite himself. "They seemed like nice people."

She turned serious. "Peter, I'm sorry, you should be going with them. It's not fair…"

He shook his head. "Are you kidding? Go live with those murdering savages?"

"Don't," she said. "I know you would be there now if it wasn't for me."

"Maybe," he admitted. "But I don't think so." And he knew it was true, though he wondered why. After the isolation he had endured, he should be desperate to be around people, but he wasn't.

She smiled at him, but it was a sad smile.

"Where to now?" she asked. "Do we continue on the road?"

"Why not?"

"Those skin heads…"

"We'll keep an eye out," he said. "Go slowly, that way no one will hear us coming the way we did those two. It'll save us some gas too. Which reminds me, we need to look out for abandoned cars. I've got a siphon."

"Okay, will do. Where are we going, anyway? I assumed you had a plan, but you weren't talking to me, so..."

"Honestly I'm not sure," he admitted. "I know I want to eventually find an abandoned house, far away from here, but I'd like to take a look around first. Maybe we can figure out what happened if we had more information."

"Yeah," she said. "It's weird, the constant precipitation." She looked up at the sky, frowning. It was still drizzling, but the clouds were moving quickly, and that probably meant it would get worse.

"You mean the rain? What about it?" It was indeed peculiar that constant snow was replaced by nearly constant rain.

"Not just the rain," she said. "Rain and snow are the same thing, only temperature separates them. That much water in the atmosphere, it had to come from somewhere, and I doubt this is just a localized phenomenon. Something really bad happened, Peter, and it wasn't a nuclear war."

"Are you sure?" he asked, feeling foolish as soon as he did. He knew what she would say. "I mean I know what you said before, but…"

"Of course not, we can't be completely sure about something that's never happened before, too many variables. But that's not what I'd put money on."

"I'll place my bet with you, then," he said, and she rewarded him with a smile.

They got back in the jeep and continued east on 28, keeping their speed under twenty miles per hour, at least in those places where it was safe to go even that fast. Much of the road was damaged, and some of the potholes were quite big. About ten minutes later they came to a section of road that had completely collapsed. Peter had never realized that this part of 28 was an actual bridge over a branch of the Delaware River, but that fact was now readily apparent by the thirty foot drop to the rushing water below.

"We'll have to go down that bank and cross the river," he said.

"We have to leave the jeep?" she sounded disappointed this time.

"No, I mean cross in the jeep."

"Are you serious?" Penny asked, looking down at the frothing current. "We'll get washed away. The current is insane!"

"Nah. It's not that bad. It's a lot deeper than I remember, but I can see a shallow spot over there." He pointed. "The runoff widened it quite a bit, spread it out some. The hard part will be getting up the other side. May have to winch it. Those people we just passed, they made it. I can see their tracks, though of course they didn't have a trailer." He wondered why there wasn't a lot more water. Most of the floodwaters had receded, but the reservoirs couldn't possibly hold all the melted snow. Where had it all gone so quickly?

"You have a winch?" she asked.

He gave her an amused look. "No, that big thing in the front bumper is actually a grenade launcher."

She punched him in the arm. "Hilarious. I suppose I'm getting out?"

"Not this time. Unless you want to swim across."

The descent down the rocky slope would have been easy for the jeep alone, but was extremely nerve wracking with the trailer. Peter had wondered why he'd had to pay extra for brakes on his "off road" cargo trailer, but he was glad he did. Even with the brakes, though, the trailer almost slid sideways as he rolled down the rocks in low gear, though he was able to save it by easing off the brakes and speeding up a bit.

Only the tops of his tires showed above the water as he entered the river, but the jeep could easily handle that and more. Crossing was no more difficult than he expected, despite the scare he had when Penny started screaming that they were being washed away. The jeep slid sideways in the aggressive current, but the river wasn't very wide, maybe two hundred feet, and they were on the rocks on the opposite bank in seconds. His prediction about climbing up the far side turned out to be correct—all four tires spun on the wet rocks and the jeep didn't move. This was another case of the trailer holding him back, and its brakes weren't going to help him this time. He climbed out, rigged the winch and walked the jeep up, working the remote while Penny drove.

"Let's never do that again," she said as they got under way.

"Agreed."

The road was nice and flat for the next few miles, then got bad again when they approached the remains of a fair sized village.

"Margaretville," he said. "I used to do my grocery shopping here."

There'd been a video store there too, and an inexpensive local diner where he liked to eat. Jennifer hated the place, called it "peasant food." He hoped to spot something familiar as they drove up, but not a single building was still standing. Peter was not surprised. Another branch of the Delaware twisted and turned throughout the entire town. Whatever the snow hadn't crushed, the runoff would have destroyed. He saw wrecked cars, but the bridge across the river was washed out, and the banks were far too steep to climb.

"I want to search those cars," he said. "There's another way into town half a mile back, by that smashed up store with the Christmas sign."

"You think there will be people there?" she asked, eyeing the ruined streets nervously.

"Nah. Not unless they're scavengers like us. You have to remember that all of this was under twenty, maybe thirty feet of snow, and then got washed away in the thaw. No one could have survived."

"I guess." She didn't sound convinced.

They turned around, which wasn't easy on a narrow road with a trailer. Peter couldn't risk driving onto the shoulder; with all of the flooding, the ground along the road could be very unstable. The road itself could be unstable, but they didn't have much choice there.

When they got to the collapsed store, he remembered there was another river crossing there too.

"Shit," he swore. "I forgot about that one."

"Look," she said, pointing at what was left of the bridge. "There's a car under there."

"Worth a look, I guess." Leaving the jeep, they made their way down the rocky bank to the smashed Subaru. It was right side up at the base of the small river, only a couple of feet under water, though the entire tail end was high and dry on the rocks.

Penny saw them first, and froze. She clutched Peter so suddenly he almost slipped on the loose stones. The station wagon was full of bodies. A whole family of bodies, and they were only now starting to rot. He wondered why he hadn't smelled anything, then realized the car would be almost air tight.

"Don't look at them," he said. "Let's just check the tank and go." There could be something of value in the cab, but he wasn't about to find out. If he so much as cracked a window, all that horrid stench would escape.

"I can't," she said, starting to back up the bank. She looked pale and her footing appeared unsteady.

"Don't worry, I'll do it. You go back up there and keep an eye out, okay?"

"Okay. Thank you."

He descended the rest of the way to the car and used a knife to pop open the gas cover. Removing the cap, he bent down and smelled the opening. He was rewarded by the smell of gasoline, but there was an undertone of something much worse.

By the time he was done he had almost three five gallon jugs full of gas. The family had probably been coming from the gas station in town. Perhaps the bridge had collapsed in the first quake. He emptied one of the jugs into his jeep and secured the rest in the trailer.

"Let's get out of here," he said, eager to put as much distance between them and that Subaru as he could.

Penny nodded, looking pale.

"Merely mortal dross," he said, quoting the Milton poem they had recited back at the house. "They are long gone."

She managed a weak smile.

The next town was just around the corner and had not fared any better. They didn't see anyone, and Peter wasn't surprised. If someone did manage to survive, there was little reason to stay.

The road was cluttered with debris, and Penny had to get out a couple of times to guide the jeep over or around felled power line poles and other wreckage. There were a bunch of cars, though most of their tanks were nearly empty, and those that weren't had too much water in the gas. A couple of hours of searching yielded one more gas jug, bringing the count back up to three.

Continuing on their way, they drove steadily for the next hour or so. There wasn't much to see on the side of the road except ruined buildings. Just before they got to where Phoenicia was supposed to be, the damage that they had gotten used to seeing changed. It became gradually more intense until the fallen trees outnumbered the standing ones. The road got worse, but the damage to it was spread out. It was cracked, uneven, but not completely destroyed in any one place. Driving was slow, but not difficult. There were no surviving buildings at all, and what should have been a familiar environment was almost completely alien to him.

"This is weird," he said. "It doesn't look like flood damage anymore."

"It still looks like water damage, though," she said. "Maybe all the runoff passed through here. Is this a lower elevation?"

"Yeah, it's about a thousand feet, maybe less. In a little bit there's a sharp elevation drop down to four or five hundred," he said.

"You're thinking they had less snowfall?" she asked.

"It's possible. That was always the case before."

"It would be interesting," she admitted. "There may be a lot more survivors if they were spared the worst of the snow. Assuming that what happened here is localized, which I don't think it is."

They crested the last hill before the drop off and coasted down in neutral, trying to conserve gas. He was looking up at a mountain in the distance when he heard Penny gasp.

"Peter stop the car!" she cried, and he hit the brakes just as he saw what had alarmed her. The mountain he was looking at was an island.

"My god," he swore, unable to take his eyes off the scene before him.

They had come to the shore of an ocean, a hundred miles inland from New York City.

Chapter 11 – Discovery

But if it had to perish twice, I think I know enough of hate
To say that for destruction ice, is also great
And would suffice.
- Robert Frost

"They're all dead, aren't they?" Penny said, her voice barely above a whisper. They stood by the road where it disappeared beneath the gently lapping water and stared at the strange horizon. The sun was coming to rest behind them, setting the young sea aglow with scintillating filaments of orange and purple.

"Yes," Peter said hoarsely, breathing in the familiar ocean air. He remembered a time not too long ago when the salty breeze had filled the sails of his sloop, pushing him towards the blue horizon in search of adventure. He had sold the boat long ago, right after Jennifer started getting sea sick. The house in the Catskills had been her concession, and he had forgotten all about the call of the sea, lost in the majestic beauty of the mountain wilderness. Now the two were one.

"My mom, my dad," she continued, lost in her own thoughts. "Everyone."

"Everyone," he agreed, mesmerized by the terrible beauty before him. Numerous islands rose out of the water, peaks of mountains too tall to be drowned by the tides of the apocalypse. Were there survivors on the shores of each of these new landmasses, staring out over the water, weeping for all the loved ones drowned beneath?

They were silent for several minutes. Penny drew close to him and he put his arm around her. How was he supposed to comfort someone else when his own emotions were such a mess? He had known for months now that something bad had happened to the world, but this? He had never imagined—never could have imagined. He had known, on some level, that everyone he knew was dead, but he had never been forced to accept it. After all, he hadn't been sure, and if he wasn't sure then it was just speculation. He could just as easily have chosen to believe that they were all alive, being taken care of in some FEMA shelter or living normal lives while he alone suffered from some localized disaster. All that was over. Now he *knew.*

He felt her hand slide into his and he gripped it, squeezing firmly but gently. They stood there for a few more seconds in silence, staring out at the magnificent horror before them.

"What's the elevation here?" she asked, suddenly pulling away from him. She walked down to the edge of the water and reached down to touch it. She brought her hand to her tongue, tasting it.

"Sea water," she said.

"I don't know," he admitted. "Maybe six, seven hundred feet. Maybe less. If my phone still works, we can check our GPS coordinates."

"Let's see," she said, walking back towards the jeep. He caught up to her and fished his smart phone out of the glove compartment. The battery was dead, so he plugged it into the car charger and turned it on. After it booted, he opened his GPS app and selected the signal screen. There was nothing.

"Let's wait a bit," she said. Suddenly an orange bar appeared on the screen, then another, and another. Soon there were eight bars, and three of them turned green. It took the app a second to find their location. Peter pressed the top left corner of the screen.

"May seventeenth," he whispered, stunned by the sudden disparity of standing on the visible fringe of an extinction level event while holding a working smartphone.

"Four hundred and twenty four feet," Penny said. "That's not possible."

"Why not?" He had never cancelled the last route he keyed in, and the app was telling him to drive straight on route 28 for fifteen miles. Straight, into the ocean.

"There isn't that much water in the whole world."

"What about the ice caps?" he asked, still staring at the screen, mesmerized by pictures and numbers. Had it been only four months ago that he took such wonders for granted?

She shook her head. "Not even close. If all the ice on the planet melted, that would only raise sea levels by like two hundred feet."

He looked up, his curiosity piqued. "How do you know?"

"I don't know, I only know what I've read. There are only thirty million cubic kilometers of ice on the whole planet, about twenty nine and a half of which are grounded."

"Grounded?"

"Part of the ground, coming up from the crust. Floating ice doesn't affect sea levels one way or the other, because it's floating and already displacing water."

"I see." That part should have been obvious, but he had been thrown by the terminology. "How do they know how much ice there is? Isn't it a bit of a stretch to measure something like that accurately?"

She shrugged. "They say it's accurate to within ten or fifteen percent. They measure the surface with radar and laser altimetry, then calculate the depth using seismic soundings."

"Makes sense," he said. "But whether the ice is grounded or not, wouldn't it only count if it were above sea level? I mean if it wasn't, wouldn't the water just take its place if it melted? And isn't ice less dense than water?"

"Yes, that's very good. Only about two million cubic kilometers are below sea level, though. Between that and the loss of density, you're looking at about twenty four million cubic kilometers of net increase, which is what was used to calculate the rise in sea level. But all this is irrelevant."

"Why?"

"Because it would take an average global temperature increase of almost forty degrees Fahrenheit to melt all the world's ice, and it would take decades."

He nodded. "More mysteries. Could it have been a comet?"

"A lot could be explained by a comet. For one, the extra water. It would have to be a really, really big comet though."

"Do you think…"

"No. If a comet were to hit the Earth, we would have known about it for years. Even in the worst case scenario, months or weeks. Did you see anything on the news about a giant comet coming to kill us? And that's not even considering that a comet with enough ice to do this would wipe out all life on Earth, assuming it didn't crack the planet in half."

"I guess you're right."

"Peter," she said. "When you checked the TV satellites, did you get a signal? Was it weak?"

"No," he said. "Not at all. Full signal, on all transponders. There was just nothing coming through. Otherwise I would have just assumed that the quake shook the dish out of alignment."

She nodded, satisfied. "So maybe it wasn't the satellites then."

"What do you mean?"

"Maybe it was the ground based transmitters that went dead. When did you check?"

"Not long after the quake, when I fired up the generator." He had considered the possibility, but for that to happen...

"That means," she continued. "They would have to have been destroyed, or damaged, all at pretty much the same time. Where are the broadcast centers? Do you know?"

He shook his head. "No idea, sorry."

"I'm hungry," she said, suddenly changing the subject. "Can we eat?" She placed a hand on her stomach through her unzipped jacket.

"Of course. Let's figure out where we're going to spend the night first, though. We'll need to take turns on watch, too."

They set up a camp a few hundred feet off of the road behind a clump of trees. He pitched the smaller of the two tents he had brought with them, but decided against starting a fire. It wasn't much of a decision. Even if it weren't drizzling, all the wood in the area would still be wet from the spring melt.

"No fire, okay?" he said. "We'll have some heater meals instead." He was afraid that she would complain. "I brought some sub zero sleeping bags, so we'll be fine in the tent."

"Okay," she agreed. "Better alive and cold than dead and warm."

He smiled, relieved that she had taken it in stride. "Yeah, that's one way of looking at it."

"Do you think we'll ever be able to relax again?" she said wistfully. "To just sleep without standing watch?"

"I don't know," he admitted. "But I hope so."

They hadn't eaten since before leaving the house, both too

caught up in the events of the day to think about food. After decid-ing a heater meal a piece wasn't enough, Peter opened a can of Spam. Gradually the dusk of evening was replaced by absolute black of night. He took out a flashlight with a red lens filter and set it down on the ground. Penny looked strange under the ominous crimson glow.

"I'll take first watch," Peter volunteered. "You go on to sleep."

"Okay," she said, then her eyes widened. "Peter look!"

He turned around. At first he didn't notice anything, then he spotted it. A small fire in the distance, maybe half a kilometer.

"That's interesting," he said. "We should probably check it out."

"But it's so dark," she said. "Either there's no moon or it's hidden by the clouds, but either way, we can't see anything."

He smiled. "You forgot who you're dealing with," he said.

"Don't tell me, I'm afraid to ask."

"Gen three night vision," he said. "I only have one. The other is first gen, not nearly as good. Real gen one though, not the con-sumer crap."

"I don't know what that means."

"Third generation night vision," he explained. "Among the best available. Very clear, very bright image even on a night like this. The first generation device will do, but it's not nearly as good."

"How do you have all this stuff?" she asked. "I mean…you're like the Punisher."

"The who?"

"The Punisher? Comic book superhero vigilante? Kills bad guys?"

"I don't kill—" he started to say, then stopped as his gut tight-ened.

"I'm sorry, I didn't mean to—" She put a hand on his arm and squeezed gently, then seemed to realize it and pulled it away hasti-ly.

He tried to smile. "No, it's okay. Honestly I don't know why I have all this stuff. I'd say it was my hobby, but I've always known it was more than that. I can't explain it."

"I think I understand," she said. "It's a part of who you should have been."

He blinked, taken aback by her astuteness. "Yeah, I guess that's true." It wasn't easy to admit, not to himself, and not to her.

"You take the good one," she said. "I'll be okay with the other."

He got the goggles out of the cargo trailer and put the better one on. He flipped the switch and lowered the eyepieces. He heard the familiar whine, then the world around him switched on as though a green sun had dawned. The flashlight was like a glaring spotlight, uncomfortable to look at. He reached down and turned it off.

"Hey," Penny said. "I can't see anything." She smiled and tilted her head. "You'd better not take advantage."

"Here," he said, handing her the other one. She fumbled for it in the dark and he pressed it into her hands. Her breath tickled his neck.

"Help me," she said, struggling with the straps. He placed the goggles on her head and turned them on.

"How is it?"

"Wow!" she said. "I can see! It's not very clear, but I can actually see where I'm going." She picked up her rifle and turned on the red dot sight. "Ouch. Way too bright."

"You'll need to adjust for the goggles," he explained. "Just turn it one or two clicks."

"Better. It's hard to aim, though…"

"Shoot with both eyes open. You don't have to look into the sight, just look behind it."

"Ah," she said, getting the hang of it. "Do you think we'll need to…you know…"

"No, but you can't be too careful."

After adjusting the reticle of his own weapon, he reached in the back of the jeep and pulled out a tactical vest filled with spare magazines for his rifle. Fishing out the old laptop bag, he took some more magazines from a plastic box behind the seats and put them inside.

"Here," he said, handing the bag to Penny. "If you need to reload."

"Thanks. But I want a cool vest like yours," she said as she took the bag.

"I have some spares, but they're not set up."

"Why did I ever doubt you?"

"Actually," he said. "I have a better idea. Put your rifle away, and give me that bag."

"Why?"

"You're going to take the big one. If something happens, I don't want you in harm's way."

"If something happens? You mean if those are the…"

"Yes."

"Then why go?"

"It's probably nothing, but if it is them, we need to find them before they find us. We can't stay here without knowing who that is, and if we leave, we risk attracting their attention."

She put her rifle in the jeep while he replaced the contents of the laptop bag with two drum magazines. He took the "big guy" out of the trailer and handed it to her.

"It's heavy," she complained. "The bag is heavy too."

"Don't carry it, use the sling, wear it on your back."

She did as he instructed and they set out, heading in the direction of the fire.

Away from the road, movement was very difficult. There was a lot of mud, and sometimes their boots would sink in and not want to come back out. Penny was wearing Jennifer's boots and they didn't fit very well. One popped off her feet a few times. Peter held her up while she got her foot back inside, and they continued along.

"The jeep wouldn't make it here," he whispered.

"*We're* barely making it here," Penny replied. Just as she stopped whispering, Peter thought he heard something from the direction of the fire.

"Did you hear that?" he asked, then listened more carefully. He heard voices, laughter, general revelry. He also heard a woman scream. "I don't like this."

"Should we go back?" she asked nervously.

"No. We should see who it is. If we stay quiet, there's no way they're going to see us."

"What if they have night vision too?"

A good question. "Unlikely. How many people do you know who do?"

"Only you."

"I rest my case." He smiled, though he wasn't sure if she saw him.

They continued walking, moving closer to the fire, until Peter could make out some distinct shapes. There were a bunch of them. He couldn't be sure how many because a good number were obscured by the fire's blinding glare. The goggles had a relatively short useable range in dense woods, and the closer they were to the fire, the less he could see. The brightness was adjustable, but the more he turned it down, the less the range.

He saw several men walking around, laughing and shouting. Some held bottles, presumably beer. There were two sitting upright next to some trees, perhaps tied to them, perhaps not. Two more were standing over a woman, though he couldn't see what they were doing. The woman screamed.

"The skinheads," he cursed, though he couldn't make out any details of their appearance. It seemed as good a label as any.

Chapter 12 – Vengeance

Theirs not to make reply, theirs not to reason why,
Theirs but to do and die: Into the valley of Death
Rode the six hundred.
– Alfred, Lord Tennyson

"What do we do?" Penny whispered, obviously frightened. "What are they doing to that woman?"

Peter didn't answer. Instead, he dialed up the goggles to full brightness and surveyed the woods around the skinhead camp.

"See that clearing over there?" he asked her. He kept his voice down, but at this range there was little danger of them hearing him—the skinheads were making a lot of noise.

"No."

"What about that big stump?" He wasn't sure how much better his goggles were than the ones she was wearing. It had been years since he'd done a side by side comparison.

"Yeah."

"Okay, well past that stump is a clearing. It's between us and the camp. We're going to go to the edge, and you're going to set up the big guy behind that stump. Do you understand?"

She nodded. "But why? Shouldn't we get out of here?"

"No," he said. "I can't just leave those people. I have to see if there's some way we can save them. Besides, we need to know what we're up against, and we're in no danger as long as we stay quiet. They're making enough noise to drown out a helicopter."

"Peter…" she started to say, then changed her mind. "Okay. I understand."

"You do?"

"No," she admitted. "But I trust you. Do what you have to do."

"I'm going to get closer to the camp. My plan is to come right back so we can decide what to do, but if anything goes wrong, I am going to fall back across that clearing, across your line of fire. When they chase me…"

"Light 'em up."

"Yes," he said, impressed with her courage. Most people he had known would be hysterical in her place. "Just open up on them and don't stop. If you don't hit them, keep them down. Don't shoot too fast. Tap, tap, tap, tap. Keep it steady. You have a hundred shots, and when that runs out, there are two more drums in that bag…change them just like you would a regular magazine, they work the same way, they're just fatter on the bottom. Keep your head, don't panic. Don't worry about the empty ones, just drop them, we'll find them later."

"Okay. I can do it." She made an effort to sound brave, but he could hear the uncertainty in her voice. She was afraid, but she would do what she needed to do.

"And take off your goggles. The big guy has a gen three night vision scope." He reached behind her and turned the sight on.

"That's some wicked Call of Duty shit, Peter."

"What?"

She sighed. "Never mind."

"It's going to get confusing," he warned. "You're going to wonder if it's okay to shoot, you're going to question who the bad guys are. Make it real easy on yourself. You know what I look like, right? Anyone who is not me is dead. Understand?"

"Yes."

"If they don't pursue," he said, afraid to alarm her but realizing it was necessary. "If they shoot me, or capture me, don't do anything. Go back to the jeep, get back on the road and get the hell out of here."

She nodded. "Peter…"

"Yeah?"

"You're one hell of an almost fucking Seal."

He smiled. "Thanks. Don't do anything stupid. Do you understand?"

She nodded. "I do."

"I'm counting on you," he said.

"I won't let you down."

They made their way to the stump, slowly, cautiously, careful not to make too much noise. The wet branches didn't crackle under their boots but sank into the mud instead. A mixed blessing, but one that could save their lives.

Penny unfolded her rifle's bipod and set the weapon down on the stump, crouching behind it. Peter was about to tell her to set up on the ground, but realized the bipod would sink into the mud just like the sticks. This was his show, but she was still smarter than he was.

His resolve faltered. Was he right to risk her life? Over the lives of a few strangers? Sun Tzu wrote, *Who wishes to fight must first count the cost*. No, he decided, it wasn't worth it, but he would still do it.

He could convince himself that there were good reasons to attack these men. Assuming they were who and what he thought they were. There was much more at stake than their immediate safety. The people in that camp were predators, and so long as they ran free, they were a threat. What good would it do to run from them now, to find an empty house and make a new life, only to have that life destroyed? All of those things were true, but he knew that none of them were the reason he was moving toward the camp rather than running away.

The canvas of the world had been painted over, the old world lost, gone forever. And with it, his failings were erased from existence, save within himself. Penny had been right. He had been denied the life he should have led, denied the chance to be the man he should have been. None of that mattered anymore. There were people who needed his help. There were bad people who needed to be stopped. This was his chance to become something more than what he was. And, perhaps, to redeem himself in the only way left that mattered—in his own eyes. All was lost, the whole damned world, but he could have *that*. And he wanted it, wanted it so badly that he couldn't stop himself.

"What though the field be lost?" he said softly, quoting Milton. "All is not Lost. The unconquerable will, and study of revenge, immortal hate, and the courage never to submit or yield."

He advanced slowly across the clearing, making sure that Penny was far to the side rather than directly behind him. The closer he got, the more he dialed down the goggles' brightness. He felt exposed, as though a casual turn of the head would reveal him, but of course that wasn't so. Outside the island of light cast by the fire was absolute darkness, and he was as a ghost within.

He passed the clearing without being spotted, then slowed his approach even more as he closed to within thirty meters of the camp.

With the brightness dialed all the way down, he was finally able to get a good look at what was going on. The fire was blazing in a split steel drum, going strong despite the drizzle. The two men next to the trees were indeed tied, he could see that clearly now. One of them was young, with long hair, dressed far too sparingly for the cold. The other wore camouflage, the newest military pattern. A soldier? He was in bad shape. His head was listing and Peter could see signs of discoloration on his face.

Looking around at the others, he could see no reason why the label skinhead had been applied to them. One of them had a crew cut, but two others had long hair. Their clothes ranged from black leather with chains to camouflage hunting jackets. There was nothing cohesive at all about their appearance.

He turned his attention to the woman, and the reason for her scream became obvious. Two of the thugs had her bent over a fallen tree trunk, her jeans down around her ankles. There was one on each side of her. When the one in front pulled back momentarily, she managed a scream.

"Fuck is wrong with you," the one in front shouted at the other one. "You wanna be a fucking baby daddy?"

"Fuck you!" the other one called back as he stepped away and pulled up his pants. "You get shit on your dick if you want."

"You're a fucking idiot," the first one said.

"You're the idiot! We're probably gonna have to eat the bitch if we don't find some fucking deer soon."

The other one erupted into laughter. "Fuck yeah!" he shouted as he intensified his motions. "Eat the bitch!" He pulled back, then grabbed her hair and pulled her over the log. She screamed as she fell face first, her bound hands unable to break her fall. She lay there, shaking, while the two men went back to the fire.

"Keep it down you fucking morons," one of the men by the fire growled. He was older than the first two, judging by his voice. He wore tree bark pattern overalls and a Kalashnikov rifle slung over his shoulder. It was too far for Peter to tell which variety.

"Why? There's no one—" The older one backhanded the rapist hard across the face. Peter had lost track of which of the two it was. He was a detached observer, refusing to give in to his anger. He had to stay clear, stay focused.

"Fuck," the man cried, falling to his knees.

"When I fucking tell you to do something…" the older one said, standing over him, menacing him with a raised fist.

"Okay, okay!" the man on the ground pleaded, hands raised. "I get it!"

Peter counted seven of them: the two rapists, the older leader, three sitting on or near the hood of a pickup truck and one near the two prisoners, probably a guard. All were armed. There were some AKs, some AR-15s, a couple of shotguns and a scoped hunting rifle. Only three of them carried their weapons: the leader, the one by the prisoners and one of the two on the pickup. The rest of the guns were either leaning against a tree or lying on top of something.

His resolve faltered and he started to feel foolish for having come here, for risking Penny's life. Objectively, he knew that these men had to die, and he knew that the plan he had devised was an effective one. He could see them, they could not see him. His weapon was equipped with a sight that could be used in the dark, while none of their weapons had anything more than iron sights or scopes and were consequently almost useless. He had the element of surprise, and he had support in the form of Penny and the heavy rifle.

His fear told him to pull back, his common sense told him to engage. The growing darkness within him told him that the blood of these men would dilute the blood of those he had killed unjustly, before knowing why he should. A small, dimming fragment told him that killing was wrong, but there was no part left that would listen.

Attack him where he is unprepared, appear where you are not expected. Sun Tzu.

He lifted his carbine, put the dot on the leader's head, and fired.

The blast slammed into his ears, filling them with an all too familiar ringing. The flash of his rifle amplified by the goggles blinded him for a split second, but he recovered quickly enough to put the dot on one of the remaining two armed men. He fired. The man went down, joining his leader.

The third opened fire, filling the night with the cracks and booms of projectiles breaking the sound barrier while the rest scrambled for their weapons. Peter dropped down to the ground, but the bullets weren't coming anywhere near him. The man had been too surprised to look for the flash and was shooting wildly. They still had no idea where Peter was. The sound of automatic gunfire roared from the camp—one of them had a military weapon, though he didn't know how to use it and would waste his ammo faster than the others. He heard the boom of a shotgun as a tree branch not far above his head exploded and showered him with pine needles. He almost panicked and ran, but managed to hold still. It had been a lucky shot, nothing more.

Rising into a crouch, he found the nearest of the bunch and aimed, fired twice in rapid succession, then turned and ran, zigzagging through the clearing.

"I see him!" one of the men shouted over the gunfire. Peter kept his head, realizing that the only thing the man saw was where his muzzle flash had been, not where he was now. Bullets broke branches and smashed into trunks all around him, but none came close, it was random fire. Penny was safe, at least for now, as he had put her out of the way. He made no effort to avoid making noise as he ran. He needed to get them to chase him.

Flashlight beams lit the night, but none found him.

"It's just one guy," someone shouted. "Kill him!"

They started to give chase, exactly as Peter had hoped. Then one of the beams struck him as it chanced over his position, then quickly reoriented and fixed on his back.

"There he is!" a voice shouted.

Peter had no choice. He hit the ground hard, diving behind a narrow tree. Muddy soil and bark erupted all around as his pursuers fired on the light, focused squarely on the tree he was behind. It wasn't enough cover. As soon as the idiot with the light lowered the beam, they would get him. He started to roll away, hoping to find a better position, when the light came down and hit him right in the face. A steady stream of gunfire erupted, and Peter knew he was done for. If that beam hadn't found him, his plan would have worked.

He spun around, hoping to lay down enough fire to force them to take cover, and immediately realized that they were already behind cover, and they weren't the ones shooting.

It was Penny. The big rifle rocked the night with a steady rat-tat-tat as she fired on the thug's position in exactly the manner he had instructed. Wasting no time, he brought up his weapon and gauged the situation. Penny was firing from his left, and they taken cover against that fire, foolishly forgetting about Peter. He had killed or wounded three of them in the camp and there were four huddled in front of him.

He took aim, fired. Took aim, fired. Two of them dropped while a third flattened himself against the ground. The fourth whirled on Peter, forgetting about Penny. The suppressive fire died, and Peter was momentarily overcome with dread. Had there been another one? Had he gotten to Penny?

A single shot, and the fourth man's head split like a coconut, a large piece of skull detaching from the whole, then the suppressive fire resumed. She had been aiming.

"Hot damn, woman," Peter murmured, then aimed at the last one, lying prone, protected from Penny's fire, but not from him. He fired three times.

Climbing to his feet, he advanced on the thugs' position, weapon held at the ready.

"Penny cease fire!" he yelled, waving his left hand. "Cease fire!" Somehow she heard him, or saw him approaching, and stopped shooting. Two of the thugs were crawling. He fired, four times into each man, then dropped his magazine, fishing for a new one from a vest pocket. He managed to insert it into the magazine well despite shaking hands, then hit the bolt release and continued his advance toward their camp.

There was one still alive there, bleeding from a shoulder wound, rifle in hand. He heard Peter, but never saw him. Two shots to the torso ended him. Taking cover just outside the camp, Peter waited, and listened. The only thing he heard were the woman's sobs.

He doubled back to Penny's position, relieved to find that she was alright.

"You were amazing," he said. "Absolutely brilliant."

He saw her smile, but also noticed the way she trembled. "Thank you." She pulled off her goggles and wiped her brow with the sleeve of her jacket.

"You saved my life," he said, then lifted his goggles, leaned close and kissed her on the cheek. Or at least he tried to. In the darkness he found her lips instead. Had she moved to meet him? The kiss had been an impulse that he hadn't thought to resist in the excitement of the moment. As her lips met his, he felt the rapid beating of her heart. She was terrified.

"Oh shit," he said, pulling away quickly. "I'm sorry. I don't know what I was thinking."

"No," she said. "It's okay."

"I'm just, you know, I mean…the fighting—"

"Peter, it's okay."

He could barely make out her face, let alone gauge her expression. He tried to read her tone, but there was too much going on in his head, so he just stared at her stupidly in the darkness. After a moment that seemed to last an eternity, he took the big rifle from her, swapped the almost empty magazine and handed the weapon back to her.

"Come on," he said. "We're going to reposition you. It'll be safer that way. I think they're all dead, but better safe than sorry."

She nodded, slung the weapon over her shoulder and followed him.

They made their way to the other side of the clearing, where Peter left her near a large gray boulder. She set up her weapon and crouched behind it, watching as he started to move towards the camp.

When he was near enough to see clearly, he stopped and waited, watching and listening.

The woman was still sobbing, oblivious to the shooting. She was in really bad shape, he realized, and wouldn't be easy to deal with. The soldier was struggling with his ropes, but he had no chance to free himself. The thugs had done a good job.

"What about you?" the soldier said to the other prisoner. "Can you get loose?"

"No," Long Hair replied. "Not a chance."

"Miss," the soldier said, turning to the girl. "Miss, please. We need to get loose. We don't know who that was they were shooting at, and we don't know who won. They could be back here at any minute. Don't you want to get away?"

The woman ignored him and continued sobbing.

"Fuck," the one with long hair said. "What the hell is wrong with her?"

"Give her a break," replied the soldier. "What those fucking animals did to her—"

"Her break is going to get us killed."

Deciding it was safe, Peter advanced into the camp, raising his goggles as he came near the fire. The soldier saw him right away.

"Who are you?" he demanded, his voice confident, projecting authority, as ludicrous as that seemed in his position.

"A friend," Peter said. "Are there any more of them?"

"How many did you kill?" he asked, wasting no time with stupid questions.

"Seven."

"That's all of them then."

"How sure are you?" Peter asked.

"One hundred percent."

Peter approached him, freed his knife from its sheath and cut the man's ropes. He noticed his name tag, but couldn't quite make it out in the dim light. The yellow bar in the center of his chest was clear though, as was the "US ARMY" patch. What the hell was an army lieutenant doing here, in uniform?

Once the soldier was free, Peter gave him the knife.

"Cut the other guy loose. I'll go check on the girl."

"Right," the lieutenant said as he climbed to his feet. Peter noticed him cringe and grab a hold of his ribs. They had probably beaten him, pretty badly by the look of it.

"Who are you, man?" the one with the long hair asked, but Peter ignored him. He walked over to the woman and knelt down. The firelight didn't reach there, so he flipped his goggles back down. She was worse off than he realized. Her face was badly discolored and swollen, and she had numerous bruises on her legs and buttocks. She was young, probably in her late twenties.

"Miss," he said, trying to keep his voice soft. "It's over now, they're dead."

A flash of light overwhelmed the goggles for a split second, followed by the loud pop of a distant explosion. A woman's scream filled the night.

Penny.

He wasn't aware of getting to his feet, but suddenly he was running, almost flying through the night. His weapon was held before him, the sight's red dot a glyph of death, ready to lay waste to everything in its path.

Another flash of light, and the world around him exploded. A crack of thunder so loud it was suddenly silent stopped him in his tracks. Everything was white. He was confused. He flipped up the goggles, but nothing changed. Slowly, shapes took form all around him. Crouching shapes, holding weapons, coming towards him. He felt his rifle yanked out of his hands, and before he could react he was knocked to the ground, face down in the mud. A needle pierced the skin behind his neck, and the white turned to black.

Chapter 13 – Fellowship

Ay, War, they say, is hell; it's heaven, too.
It lets a man discover what he's worth.
It takes his measure, shows what he can do,
Gives him a joy like nothing else on earth.
— Robert William Service

He woke slowly, looking around at the strange green walls. He was on a folding cot, also green, still dressed but without his weapons or vest. There were several other cots, all empty. He felt strange, as though coming down from a high. The room he was in resounded with rhythmic tapping, like an amplified recording of a thousand marching insects.

His first thought was that he had killed people, again. It was a strange sensation, like a pressure from some distant corner of his mind that was trying to force its way in. He could open the door and face what he had done, or he could push it aside, but in doing so leave it loose in the wilderness of his subconscious where it would be free to rampage unchecked.

I beheld the wretch — the miserable monster whom I had created. The words came to mind unbidden, not tangibly but as a fleeting thought, a companion to those remembered earlier, like a glimpse of a leaf carried away in the swirling eddies of gale force emotions. Freedom and power had a price.

He pushed the disturbing thought aside, and remembered that he had not been alone.

"Penny!" he shouted out as soon as he regained control of his mouth. "Penny!"

A canvas flap parted and a man walked in, a soldier, in full kit, covered almost head to toe in a digital pattern camouflage poncho. He had a rifle that he held casually at his side. Peter realized that they were in a tent, and that the tapping was rain. The soldier was dripping wet.

"Where's Penny?" Peter demanded as soon as he saw him. "Where the hell am I?" The soldier's poncho bulged around the shoulders and chest, indicating body armor. His uncovered Kevlar helmet dripped onto his shoulders.

"Relax, guy," the soldier said. "Your girlfriend's fine. She's with the doc." There wasn't much Peter could distinguish about the man's face by what was visible past the helmet, but he did notice that he was very young.

"Is she hurt?" Peter jumped to his feet, but his head rebelled, vision reeling, and he felt himself collapse. The soldier reached out to steady him, but couldn't stop him without dropping his weapon. Instead he guided Peter back onto the bunk, holding onto his collar.

"Take it easy, man. She's fine, I told you," the soldier explained. "The doc just wants to check her hearing, 'cause of the flashbang. He'll want to see you too."

"Flashbang? What's wrong with me? Why do I feel like shit?"

"The Rangers gave you guys a sedative. Should've worn off by now, you two slept through the night. Come on, sit up, I'll give you a hand." After helping him, the man turned his head to the tent entrance.

"Sergeant!" he shouted. Another soldier peeked inside and looked at Peter. His face was wider and harsher than the first soldier's, but Peter didn't care to notice anything beyond that. Where was Penny?

"Stay with him," the sergeant ordered. "I'll tell the colonel."

"I want to see Penny," Peter demanded.

The sergeant hesitated, annoyed. "I'll get her." He disappeared behind the flap.

"What's going on here?" Peter asked.

"The colonel will tell you."

Before he could say anything else, the tent flap parted and Penny rushed in. She ran to the bunk and threw herself into him, almost knocking him over. He grabbed her, feeling intense relief wash over him. She was wearing the same kind of poncho as the soldier was, hood down. He ran his hands through her wet hair.

"You're okay," he whispered, feeling a tear roll down her face.

She held him tightly, rocking back and forth on the cot.

"I was worried about you," he said.

"Everything's okay," she explained. "They're not going to hurt us."

"Who are these people," he asked her, pulling away just enough to look at her. "Why did they attack us?"

"Dude we didn't attack you," the soldier said irritably. "You're alive, aren't you?" Peter ignored him.

"I don't know," Penny said. "I only woke up a little while ago. They took me to their doctor."

"Are you hurt?"

"I'm fine, Peter, don't worry. And…you're like totally the goddamned Punisher! So fucking badass."

"The who?"

"Jesus Christ, Peter!"

The sergeant came back through the tent flap. "Sir," he said to Peter. "The colonel wants to see you."

He reached out to him, and Penny let him go, allowing the sergeant to help him to his feet. He felt unsteady, but didn't collapse again.

"Shouldn't he see the doctor?" Penny asked.

"He will," the sergeant explained. "After." He turned to the soldier. "Haggerdy, get this man a poncho, then you're relieved. Go get some chow."

"Thanks, Sarge," the soldier said, grabbing a folded poncho from a plastic container in the corner. He helped get it over Peter's head, then left the tent.

"What about you, miss?" the sergeant asked Penny. "Are you hungry?"

"I'll wait. I'm coming with him."

The man nodded, then put his hand under Peter's elbow, guiding him outside. The light was blinding, painful, but his eyes gradually adjusted, allowing him to take a look around. It wasn't as bright as he'd thought. Gray clouds rolled quickly across the sky, assaulting the camp with a heavy barrage of rain. There were several tents and many soldiers walking around, some in full kit, others in uniform and poncho. There were several humvees, a working generator, trucks—he even saw an Abrams tank in the distance. The aftereffects of the drug combined with the bizarre backdrop lulled him into a dreamlike fog. He stumbled on a small stone and almost fell, but Penny caught him in time.

"Maybe he *should* see the doc," the sergeant grumbled.

"No," Peter insisted. "I'm okay. Just a little light headed." The footing here was treacherous. The soil was muddy under the grass, and the constant runoff from the endless rain was carving channels into the earth, most of which overflowed into massive puddles that covered rocks and depressions.

The sergeant led them to another tent, smaller than the first. Inside was a man seated behind a table, shuffling through a stack of papers. About a dozen folding chairs stood in rows in front of the desk, and a whiteboard with some sort of intricate hand drawn grid occupied the space behind it. The man, a full bird colonel, looked up at them as they entered. He was narrow faced with short cropped gray hair, probably in his fifties. Hard eyes, but not unkind, with lines around the edges that suggested he was used to smiling. His skin was deeply tanned, and Peter realized for the first time that most of the soldiers he'd seen were wearing desert pattern camouflage under their digital green rain gear.

"Thank you sergeant," the colonel said, his voice surprisingly soft, yet giving up none of the authority Peter would expect from someone of his rank. "You're dismissed."

"Yes sir." The sergeant spun on his feet and left the tent.

"Please," the colonel said. "Have a seat. Anywhere you'd like."

Exchanging nervous glances with Penny, Peter approached the front row of chairs. Before he could sit, the colonel stood and extended his hand from across the table. Peter took it. The man's grip was firm, but not overbearing.

"I'm Colonel Hamilton," he said. "United States Army." He let go of Peter's hand and extended his to Penny, who shook it hesitantly.

"Peter," he said as he and Penny sat down. "Peter Anderson."

"And you, young lady?" the colonel asked Penny.

"Penny," she said, and didn't offer anything else. Peter understood her hesitation, and hoped the colonel wouldn't press.

"I'm very pleased to meet the both of you," he said, motioning for them to sit. "I understand I am in your debt."

"You are?" Peter asked, confused. "I don't understand…we were attacked, drugged…"

"Necessary precautions," the colonel explained. "We were mounting a rescue operation of our own, but you got there first. We saw you free my officer, but we couldn't take any chances."

"The lieutenant?" Peter asked.

The colonel nodded. "We lost one of our birds a week ago…it's hard to keep them in the air without proper facilities. The pilot was killed, but the lieutenant survived. He was trying to make his way back when our friends got their hands on him. I understand he was not particularly well treated."

"One of your birds? You had a helicopter?"

"We have a few," the colonel said. "I pieced together whatever I could. We're a mish-mashed outfit, but we're all that's left, at least here on the east coast."

Peter shook his head. "I don't understand…how did you survive the snow? Do you know what happened? Are there others? Can you contact anyone?"

The colonel held up his hands defensively and smiled. "Mr. Anderson, please. I don't have the answers you're looking for. We had advance warning of the tsunami and were able to make it to higher elevations. We had no idea how bad it was going to be…a lot of us just didn't get high enough."

A tsunami! That explained the damaged they had seen on the road before the new coast. Not a single building left standing, but roads still passable. That was typical of the photos he'd seen from the tsunami in Japan in 2011.

"Tsunami?" Penny said, suddenly animate. "There was a tsunami? What was the amplitude? Do you know what caused it?"

The colonel shook his head, still smiling. "Miss, I'm a mechanical engineer, I don't know anything about tsunamis." He turned to Peter. "National Guard," he explained. "A lot of us are regular army, air force…we even have some marines and navy. Most of us were just back from deployment."

"So a tsunami caused all this?" Peter asked, fighting disappointment. He had lived with the mystery for so long, such a simple answer was a letdown. It was a ridiculous reaction, he knew that, but he couldn't help it.

"Oh no," the colonel said, shaking his head. "That much I do know. The tsunami was just a symptom. Whatever caused this created tsunamis all over the world. I don't think there's anyone left alive who was at less than a thousand feet up on the whole damned planet."

"It reached that high?" Penny asked, her mouth hanging open. "That's not possible!"

"Oh, it *is* possible," he said. "Because it happened. I was in a helicopter over New York City, after the blast wave…"

"Blast wave?" Penny said. Her mouth was dropping lower with every word the colonel said. "Was it an asteroid? A bomb of some kind?"

The colonel continued to shake his head. "Miss, I want answers as badly as you do. All I know is that there was an event, somewhere in the southern hemisphere. The event caused blast waves traveling at supersonic speeds. There wasn't enough time to ground the airliners…" he trailed off, looking pained. "Not that it would have made a difference. There were also seismic events, but those were barely more than minor tremors by the time they got here. God knows how bad it was further south." He spoke with clearly defined words and carefully calculated pauses. He didn't string syllables together or use filler words the way most people did. Despite his surroundings, the colonel was neatly shaven, his hair combed, uniform clean and pressed. An impressive man.

"You said you were over New York City?" Peter asked, though it was hard to force the words. He didn't want to know.

The colonel looked distant. "Narrows bay was dry," he said, speaking softly. "I'd never seen anything like it. Then the water came. It was high, massive, like you'd see in the movies, not like it's supposed to be, not a gradual rise. It smashed and just kept going, around all the buildings, and as it got closer inland it just kept getting higher and higher. We followed it up to Bear Mountain by West Point, but it just kept going. It stopped just past the academy. Before it had much of a chance to fall back, another one came, then another. By the time they stopped…" He turned away.

"How far did the water get?" Penny asked. "In relation to where it is now?"

"Much higher, several hundred feet, maybe as much as a thousand."

"What about after it receded?"

"I don't have exact figures, but definitely a lot lower than it is now," the colonel explained. "The snow and the runoff brought it up to its current level."

"That's just not possible," she said softly, but the colonel misunderstood her objection and didn't respond.

"So it's not just here," Peter mumbled, struggling to imagine such devastation on a global scale.

"No," the colonel said somberly. "Not just here. We've been able to contact some other units on satellite phones. Some out by Colorado, Idaho, Wyoming, California. Things are a little better over there, a lot more infrastructure survived, but the human casualties were almost total, like here. Everywhere there are mountains high enough, though, some people survived."

"What about the Navy?" Peter asked.

The colonel stared at him, head tilted sideways as though waiting for him to come to his own conclusion.

"Tsunamis aren't dangerous to ships…" Penny started to say, then looked away, her lips moving silently like she was trying to figure something out.

"This one was," the colonel said simply. "We've been able to make contact with a few ships, submarines, smaller vessels, maybe there are more, but…we'll just have to wait and see."

They sat in silence for a moment, absorbing.

"Are we prisoners?" Peter asked, finally able to let go of the grim picture the colonel had painted.

"Of course not. You risked your lives to save my officer, and that's not something I'll soon forget. In any case, we're not here to take prisoners, we're here to establish order. Make sure animals like those don't have the run of things. That poor young lady…"

"Is she okay?" Peter asked.

"Physically," the colonel said. "She'll recover, but as to the rest, I can't say. She's with the doc. He has her sedated."

"So we can have our weapons back?" Peter asked.

"This is still America." The colonel smiled sadly. "Maybe now more than ever. We have your vehicle as well. We put your things in the trailer."

"Thank you. Can you tell us where we are?"

"Not far from where you were, about two miles. We're pulling

up camp soon, heading inland. We've heard of communities forming, and we're going to see what we can do to help. Rebuild roads,
that sort of thing."

Peter cringed, thinking back to the people from whom they
were running.

"The other one," the colonel said. "The one with the long hair,
was he with you?"

"No," Peter said. "We don't know him."

"You knew the girl then? I'm very sorry…"

"No."

The colonel frowned. "You didn't know any of them? Why did
you engage then?"

Peter shrugged. "It had to be done."

"Indeed." The colonel got to his feet. "You two must be hungry. I insist you have dinner with me and my officers."

"Thank you sir," Peter said. "We'd like that."

After donning a poncho, the colonel led them to a larger tent
arrayed with tables and chairs. It was noisy, dozens of voices
clamoring over one another in a cacophony of concordant rhythms.
It was one of the most beautiful and frightening sounds Peter had
ever heard. His survival instincts, focused on the safety of solitude,
screamed at him to flee, while nostalgia and the sheer joy of seeing
so many human beings in one place were almost overwhelming.
He looked at Penny, and noticed that her eyes were moist. He took
her hand in his, and she squeezed it tightly.

Chapter 14 – Remittance

Not yet will those measureless fields be green again
Where only yesterday the wild sweet blood
of wonderful youth was shed;
There is a grave whose earth must hold too long,
too deep a stain,
Though for ever over it we may speak
as proudly as we may tread.
- Charlotte Mary Mew

"You're ex-military, aren't you?" the colonel asked, holding a piece of baguette dripping with gravy. They had a fully functioning field kitchen, and Peter was eating real food for the first time since he could remember. It was just meat loaf and mashed potatoes, but it was wonderful. Penny, sitting next to him, seemed lost in her meal, perhaps afraid to call attention to herself.

"Just a little bit," he explained.

"A little bit?" said Sullivan, an air force major the colonel had introduced as his executive officer. "Isn't that like being a little bit pregnant?" He was a balding man with a thin mustache and a friendly face.

A few of the others laughed. The lieutenant that Peter had rescued was nowhere in sight, but that didn't surprise him. The man had been badly hurt. He was probably in the medical pavilion with the other rescued prisoners.

"Lieutenant J.G.," Peter said. "Navy. Public Relations."

"You did good work," the colonel said. "We saw the tail end, how you led them across the young lady's field of fire. That heavy barreled rifle of yours can lay down some serious fire for a civilian weapon. They teach you that in public relations school?"

"No sir," Peter said. "I, uh, I was almost a Seal."

"Almost?"

"I injured out of SQT, two weeks to go."

The colonel nodded. "Special warfare training. That's good. I could use a man like you. You're handy with a carbine, and your heart's in the right place. We're going to be building something here, working with local communities. There aren't many survivors, but I hope there are enough."

"Enough?" Peter asked, not sure what he meant.

"To rebuild," the colonel explained. "To grow food, to survive. A third of the world's population lived at less than one hundred meters above sea level, the old sea level. If I've done my math correctly, that would mean that about fifty perfect lived at two hundred meters. That accounts for everyone either drowned or killed by the tsunami, though that's being conservative. As I've said, I think it reached higher than that. The rest have had to survive four months of snow or rain, depending on where they were, and a complete breakdown of the global distribution system. Not to mention the fact that I don't think too many people in the southern hemisphere survived the event itself."

"Distribution system?" Peter asked. "You mean like deliveries? Supplies?"

"Everything," the colonel explained. "Food, medicine, electricity. Most of the world is divided into specialized zones…agriculture, industry. You can raise enough cattle in Texas to feed the whole country, but what good would that do Rhode Island if there's no way to get it there? How long do you think a big city like New York would last if it was cut off from the outside? Or Denver, since that one probably survived the tsunami."

"I guess until the food ran out, then…" he stopped, not wanting to imagine what would happen after that. Once all the pets were gone, there would be only one thing left to eat.

"You're starting to see the big picture," Major Sullivan said, looking grim. "North of here we…"

The colonel cleared his throat and raised an eyebrow, and the major stopped talking immediately.

"Sorry sir."

"What is it?" Peter asked. "What don't you want us to hear?"

The colonel looked at Penny, then at Peter. "Spare the grizzly details, Hank," he said after a moment of contemplation. "But I suppose they have a right to know."

Penny looked up, curious.

The major nodded. "We were crossing the Twin Cities Channel about a week ago—"

"Twin Cities?" Peter asked. "Minneapolis and St. Paul?"

"Not quite," the colonel explained. "It's a macabre name the men have taken to calling the channel between the two islands."

"I'm confused," Peter confessed. "What islands?"

"You mean the mountain ranges, don't you?" Penny asked grimly.

The colonel nodded. "Yes, miss, the mountain ranges."

"There are three major islands in our new world," Major Sullivan explained. "The Adirondacks, the Green and Taconic mountains, and the Catskills, though the Greens and the Catskills aren't discreet land masses. They merge into the Appalachians running northeast in to Canada and southwest into Pennsyltucky."

"Pennsyltucky?" It was Penny's turn to be confused.

Peter smiled. "It's what some people call western Pennsylvania. Because it's so rural and remote. Like Kentucky."

"Oh."

"My apologies," the major said. "I'll try to refrain from colloquialisms."

"Why do you call it the Twin Cities Channel?" Peter asked. "The crossing between the islands…"

"It…" The major hesitated. "It goes right over what used to be Albany and Schenectady. There are some parts of Albany that are still above sea level, like scattered little islands. Our navy guys sent divers down into the cities, they brought up video..."

"It was one of the most disturbing things I've ever seen," the colonel cut in. "After the tsunami, that is. An American city, underwater. Most of the concrete and stone buildings are still standing down there."

Peter tried to picture the new landscape of the American northeast, but his imagination balked. Life had been much simpler when it was just him and his rifle in the cabin. Turning to Penny, he quashed what little nostalgia he had left. His life had been almost unbearable before she came. Why did he have to keep reminding himself of that?

"So we crossed the channel," the major continued. "Our plan was to head south along the eastern coast, look for survivors, but we found people close to our landing site. There was a university there, and..." the major stopped, looking pained. "What we saw..."

"Just say it," the colonel said.

"They were eating each other," the major said hoarsely, his throat dry. "There was a group of kids that took over, locked the rest up, like farm animals. Some of them..."

"No details, major," the colonel warned.

"Sorry sir," the major apologized. Peter was surprised to see the hint of tears in the man's eyes. Even the colonel looked stricken. What could they have seen that had so horrified men like these?

"What did you do?" Peter asked. His imagination was tormenting him, trying to fill in the details they were leaving out. He tried not to remember that Penny had been a college student.

"We fucking killed them," the colonel said coldly. Peter blinked, not expecting such language or such harshness from the colonel.

"We put them in an abandoned house and set it on fire," the major explained. The colonel did not object. This detail, it seemed, was okay. "They weren't worth the bullets it would have taken."

"Did any of the..." Peter hesitated. "You know, the victims...did any of the victims make it?"

"They were pretty bad," the major explained. "They didn't feed them much...they looked like concentration camp survivors, but yeah, most of them made it. There was another band of survivors in a nearby town, and they took them in."

They ate in silence for a few minutes. Peter wanted to ask questions, wanted more details, but he knew he was better off not knowing. He wished they had never told him in the first place.

"So as I said," the colonel said suddenly. "I could use a man like you. What do you say?"

"What?" Peter didn't understand what he meant, lost in his thoughts. "Oh, sorry, colonel I was just...trying not to think. Thank you, sir, but I don't think so. Penny and I just want to build a quiet life for ourselves, away from people. At least for a while..."

"I understand," the colonel said. "I wish you the best of luck. If you change your mind, you let me know. I'm sure we'll be seeing each other again. It's a small world now, literally."

"Thank you, sir. Where will you go, exactly?"

"There's a town not far from here," the major said. "One of the larger clumps of survivors is congregated there."

"I know the one," Peter said, scowling to himself. Why did the universe seem hell-bent on leading him back to that infernal place? "My house is near there. Part of the town, technically. At least it *was* my house. What will you do?"

"Keep order, let the people do their thing. We have over two hundred men here, and those men will need food once our supplies run out. We plan to establish communications among all the settlements, maybe move some closer together. We need to get people farming again, raising livestock."

"I wish you luck," Peter said. "We're fortunate to have you."

"This house of yours," the colonel said, looking like he just had an idea. "Is there a lot of open land around it?"

"Yes, why?"

"How many open, flat acres? Mostly flat, at least."

"Eight, nine."

"How far from the town center?"

"Three miles from the village, but—"

"How about you do me another favor?"

"Name it," Peter said.

"I'm going to need a command center in the area," the colonel explained. "At least temporarily. I was going to seize an abandoned house, but it would go over better with the locals if we had an owner's permission. They wouldn't take kindly to us just seizing something they probably see as their property, and we need all the good will we can get right now. How about I use your place? It sounds perfect for what I need…lots of space to pitch the tents and land my birds. We won't damage anything and we'll even make repairs for when you come back."

Peter shrugged. "Sure, I guess. I just don't understand…how could someone's permission make much difference? I mean with the way things are…" He had wanted to say he had no intention of ever returning, but stopped himself, afraid that it would sound suspicious. Why leave a perfectly good house next to a band of survivors? The colonel was being polite and not asking any questions. It would be best not to give him any more reasons to be curious.

"It does to me. If we're going to restore order, we need to foster respect for property. If I tell people I have your permission, that shows that we respect their property, which will build trust. Trust is the most important commodity now."

Peter thought about it, liking the idea. He knew he would never see the house again, but just knowing that it was still there, still his, made him feel a lot better.

"That would be great, actually," he said. "Thank you, sir. Just don't use too much of my propane." He smiled, intending it as a joke, but the colonel took him seriously.

"We won't."

After the meal, the colonel sent a soldier to show them to the jeep, which they had moved to the outskirts of their camp. They had set up on what was once a cornfield, now just a muddy patch of flat ground by the side of the road. Soldiers were busy tearing down the tents, preparing for departure. The rain had come to a complete stop, and the sun shone down from a clear blue sky. Their escort left them at the jeep, parked next to a cargo humvee being loaded with large stainless steel cooking pots.

"It's beautiful," Peter said, looking up at the fiery orb, feeling its warmth on his face.

"That's twice," Penny said once they were alone, a trace of sadness in her voice. He remembered saying that same thing to her, though he doubted the context was related.

"Twice what?"

"Twice you've had to give up a better life because of me."

"No way," he said. "The colonel is a nice guy, but I like my independence. I'm looking forward to being back on the road, just the two of us."

"Really?"

"Really."

"Mr. Anderson?" a familiar voice called out. Peter turned to look and saw the lieutenant he had saved from the skinheads. He was walking towards him, leading a column of soldiers. He walked with a slight limp, but seemed all right otherwise.

"Hello again, lieutenant..." Peter said with an exaggerated pause. The man was still wearing his poncho and he couldn't see his name. As he neared them, the soldiers following him came to a crisp halt.

"Goldstein," he said.

"Peter Anderson."

"Penny."

"Pleased to meet you both," the lieutenant said. He spoke in a pleasant southern drawl, something Peter had never noticed before.

"How are you holding up?" Peter asked. His face was badly discolored on one side, the wounds partially obscured by clean white bandages.

"Fine," he said. "A couple of broken ribs, but I'll live. I wanted to thank you before we pulled out. Both of you," he said, turning to look at Penny. "On behalf of me and my men. They asked me to express their appreciation. You saved my life."

Peter waved it off. "Nah. Your guys were just about to rescue you anyway. We didn't do anything."

"You didn't know that, and it doesn't matter. I'm in your debt. Yours too, miss."

"Glad to help," Penny said, smiling at him. Even under the bandages, the man was very handsome. He had sharply defined features, short sandy hair and piercing eyes. For just a brief moment, Peter almost wanted to put him back where he found him. He looked back at his soldiers, and noticed something different about their uniforms.

"Aren't those…"

"Jarheads?" the lieutenant said, grinning. "They were strays. I sort of adopted them."

"Oohrah!" the marines shouted in unison, startling Penny. Their combined voice was formidable.

"I wish I could get them to stop doing that," Goldstein said.

"OOHRAH!" the marines shouted again, even louder.

"I can see how that can get annoying," Peter said, and found himself liking Lieutenant Goldstein.

"What were they going to do with you?" Penny said. "The skinheads, or whatever they were. No offense, but why keep you alive?"

"I'm pretty certain they were going to eat us," Goldstein said. "Either that or…well, I think I'd rather be eaten." He laughed. Peter smiled, appreciating the man's ability to find humor in a situation that had almost killed him, or worse.

"Best of luck to you, lieutenant," Peter said. "Your colonel seems like a good man, and the work he's doing is important."

"Thank you. We couldn't have asked for a better CO." The lieutenant reached out to shake Peter's hand, then turned to Penny, took her hand in his and kissed it.

"Stay safe you two," he said, then turned to his men. "Move out, marines!"

"Oohrah!"

Peter watched them march away and muttered, "Jarheads."

Once they were gone, he looked in the back of their trailer. The colonel had told the truth, as he had expected. All of their weapons and equipment had been returned, even the empty magazines he had dropped in the mud. He was also surprised to find three cases of MREs.

By the time he turned his attention back to the soldiers, they had broken their camp and were rolling out slowly, moving onto the road and heading west. Penny walked up to him and they stood close together as they watched the convoy pull off of the field and onto the cracked asphalt, spitting up mud as the humvees and trucks struggled for traction. Peter also counted four Abrams tanks and five Bradley fighting vehicles along with several fuel tankers and cargo trucks—an impressive fleet. The helicopters had been nowhere in sight, but as the convoy got under way he heard their rotors and soon counted a pair of gunships and a Blackhawk cargo bird as they flew overhead and disappeared over the treetops to the west.

He noticed a pile of junk the convoy had left behind, mostly cardboard boxes, and was about to go see if any of it could be useful when Penny pulled on his sleeve.

"Peter look," she said, pointing to the empty camp. They were not the only ones left behind. The long haired man they'd rescued was walking towards them, waving.

Chapter 15 – Opportunity

He rose at dawn and, fired with hope,
Shot o'er the seething harbour-bar,
And reach'd the ship and caught the rope,
And whistled to the morning star.
- Alfred, Lord Tennyson

Peter hated him right away. He was tall, several inches over six feet and not at all lanky. His shoulder length blond hair fell artfully around a face with high cheek bones and a strong nose. The worst thing about him were his eyes, brilliant green, looking both intelligent and expressive. He carried a yellow fuel jug, presumably filled with diesel. Peter noticed Penny studying him as he approached.

"Heya," he said cheerfully. "Thought I'd be the only one left behind." His voice was vigorous and friendly. He was probably in his mid to late twenties. His gaze lingered on Penny.

When Peter didn't reply, Penny introduced them. "Brad, this is Peter, Peter, this is Brad. Brad and I met briefly, when the doctor was examining me."

"Where are you headed?" Peter asked, studying him carefully. He did not appear to be armed, which was odd, considering the colonel would have had no problem giving him one of the captured weapons if he had claimed it as his own. What was he doing wandering around without the ability to defend himself? Or, for that matter, with a jug of diesel fuel without a truck to put it in?

"Nowhere specific," he said. "Need to find some things, then I'm heading back home. I just wanted to thank the two of you for saving me, I know you didn't have to, and I want you to know I appreciate it very much, for what it's worth."

"You're very welcome," Penny said, smiling.

"Yeah," Peter echoed without much enthusiasm.

"Well," Brad continued. "I'd love to stay and chat, but unless you have some diesel fuel you want to part with or one of you knows how to sail a boat, I've got to get going. My little brush with death has already cost me too much time."

He turned to leave, and Peter almost didn't say anything. Had his time in solitude not compromised his brain-to-mouth filter, he probably would have kept quiet.

"I know how to sail," he said, regretting it even as the words left his mouth. Brad whirled on him.

"Really? I just asked as a joke, actually, but…like a casual sailor?" he asked. "Or…"

"I can sail the pope into a whorehouse on Sunday morning." It was something he used to say, back when he had his boat. He hadn't wanted to say it, but it came out, and the words were accompanied by brief but powerful memories. The feel of the deck dropping under his feet as he crested a breaker, the strain of the rigging as the wind caught the sails. It had been too easy to pretend he hadn't missed it.

"Seriously?" Brad asked, seeming hesitant to accept it.

"Seriously," Peter explained patiently. "I owned a boat for many years, sailed all over the place."

"*Sail* sail?" he asked. It wasn't a stupid question, some people used the word "sail" whether their boat was powered by wind or diesel. Ah, diesel. Now it made sense—the larger sailboats had auxiliary diesel engines.

"As in the big white things that fill with wind, yes."

"You *sail* too?" Penny asked, shaking her head. "Is there anything you don't know how to do? How come you never told me?"

He shrugged. "I guess it never came up. Plus what possible use…" he hesitated. "I'm a moron, aren't I?" They were living on what was essentially a chain of small islands, and Peter never bothered to recognize the importance of knowing how to sail a boat. He had to get his mind around the fact that they weren't in the mountains anymore.

Penny smiled. "Little bit, yeah."

Brad hesitated, contemplating something. "Do you think you could….we have a…I guess I can trust you, right? I mean you saved my life and all that…"

"Spit it out," Peter said. "What do you need?"

"Our boat ran aground," he blurted out. "Not far from here. I took the dinghy and went to look for diesel fuel, that's when…you know…"

"Who's we?" Penny asked.

"Some friends, colleagues…"

"Why diesel fuel?" Peter asked. "You wanted to power off?"

"Yeah. The others thought that would be the only way. We burned through all our diesel getting up here, so…"

"What about the tides?"

"The keel punched through a roof," he explained. "It just goes up and down, deeper into the house. It happened during high tide, so that's no help."

"You dove under the boat?" Peter was surprised. "Isn't the water freezing?"

Brad shook his head. "No need. We had a camera we lowered down."

"I see. How far in is it at high tide?"

"The keel? I'm not sure, a good couple of feet, I think."

"That doesn't sound like much of a problem. Is there no one on this boat of yours that knows what he's doing?"

Brad frowned, as though about to protest, but changed his mind. "Not so much, no. I can put up the sails and get the boat moving if the wind is right, but none of us are sailors. That's why we used up all of our fuel."

"I guess I can help," Peter said. "If it doesn't take too long. I just want to check out the stuff the soldiers left first, see if we could use any of it."

"Thanks, man," Brad said. "Take your time."

They searched through the junk and found a couple of items that Peter thought would be useful. One foam lined hard case that would fit several full sized rifles, and a fragment of camouflage netting used for concealing vehicles from aerial observation. The case was cracked, but repairable, and the net fragment was just a small piece by military standards, but more than enough to use for his jeep, though it would not cover the trailer.

After loading the loot, Peter made room in the back seat for Brad and they set off towards the coastline.

"I'm not sure I can get us there like this," Brad said. "I wasn't in a car."

"You mean where you left your dinghy?"

"Yeah."

"How were you planning on finding it?" Peter asked.

"The army guys told me where the dead assholes' camp was. I was going to go there and back track. From there, I'm pretty sure I can find it."

"We're headed there now. In the mean time, can you think of any landmarks? Most of the road signs are still standing...hard to wash them away, I guess."

"Um...yeah, there was something...I can't quite piece it together though."

"What's the first thing that comes to you?"

"Diarrhea Road?" he said, looking embarrassed. Penny laughed.

"Diandrea?"

"That's it!" Brad said excitedly. "Is that near here?"

"It's actually right down the road. There are only two signs like that, within minutes of each other. It's a small semi-private road. I knew someone that lived there..." He didn't let himself finish. That person was now dead.

"Well at least something turned out right," Brad commented. "I went south for the better part of a day before I ran into those bastards. At least they had the decency to take me almost all the way back to where I came from. That's a bit of luck right there."

Peter couldn't agree more. The faster he helped these people, the sooner he could get Penny away from this surfer-dude lookalike. He knew his feelings were irrational. It wasn't as though their relationship was a romantic one, but as long as he and Penny were alone together, things felt right, and he wanted to keep it that way for as long as possible. The thought of her leaving him alone was terrifying.

Slowing down to pass a badly damaged section of road, they once again came into view of the new coast. It was every bit as breathtaking as before, and every bit as unsettling.

"It should be right over there," Brad said, pointing. "I pulled it into some bushes, but it's pretty big, if anyone saw it..."

Peter drove the jeep down the embankment, careful not to tip the trailer, and parked it behind a cluster of trees. He covered it

with the camouflage net and some scattered branches with remnants of leaves still clinging to them. It wasn't the best hiding
place, but at least it wasn't in plain sight.

"How far away is the boat? Will we be gone long?" Peter
asked as they got out.

"It's about a ten minute ride by tender."

"Should be fine," Peter mumbled.

"You guys pack some serious firepower," Brad commented as
Peter handed Penny her rifle and clipped his own into his tactical
sling.

"Haven't you heard?" Penny said. "There's an apocalypse on."

"Cheeky," Brad said, grinning. "I like that." He turned to Peter. "You should keep an eye on your daughter, sir, a pretty girl
like that is bound to cause trouble."

Peter recoiled as though struck. His *daughter*?

"He's not my father you idiot!" Penny snapped. Peter could
hear the anger in her voice, but was there something else? Shame?
He felt a profound sense of despair starting to take root as he
walked, staring straight ahead, not wanting to look at anyone.

"Oh man I'm sorry…" Brad started.

"He was a small child when I was born," she continued, still
angry.

"No, you're right, I'm sorry, I just wasn't thinking. So you two
are…"

"I think you should shut up now," Penny said sternly.

"Right, shutting up. I'm sorry man, I didn't mean anything."
He sounded very embarrassed, but Peter didn't look at him.

"Forget it," he grumbled. "Let's just find this thing and get it
over with."

They walked for several minutes before they spotted the boat.
It was a large inflatable, about twenty feet long, with a rigid fiber-
glass bottom and a center console with a steering wheel. The words
"TT Archangel" were painted on the side.

"That's some dinghy," Peter said, admiring the boat despite his
sour mood. His own had been a fraction of that size and lacked a
rigid hull. Where his modest tender got by with a two horsepower
outboard, this dinghy sported a seventy five horsepower fuel-
injected Honda four stroke. "This thing must fly."

"Strange name for a little boat," Penny said. "Archangel."

"TT stands for 'tender to,'" Peter explained. "This boat is just a yacht tender, people use them to get to shore and ferry supplies and stuff. The yacht it tenders is called Archangel."

"My turn I guess," she said, grinning.

"Your turn?"

"To be a moron." She smiled at him. "I can't say I didn't have it coming." She turned to Brad. "Sorry I called you an idiot, before."

"Nah," he said, sounding sincere. "I deserved it."

Looking at Penny, Peter said, "A very smart person I know once said 'knowledge and brains aren't the same thing.'"

"Who was that?" she asked.

"You."

She beamed at him. "Now you know why I like you."

He opened his mouth to respond, but she had already walked off to get on the other side of the inflatable. He noticed Brad looking at him, but he turned away as soon as he was spotted. Not very difficult to see what was going on. He should have kept his mouth shut about knowing how to sail.

Pushing the tender back into the water proved a lot harder than Peter imagined. The three of them barely managed it. It wasn't much easier to board the boat without getting their feet wet, but they managed that too. The motor came to life with the push of a button, and in moments they were flying across the mostly calm water, hair flapping wildly in the wind. It wasn't particularly cold out. The rain had not returned, and the wind actually brought some relief from the overly heavy jacket Peter was wearing.

In just a few minutes they had crossed the bay between two mountain islands, losing sight of their starting point. A spray of icy water rewarded an overly aggressive turn as Brad took the tender around the edge of a natural jetty formed by a narrow ridge of rock that had once been the top of a terrestrial formation.

"I hope you know how to get back," Penny shouted over the engine's roar.

"No problem," Brad assured her.

Peter felt a nudge and turned to Penny, who was holding his phone with the GPS app active. She had apparently charged the battery.

"Look," she said, handing it to him.

"Sawkill," he said, fascinated by the display, which showed them moving across county route 30.

"It's crazy, isn't it?" she said.

"That about sums it up," he agreed.

"How are we going to live?" she asked suddenly. He looked at her, saw the doubt, the fear.

"We're going to be okay," he said. "Don't you worry about it."

"I can't not worry."

"Then let me worry for you," he said. "I'm better at it than you are." He smiled, and so did she.

"Do you have a plan?" she said.

"Not yet," he continued. "But for starters, I think we're going to be fishing a lot."

She laughed, then her expression turned serious. "Are *you* okay?" she asked him.

"What do you mean?"

"About what he said…"

He shrugged. "Yeah, sure, I'm fine." He wondered why she would ask him, why she cared.

"Liar. Forget what he said. It's not important. It doesn't matter to me, and it shouldn't matter to you. Besides, I'd bet he never even thought that and was just fishing for information."

"There she is!" Brad shouted, pointing with his free hand. Peter looked, and gaped. Brad pulled back on the throttle and the tender settled into the water, quietly gliding forward. Peter stared at the approaching yacht, a stately bastion of civilization sitting calmly among the aftermath of Armageddon.

"That's the biggest sloop I've ever seen," he said. "It must be a hundred feet long and as wide as my house."

"Ninety five," Brad corrected. "With a twenty three foot beam."

"What's a sloop?" Penny asked.

"It's a type of rig," Peter explained. "One headsail, one mainsail. It's the typical triangle shape you see in most small sailboats. Although technically that's a cutter rigged sloop. See the multiple headsails?"

"What am I looking for?"

"See those thick tubes going from the top of the mast to the bow…the front of the boat?"

"Yeah, there are three of them. Those are sails?"

"Yes," he explained. "They're rolled up."

"She's a beauty," Brad said proudly. "Isn't she?"

"Yes," Peter agreed. "Why is the deck so cluttered? What is all that stuff?"

"Archangel is a research vessel," he explained. "Marine biology."

"You're a marine biologist?" Penny asked.

"Well yeah, most of us were. I'll fill you in once we're on board." Another almost physical blow. Not only was he young and handsome, he was also a scientist. As excited as he was to get a close look at the boat, he once again wished that he had just let him walk away.

"Marine biologists who don't know how to sail?" Peter asked.

"It's not as rare as you think," Brad explained. "Archangel is one of only two sail powered research vessels in the world…" he stopped suddenly, frowning. "Was, I mean. She's probably the only one now."

As they neared the boat, Peter saw people up on the deck. At first there were two men, then a woman came up from below. All made their way to the stern, where a tender lift was mounted above the transom. They looked apprehensively at Peter and Penny, and he quickly realized why. No one on the boat seemed to be armed.

"Ahoy there!" Brad called as he waved to them. "I brought help!" They exchanged anxious glances, but seemed to relax a bit. Two of them were older, a bearded man with thinning white hair and a woman with gray, while the third looked only a little older than Peter and had a full head of brown curls. They wore ill-fitting offshore sailing jackets, bright red with reflective patches.

"Who are your friends?" the oldest asked, eyeing Peter's rifle nervously. He was such a distinguished looking man that Peter had expected a British accent and was disappointed, though he did speak in a clear deep voice that would have made Colonel Hamilton jealous. He wore a pair of wire rimmed glasses over intense brown eyes that were in almost constant motion.

"Dad," Brad said as he pulled the tender up to the transom. "This gentleman is Peter, and the young lady is Penelope. Guys, this is Dr. Gable, my father."

Peter momentarily narrowed his eyes at Penny. She had never spoken her full name to him, but she must have told Brad. When had she had time? While he had been asleep in the military tent? She seemed embarrassed and was about to say something when Brad cut her off.

"They saved my life," he continued. "Peter is a sailor. He can help us."

"We thought something happened to you," the woman said. "We were so worried!" She was pleasant looking, though she wore no makeup and had her dark gray hair pulled back in a simple ponytail. She reminded Peter of one of his aunts.

"Something did happen to me, Di," Brad said. "But we can talk about that later." He turned to Peter. "This is Diana. Dr. Foster."

"A lot of doctors," Peter murmured, but no one heard him. The more things changed, the more they stayed the same. From military combat troops to PhDs, Peter once again found himself surrounded by people who had accomplished all the things that he had failed at.

"Let's get this thing stowed," Brad said. Peter supposed that he had a PhD also.

Between Brad and three on the boat, they got the tender secured to the lift and lowered a ladder. Peter set foot onto a sailboat for the first time in more than five years, and felt completely at home.

"Let's get to it," he said. "We've got a boat to move."

Chapter 16 – Destiny

And there is a Catskill eagle in some souls that can alike di-
ve down into the blackest gorges, and soar out of them again
and become invisible in the sunny spaces. And even if he for ev-
er flies within the gorge, that gorge is in the mountains; so that
even in his lowest swoop the mountain eagle is still higher than
other birds upon the plain,
even though they soar.
— Herman Melville

"First things first," Peter said as soon as he had everyone's attention. "I need to see what we're dealing with. Let's get that camera of yours down there."

The brown haired man, whom Brad had introduced as Dr. Burgoyne, looked displeased, but soon disappeared into the aft hatch. Peter was not familiar with the layout of the boat yet, but he did see that there were multiple egresses from the cabin. One in the center cockpit where the control pedestal was located and one in the aft cockpit that seemed to lead directly to the owner's stateroom, which as far as Peter could tell was filled with boxes and sail bags.

"Do you think you will be able to get us going?" Dr. Gable asked. Peter supposed they were both Dr. Gable, but he decided that Brad would just be Brad.

"The simple answer is yes," he said. "The only question is how." He noticed that they were all staring at his rifle, which hung muzzle down in front of his chest. When they weren't fixated on his, they were staring at Penny's, slung over her shoulder. She was looking around the boat, oblivious to their scrutiny.

"What are those?" she asked, pointing to large white drums mounted on the gunwale in the aft cockpit. There were lots of tubes all over the deck. Some ran from the drums to what looked like racks of polished aluminum disks covered with multiple blue anodized knobs. Various tubes were coiled around the discs as well. There was other equipment too, canisters, hoses, all manner of strange gear he couldn't identify. Peter would have thought that all this junk would make sailing the boat very difficult, but it was all positioned out of the way of the running rigging.

"Those are filters connected to pumps," Brad said. "They filter the larger particles out of the sea water…it's a twenty micron mesh. We used them to collect microorganisms. Those," he indicated the disks with the blue knobs. "Are the fine filters, progressively finer: three microns, point eight and point one. That's where we get our actual samples."

"I read about your expedition, I think," Penny said. "You wanted to decode the genomes of marine microorganisms, right?"

"Yes," Brad said, smiling broadly. Peter supposed it gratified him that she was familiar with his work. "We wanted to find new species and get a better idea of the roles they play. We actually know surprisingly little about them, considering how important they are. We were almost done too, on our last leg, when..."

"Brad," Burgoyne said, having emerged from the hatch with a small camera. "Help me rig it."

"Duty calls!" Brad said, and went to help Burgoyne. The two of them mounted the camera on a folding aluminum arm and lowered it over the side. Burgoyne produced a small monitor and Peter watched as he adjusted the arm to point the camera at the keel. The picture was very dark, but Brad flipped a knob on the arm and a powerful light revealed Archangel's deep fin keel poking through the peaked roof of a three story colonial, its pillars intact.

"Do you know the tide level?" Peter asked. "Is there a bulb on the tip of that keel?"

"The tide is close to its highest point," Burgoyne said. "We don't know about the keel. We only looked at it after it was stuck." He was definitely older than Peter, but not by much. Mid forties, if he had to guess. He was clean shaven with nondescript hair and eyes, both brown. His one distinguishing feature were his overly large teeth, which contributed to a slight lisp when he spoke.

"I don't get it," Peter said, slightly exasperated. "You guys are marine biologists, supposedly working off of this boat, but none of you seems to know much about it."

"None of us are sailors," Burgoyne explained, sounding annoyed. "The only people that really knew how to sail this boat were Devon and the crew, Matt, John and Ying Chih. They were all topside when it hit us."

"When what hit you?"

"Tsunami," the woman, Dr. Foster, said as she came up behind them. "Devon Howard was the leader of the expedition. He was at the helm when the first one hit." She didn't look comfortable talking about it, but there was a lot of that going around these days.

"Tsunami aren't supposed to be dangerous to boats at sea," Penny said. "In fact you're hardly supposed to notice them." Peter knew that she was fishing for information. She had heard what the colonel said about the naval ships and was probably curious. Peter's own curiosity flared when he realized that they were about to hear a firsthand account.

"This one was," Foster continued. "And it wasn't just the tsunami, there were blast waves. We were about twenty miles off the northern coast of Brazil, which I suppose didn't help. The first one wasn't so bad, although it jolted the hell out of us...we were all down below. The second one nearly capsized the boat. Then the tsunamis hit, and they did capsize us."

"That must have been some wave." Peter said, trying to imagine it.

"The boat rolled," she said. "There was a lot of wind. A normal tsunami is a big swell out on the open sea, this one was enormous. She righted herself, of course, as I understand keel boats are supposed to, but we were capsized twice more after that. No one who was out on deck managed to stay aboard. We looked for them for days, but..."

They were all silent for a moment, remembering, then Peter said, "Alright, let's get you people out of this hole and wherever the hell it is you're going. Brad, get that tender back in the water and bring it around to the bow. Penny, get me my phone please, I'd like to check the topo map for the area. Which of you is most familiar with the anchor windlass?"

"I am," Burgoyne said.

"Okay, go lower the smallest anchor you have into the tender. Don't actually drop it in, let it go until it's just in the water and have Brad scoop it up. Then set the windlass to free fall and leave it."

"The tender?" he asked. "What for?"

"Do you want to get moving or don't you?"

"I hope you know what you're doing," he grumbled, then headed forward.

"Is it bad?" Dr. Foster said suddenly. "Out there?" She was back to staring at his rifle. She was prettier up close than she had seemed before, and not quite as old as he had first thought, probably close to his age. Her gray hair and lack of makeup explained his initial impression.

"Out where?" Peter said. "Oh, on land. It can be, I guess. Brad certainly had a run of bad luck. There aren't that many people left out there. I'll tell you one thing, you people are crazy if you think you can get along without guns. A boat like this…you're lucky none of the nasty bastards spotted you yet."

"I don't like guns," she said.

"No offense, lady, but get real."

She didn't say anything and looked at Dr. Gable, who was approaching with uncertain steps. The old man kept looking at Brad, as though trying to get close to Peter without him noticing.

"Look, I didn't mean anything—" Peter started to apologize to Foster.

"What happened to my son?" Dr. Gable said, cutting him off. "Was he hurt?"

"Not really. We can talk about it later. Let me get you unstuck first, okay?"

The older man nodded.

"We have the anchor in the dinghy," Burgoyne shouted from the bow. "Now what?"

Peter turned to Penny and she handed him the phone. She had already pulled up the topographic map.

"Brad," Peter shouted. "Bring the anchor around to the port side."

"Aye aye skipper!" the young man shouted enthusiastically.

"I hope he knows what port is," Peter grumbled.

"He knows," Dr. Gable said.

When the dinghy was rubbing against the port hull, Peter turned to Gable.

"I'll need some snatch blocks, two should be enough."

"I don't know what those are," the man said. "I'm even less of a sailor than the others."

"If you describe them…" Dr. Foster suggested.

"They're like pulley blocks," Peter explained. "But they can open so that you can get them on a line without having to feed it in from one end."

"Got it."

Moments later, Foster brought Peter two large snatch blocks, which he clipped to the bow pulpit and the end of the boom. Archangel had an in-boom roller furling mainsail—the sail was rolled up into the boom with an electric winch, making it easy to raise and lower. Peter was hesitant to risk damaging the contraption with his plan, but decided the strain would be minor. Freeing the mainsheet, Peter swung the boom over to the edge of the boat.

He made his way to the bow, noticing the pilot house windows around the central cockpit for the first time. With its electric winches, the boat could be controlled from the inside. He briefly wondered why the expedition head and his crew hadn't been down there, but then realized there would be only so much one could do from an interior control station on a sail boat, even one as nice as this.

Once at the bow, he reached over the side and pulled up the anchor rode, then clipped it into the first snatch block. Walking back to the center of the boat, he had Brad hand him the rode and clipped it into the snatch block on the end of the boom, then swung the boom over the side of the boat so that it was perpendicular to the hull.

"Okay," he said. "Brad, take the dinghy a hundred yards out and drop the anchor."

"What are you planning?" Burgoyne asked as Brad pulled away, the outboard motor hardly above idle.

"It will be clear in a moment," Peter said. "But essentially I plan to heel the boat enough to pop it free of the house. Has someone dumped Brad's diesel into the tank?"

Burgoyne nodded.

"Good, then I'll need you to start the engine and stay at the helm. Get ready to throttle up when I tell you."

"Got it." Burgoyne went to the control pedestal and had the

engine idling quietly within seconds. When Brad signaled that the anchor was in the water, Peter went to the bow and found the windlass controls.

"Brace yourselves," he shouted, then engaged the anchor windlass.

The heavy drum began to turn, picking up the line. The snatch blocks snapped up to attention as pressure was applied, drawing the line tight. The boat began to heel almost immediately, but only a little. After a few seconds the boat lurched as the anchor bit into the bottom and held tight. The tip of Archangel's outstretched boom raced towards the water's surface as the boat's heel increased dramatically. Everyone on board scrambled around for a handhold. He felt a tremor from the hull as the keel popped free of the roof.

"Hit the throttle," Peter ordered, and just like that, Archangel was free.

* * *

"I think it's a marvelous idea," Dr. Gable said, smiling broadly. "The two of you not only endangered your own lives to save my son, a man you didn't even know, but you, Peter, are obviously an expert at sailing this boat. Your plan was so simple, I am ashamed at not having come up with it myself."

Peter picked up a piece of fish with his fork and looked it over before depositing it carefully into his mouth. They were dining together in the main salon, which was so big he had a hard time remembering he was on a boat. It was appointed in deeply lacquered wood and light tan leather upholstery, all in like-new condition. Archangel may have been used as a research vessel, but it was built as a pleasure yacht, and it showed in every richly detailed inch of her interior.

"I don't know," Peter said. "Penny and I will have to talk it over…"

"I think it's a great idea," she said. "Count me in…assuming you want to, of course. It's your decision."

Peter frowned, wishing they had never brought it up. "No, it's our decision, but as for what I want, I'll have to think about it."

They had offered him the captaincy, which he would have found irresistible if not for his growing need to get Penny away from Brad. He had long since given up chastising himself over how selfish it was, but he knew that if he didn't do it soon he might start thinking about what was best for her, and no good could come of that, at least not for him.

"No offense," Burgoyne said to Peter before turning to the others. "But I don't think it's a good idea. We have limited supplies and not all that much room."

"None taken," Peter assured him. He didn't like Burgoyne, but he was in full agreement with him in this particular case.

"Don't be ridiculous," Brad said from across the table. "What will we do the next time we run into a problem our genius IQs can't solve? Send me ashore again and hope these two show up to bail me out of trouble? Wouldn't it be easier to just keep them with us?" Peter was finding it very difficult to dislike Brad, despite how much he wanted to. He had a positive outlook and more than his share of common sense. He had obeyed orders enthusiastically and without question, which was more than he could say for Burgoyne. He did wish, however, that Brad would just shut up. He knew why he wanted them to stay, and it wasn't entirely about sailing.

"I agree," Dr. Foster said. "Look at how easily he sailed the boat."

"That's not fair," Peter protested. "Roller furling on every sail, autopilot, electric winches…this thing nearly sails itself." Nervous about his jeep, Peter had put up the sails and navigated Archangel to within sight of the coast where he had left it. The others had watched him at work, not offering to help, which he had found annoying until he realized they were evaluating him.

"What kind of fish is this?" Penny asked, savoring her meal as usual.

"Atlantic Salmon," Brad said. "We caught some shortly before I left."

"And after," Burgoyne said.

"Here?" Peter was surprised, though he supposed he shouldn't be. "I mean I guess this is the ocean now, but…"

"Do you have any equipment that can test the water?" Penny asked.

"Yes," Burgoyne said. "And we did. Oxygen and PH are normal, but salinity is down, though only a bit. Not enough to take it out of its seasonal range."

"Is there a way to calculate the amount of fresh water that would have had to be introduced to lower the salinity to its current level?" Penny asked. Peter wondered what she meant, then it hit him. She was trying to figure out how much of the polar ice had been introduced into the water, to test her hypothesis that there wasn't enough of it to cause such a drastic rise in sea level. He didn't know much about polar ice, but he did know it was mostly fresh water.

"Yes, I suppose," Brad said. "But we'd need a lot more data. One or two readings won't cut it."

"What data do you need?" she asked. "We can get the total volume of sea water before the event, accounting for increased depth by incorporating inland bodies, and salinity parts per million both old and new."

"Some of that is easy," Brad said, beaming. "One point four billion cubic kilometers of water, which includes bodies of water that weren't connected before, but about two and half percent is freshwater so you'll have to factor that. The problem is in the salinity. It's measured in parts per thousand, by the way, not million, but the problem is that it's a range, not a fixed value. And it's nothing simple like a seasonal range. The standard salinity of any given body of water varies considerably."

"I see," Penny said. "That does complicate it quite a bit."

"Yeah, it does. The Atlantic used to range from thirty three to thirty seven parts per thousand, depending on season and latitude. Proximity to freshwater runoff affects it also, among other things. Our last reading showed just under thirty four, which is well within range, even for this specific time and place, or, you know, where the ocean was near here. We'd need a lot more readings at different times and locations to even try to work it out mathematically."

"There goes that idea," she said, frowning. "Maybe we can take more readings as we go? Assuming we stay, of course."

"We sure can," he said. "And I hope you do. Stay, that is. We could really use the both of you."

"So, um, where are you people going, anyway?" Peter asked.

Gable and Foster exchanged glances before he answered. "There is a high altitude magnetometer station in Newfoundland, the Dach Caldworth Observatory. It's one of the few such facilities high enough to have survived. Its sister station is another, and that's important, because it takes two. The differential allows measurement of the field line resonance frequency. Fortunately, it's also one of the only stations that has the equipment to receive telemetry from the THEMIS satellites."

"Why?" Peter asked. "Why go there?" He had a hard time following what they were saying. These people were a lot smarter than he was, and it rankled.

"It's a bit complicated," Gable said. "We're hoping to use the facility to learn more about the event. Maybe explain some of the anomalous data that we've collected." It seemed to Peter that he wanted to say more, but was holding himself back.

"Such as?"

"The sea level, for one."

"We've noticed," Penny said. "But I'm not sure I understand how measuring the Earth's magnetic field will give you more information about the event."

Another exchange of glances, this one very brief. "It would be the final piece in a series of data we've collected," Gable explained. "We need to learn all we can about what happened."

"Fine," Peter said. "Then what?" Penny opened her mouth to ask something else, but then changed her mind.

"Then," Foster cut in. "We decide what to do with the rest of our lives. But until then, we need to know all we can, and we could use your help."

"You don't have to decide now," Gable said. "You two are welcome to spend the night. We'll clear the owner's stateroom for you." He held up his hands. "I know, I know, unfair influence, but that is where you would stay, if you agreed."

"What about Penny?" Peter asked without thinking. "Where will she stay?"

"Oh?" Brad asked, and Peter wanted to shoot him, then himself for running his mouth.

"I'll be fine with you," she said, then quickly touched Peter's arm to indicate that she had meant him and not Brad. "I'm sure there's a couch or something."

"But Devon…" Foster said, her eyes reflecting her uncertainty.

"Is dead," the older man finished for her. "We all miss him, though I know you miss him more than I do, he was your colleague, but that doesn't make him any less gone. There is ample storage space on this ship for all the things we've been keeping in there. The captain of the boat should stay in that room."

"You're right, of course," she agreed. "I just… I miss him terribly." She looked up, remembering where she was, and tried to smile away her blossoming tears. "Look at me, making a spectacle of myself. Please excuse me."

"Don't apologize on my account," Peter said. "We've all lost people dear to us."

"A drink," Gable said as he lifted his glass, his authoritative voice projecting clearly despite his subdued tone. "For all those we have lost, and for all those who have no one to remember them."

Chapter 17 – Realization

See the stars, love,
In the water much clearer and brighter
Than those above us, and whiter...
- D. H. Lawrence

Peter sat on the teak deck, leaning against the rising bulge of the pilothouse. It was surprisingly warm, considering the hour, and the rigging rattled in a gentle breeze that sent small waves lapping rhythmically against the fiberglass hull. He had enjoyed many nights like this out on the water, anchored in some secluded cove, watching the reflected stars dancing in the waves. He could almost feel that same peace now, though the weight of his decision was too heavy to ignore.

"When I move the oars, love," he whispered. "See how the stars are tossed. Distorted, the brightest lost."

He heard someone walking up to him, and he knew who it was without having to look. He was surprised to find that his ability to read the creaks and groans of a hull had transferred seamlessly to Archangel. Fate trying to tell him something, perhaps?

"Hey Penny," he said without looking up, patting the deck next to him. "Care to join me?"

"How'd you know it was me?" she asked. He felt her hand on his shoulder as she lowered herself to sit next to him. "Was it your spooky captain senses?" She smelled mildly of soap and her hair was damp enough to chill his skin through his t-shirt.

"Something like that," he said, turning to smile at her. He hadn't meant the smile to be melancholy.

"Not in the mood for jokes, huh?"

"No, it's fine, I'm just trying to figure out what to do."

"Liar!" she said. "You're struggling with something, and you're going to tell me what it is."

"I guess I am."

She turned to stare over the water. "This is a no brainer for us, Peter. We can't stay on that island. Whatever house we find, once the colonel sets things up no place will be isolated enough. These people have offered you an important job, and given us a place to live. A *very* comfortable place, by the way. Have you seen that room? It's like a luxury hotel. Running water, Peter! Cold, but still."

"You mean they didn't tell you how to turn the hot water on?" he teased.

"Bastard!" she said as her hand reached out to smack him. "You could have said something." He leaned away and she laughed as her palm slid across his cheek. She had a goofy laugh, agonizingly adorable. Every time she smiled at him, his heart raced.

"This boat is fantastic, I know that," he said. "So you want to stay then? Strictly selfishly speaking?" He was afraid of the answer.

"I would love to stay here, Peter. This boat, these people, we can sail forever and just pretend that nothing ever happened. Besides, I'm dying to know what they're up to."

"Up to?"

She raised an eyebrow. "Are you telling me you buy their story? About the magnetic observatory?"

It was a good question. "I know they were holding something back, but I don't necessarily think there has to be more to it, at least anything that would concern us." He had wondered about that, but he did have more pressing matters on his mind. Besides, it was their boat, and their business.

"They're holding something back alright, if not flat out lying. There's something fishy going on here. Did you know that Dr. Gable is not a marine biologist? He's a physicist."

"No, I didn't. You asked him?"

"Brad told me," she explained. "I was just talking to him. He wasn't part of the crew… Dr. Gable I mean. He was just visiting his son."

"You like Brad, don't you?"

"Yeah, he's great…" She hesitated. "Oh. Now I get it."

"Get what?"

"What's bothering you."

"That obvious, huh?" He had already decided that he was done being selfish. He knew what he had to do, now if only he could summon up the courage to do it.

"Not to me, no. I see no reason for it." She sat up straight and looked at him. Her eyes were intent, and beautiful.

"Penny," he said, finally deciding to do the right thing, however hard it was. "I know you must feel some sort of obligation to me. You came to me half starved, half frozen. I gave you food, shelter…"

"Combat lessons."

He chuckled, despite the pain. "And combat lessons. The point is, I saved your life, took you away from the people that wanted to hurt you, and maybe you feel that you owe me something. But the truth is, you don't. You saved me as much as I saved you, if not more. And you don't need me anymore. In fact you're better off without me. I put your life in danger to save those people, to save Brad, and I'm having a hard time forgiving myself for that. I was selfish, thinking about the sort of person I wanted to be, instead of the sort of person I should be. Someone who doesn't risk the lives of those he cares about to save strangers."

"Uh huh," she said. "Go on."

"You'd be better off here," he continued. "Safer here, with these people. You said it yourself, Brad is great. I want to hate him, but I can't. He's smarter than I am, and…"

"Younger?"

"Yeah," he said, feeling the weight of his decision crushing him. "I wish I'd never said anything to him about sailing, but here we are, and I can't be selfish anymore. I've been holding on to a fantasy, that there could be something between us." He smiled sadly. "Dumb, right? Well I'm not going to do that anymore. I have to let it go."

"Perfectly reasonable," she said flatly. "Can I ask you a question?"

He nodded, feeling miserable.

"Do I get a say in any of this, or do you and Brad get to divvy me up like a brisket?"

He blinked. "What? I don't…I mean…" She was smiling, but he wasn't sure what her smile meant.

"You think that I'm running around the apocalypse with you

because I feel like I owe you something?"

He blushed. "I didn't mean…"

"I don't owe you anything, Peter," she said. Her words were harsh, but her tone was soft, perhaps even kind. "Not anymore. We had a deal, work for food, and I kept up my end, didn't I?"

"You did."

"And yes, you saved my life, you killed for me. But, I killed for you too. I saved your ass back there when we went after those skinheads. Another decision you made without consulting me, just as you said."

He started down at the deck, miserable. "Yes."

"But it was the right one. The man you want to be, that *is* the man you should be. The man who took me in, didn't take advantage, treated me like a human being. Killed to protect me, then gave me a weapon and asked me to kill to protect him, like an equal. The man who always does the right thing, regardless of the cost."

He opened his mouth to speak, then closed it again, unsure of what to say.

She continued. "But you're being archaic in your thinking. You're from the 80s so I'll forgive you." She poked him playfully. "Stop trying to pair me off. I have a future and a life outside of who I'm with, and I would like that life to be here."

He flinched. "I'm sorry, I didn't mean—"

She put a hand on his shoulder. "I'll pair myself off, if I so choose."

"Of course, I—"

"And let's think about you, your needs," she continued. "You were brilliant today. The way you took charge, got them unstuck. It's like you were born to do this. Don't you dare throw away this opportunity just because you're worried I'll leave you for Brad. That's just not going to happen."

"Leave me?" he said. "I don't understand."

She smiled. "I guess I'm choosing. To pair myself off I mean."

"What?" He heard the words, but he couldn't process them. His mind was reeling.

"I'm assuming it's what you want too. Your 'foolish' fantasy, as you said?"

"But I'm…"

"What? Older?"

"Yes."

"You don't think I wonder if I'm old enough for you? Mature enough? Experienced enough? You don't think I worry that you'll get bored of me because I'm just a lame ass farm girl from the boonies, barely old enough to leave home, who used to gawk at skyscrapers that you took for granted? You were a Seal, for fuck's sake. A naval officer. A college professor. What am I? Just a student? Barely an adult? What have I accomplished that can compete?"

"That's ridiculous! You're amazing!" He hadn't considered that, though the idea of her wondering if she were good enough for him seemed absurd.

"I've been into you almost from the start, Peter, but I wasn't sure you felt the same. That's why I kept pushing you to tell me how you felt, you know, after you shot…ah shit. Sorry. Didn't mean to bring it up. Look, do you want to be with me or not?"

"Yes!"

"Good. Then it's settled. Unless you want to sell me to Brad for two goats and a wind turbine, stop trying to get rid of me."

"But—"

"Just shut up and kiss me."

Needing no further encouragement, Peter leaned in and her lips found his, and this time neither of them pulled away. His heart pounded fiercely, pushing hot blood that slowly spread from his chest to his extremities. He put his arms around her and she pressed close. Her nearness, her touch, awakened a passion so intense that he had forgotten that he was capable of feeling it. Yet as it returned, it was familiar and right, like an old friend that, though gone for many years, comes back as if he had never left.

After a few minutes, he pulled away and cupped her face in his hands. Her eyes glistened with captured stars, so much clearer and brighter than the ones above.

"What is it?" she said.

"A perfect moment." And so it was. Holding her, realizing the fantasy that he had harbored like a fragile ship sheltering from a savage storm, made everything else insignificant. The boat, their flight, the men he had killed—nothing mattered. All he wanted was to hold her like this forever.

He kissed her again, but this time slower, more measured, savoring every moment until he pulled away once more.

"I don't want this to end," he said.

"Do you want to talk?" Penny said. "Or make out?"

"Both."

She smiled and cocked her head. "You can't have both, it doesn't work that way."

"How great delight from those sweet lips I taste," he said. "Whether I hear them speak, or feel them kiss! Only this want I have, that being graced, with one of them, the other straight I miss. Love, since thou canst do wonders, heap my blisses. And grant her kissing words, or speaking kisses."

A pair of tears escaped Penny's eyes and left sparkling trails along her cheeks.

"Oh, Peter," she said, and put her head on his shoulder. He leaned against it, letting her hair tickle his nose and cheek as he inhaled its earthy scent.

They sat there for a long time before retiring to their stateroom. Sometimes they kissed, other times just pressed close together, almost as though afraid that letting go would mean an end to the wonder they had discovered in each other. It was indeed a perfect moment, and Peter wanted it to last. All the time that he had lost in his failed marriage faded away, and he was back where he belonged, not in his twenties, but in all the other ways that mattered.

Chapter 18 – Command

"God help me! save I take my part
Of danger on the roaring sea,
A devil rises in my heart,
Far worse than any death to me."
- Alfred, Lord Tennyson

"Have you decided?" Dr. Gable asked him as Peter climbed out of the aft hatch into the bright sunlit world above. The rain had not returned, and the temperature had to be above seventy despite the strong wind blowing out of the northeast. An amazing transformation, but perhaps with ominous implications. The warming was a little too sudden for Peter's liking.

"Yes," he said. "We're going to stay." Last night's experience had been transformative. His outlook on just about everything had changed. For the first time in as long as he could remember, he was actually happy, despite everything that had happened.

"Marvelous!" Gable said, clapping him on the back. Doctors Foster and Burgoyne were sitting behind Gable, and of the two, only Foster seemed happy that he had accepted. He couldn't spot Penny at first, but then heard her behind him in the center cockpit, with Brad. He was explaining something technical to her that Peter couldn't follow.

"Provided," Peter said, ignoring a flash of jealousy. "That you can accept my terms."

"Such as?" Burgoyne asked, crossing his arms across his chest.

"I will not accept responsibility without authority. This is your boat. You people decide where it goes and what it does, but I decide how and when, and I will not be second-guessed. If I give an order, I expect it to be obeyed, and that includes everyone." He turned his gaze momentarily to Gable, whom he had pegged as the leader. "You're asking me to take responsibility not only for the safety of this boat, but for all of your lives. I take that responsibility very seriously, and I expect you to take it seriously as well." He had given this same speech many times, both on his own boat and on others he had been asked to take charge of. It was not something he had ever taken lightly. Every time a boat set sail, lives were at stake.

"Sounds perfectly reasonable," Dr. Gable said. "I would not expect anything less. I trust there is no opposition?"

Burgoyne frowned, but didn't say anything. Dr. Foster shook her head.

"One more thing," Peter said. "If you decide you don't want me anymore, or once we conclude our business, I will sail the boat back here, to where my jeep is, and I will stay in command until we get here. Is that acceptable?"

Dr. Gable nodded. "It is. I believe that settles it?" He looked around at the others, and each nodded in turn. "In that case," he continued. "Captain Anderson, the ship is yours."

"Thank you," Peter said, and was surprised at how deeply those simple words moved him. "Now then," he said. "As the first order of business, we have to ferry my supplies from shore, then hide my jeep."

"Supplies?" Dr. Gable asked. "What sort of supplies?"

"Food, mostly, but also guns, ammunition and other equipment we're going to need to stay safe out here. I trust that will not be a problem?" he asked, turning to look at Dr. Foster.

She shook her head. "It won't, as long as you don't expect me to use one."

"I would like you to," Peter said. "But I won't push."

"I didn't realize you came with food," Gable said, smiling. "It will be much appreciated."

They spent almost an hour ferrying his things on the dinghy. Archangel had a surprising amount of storage space, most of which was sparingly filled. Supplies had been running short, it seemed.

When they were done, Peter drove the jeep as far off the road as he could. The mud had dried a bit, but it was only the second day without rain. Catskills mud was notorious for trapping trucks, and he didn't want to take any chances. He put the jeep between some dense bushes, then used the camouflage netting to further conceal it. When he was done, it was impossible to spot it from the road, and not so easy from twenty yards away, even when he knew what to look for. Since he didn't have enough netting for the trailer, he asked Brad to help him push it to another set of bushes, far enough from the jeep that no one would be able to spot the vehicle should they discover it.

Satisfied, he returned to Archangel and prepared to weigh anchor.

"I'd like someone fishing as much as possible," he said. "The less rations we eat, the more we'll be prepared should something go wrong."

"I'll start," Burgoyne said, uncharacteristically eager to volunteer. He grabbed a fishing pole from a cockpit locker and went aft, where he sat alone, working the rod.

"What should I do?" Penny asked. "Should I still carry my rifle?"

"No," Peter said. "Take one of the handguns from the box, you know the one, along with a holster." He pointed down to where his own pistol was strapped to his leg.

"Okay, but what do you want me to *do*?"

"Stay with me," he explained. "I'm going to teach you how to sail this thing."

"Awesome!" she said excitedly, and he was thrilled by her enthusiasm.

Gable came over with a map and showed him where they had to go. Peter spent a few minutes with some marine charts and his GPS topographical map, trying to figure out a safe course. His phone's charger plugged into a 12 volt socket on the control pedestal and joined a dizzying array of instruments: depth, wind speed, wind direction, radar, rudder position, speed over water, chart plotter, VHF radio, compass, autopilot, throttle, sail winch controls and, of course, a big stainless steel wheel. Peter was sure he hadn't noticed one or two, but he'd get to them in time. He didn't actually *need* any of them—he could sail the boat entirely by sight and feel—though most would be useful in their own way.

Weighing anchor proved no more difficult than holding down the button on the windlass control until the anchor clanged and rattled its way up to its roller. Another button raised the mainsail, and a third unfurled the large genoa headsail he decided to fly. The cutter rig was very useful. Each of the three forward sails was of a different size, allowing him to choose the one most appropriate for the wind. A roller furler allowed a sail to be partially unfurled in case of bad weather, but that was not an efficient option as it did not allow the sail to assume its optimal shape. Having an array of sizes at hand was much more effective, and he could even fly two or possibly three at once if his course put him at just the right angle to the wind.

In just minutes Archangel was gliding gracefully across the water on a broad reach at a respectable nine and a half knots in just over fourteen knots of wind. By his calculations, assuming a waterline length of just under ninety feet, this boat's hull speed should be about twelve knots—a speed he could only dream about in the much smaller boats he had sailed.

Letting the autopilot steer, he messed with the sails, trimming them again and again, learning how they liked to work. Each boat had its own quirks, and it would take him a while to learn how to coax the most out of a rig as complex as Archangel's.

"You're really good at that," Penny said. "So many minor adjustments. You were just being modest when you said this boat sails itself, weren't you?"

"Not at all," he admitted. "I could teach you to sail this boat in ten minutes, probably less. But to get the most out of it, that's something that takes a lifetime to learn. I'm not even all that good, to tell you the truth. Some offshore racers I knew would be able to get at least another knot out of this genoa." He smiled. "Just don't tell the others I'm a phony."

"It'll be our little secret," she said, and poked him playfully.

Although he felt a bit cold without a jacket, he decided to ignore it, at least for now. There was nothing like the feel of a sailboat caught by the wind, propelled by the struggle between the sail above and the keel below, an eternal battle between air and water that gave the vessel its forward momentum. Lift and drag, high and low pressure, all of the explanations behind why it worked were meaningless when compared to the sheer beauty of the experience. Combined with his newly discovered relationship, it filled him with a heady euphoria. He wondered how long it would last, and what would finally ruin it.

Chapter 19 – Desolation

And you as well must die, belovèd dust,
And all your beauty stand you in no stead;
This flawless, vital hand, this perfect head,
This body of flame and steel, before the gust
Of Death, or under his autumnal frost,
Shall be as any leaf, be no less dead
Than the first leaf that fell, this wonder fled,
Altered, estranged, disintegrated, lost.
- Edna St. Vincent Millay

The wind had picked up around noon and was showing no signs of letting up. Peter had swapped the big genoa for a smaller headsail but they were still flying along at just over eleven knots. Archangel rose and dipped steadily as it crested white caps that were starting to spray over the side. He had rigged safety lines earlier and insisted that everyone wear a safety harness whether they were topside or not, just in case things got really nasty.

He remembered long distance sailing as a boring, tedious affair in which the greatest concern was falling asleep at the helm. There was little danger of that now. Mountaintop islands dotted the seascape in all directions, and a morbid curiosity made it difficult to avoid staring at them, searching for the remnants of the old world. Keeping a careful eye on the depth and GPS map, Peter sneaked the occasional glance with a pair of powerful binoculars. He saw the roofs of buildings just past the waterline, and dozens of partially and fully intact houses that dotted the new islands. Sometimes he even spotted abandoned cars, some of which appeared intact.

"Captain," Dr. Gable's voice came from the central hatch as his head peeked out. The others were below, probably eating lunch. "Can I have a word?"

"Of course," Peter said without taking his eyes off the depth sounder. "There are some things I'd like to talk to you about too."

"Certainly." The old scientist came out on deck and shut the hatch behind him. "Aren't you planning on being relieved? You've been at the helm all morning." He clipped his harness onto the jack line and walked unsteadily over to a cushioned cockpit seat near the pedestal.

"Nah," Peter said. "Don't worry about it, we'll be over open sea by the time it gets dark. Then I'll just set the autopilot and take a nap. There's a nav station in the owner's stateroom, it's pretty awesome... full instrumentation, even a radar with proximity alarm. I've asked some of the others to take turns on deck throughout the night, but they'll be there just as a precaution."

"I see you have the situation under control," Gable said, satisfied. "But that's partly what I wanted to talk to you about. Why are we headed south? The research center is northeast of where we started."

"I was waiting for someone to notice," Peter said with a grin. "But there is a very good reason, doc. It's too dangerous to sail over land. We have no charts for it and there are probably tons of buildings or trees poking up to the surface or worse... just below, as you experienced earlier. We have a forward facing depth sounder, but I'd rather not rely on it if we don't have to. The first rule of sailing is that what you can't see is much more dangerous than what you can see. We're following the Hudson River, then we're going to circle Long Island and head out to open sea. We lose about a day that way, but it's the better route."

The physicist nodded appreciatively. "I apologize if I seem smug at this moment, but it was I who convinced the others that you were the man we needed. There wasn't much disagreement, of course, but I will still take credit, if it's all the same to you."

"Be my guest, Dr. Gable," Peter said, smiling. It felt good to be appreciated, something that had not been very common in his life before the event.

"Please, call me Emmet."

"Okay, Emmet, but there's something that I'm about to insist on that you may not be too happy with."

"Oh?" Gable said, raising an eyebrow.

"It's the electricity," Peter explained. "From what Brad told me, you guys mostly ran the diesel and sailed only in ideal wind. It lasted as long as it did because this boat has a two and half thousand gallon tank. But now there's just the five gallons that Brad brought back."

"Yes, that's correct, but none of us had much luck at getting her moving at a reasonable velocity without the engine, and we didn't dare try to sail in high wind. A vessel this size is not exactly an ideal learning platform."

"Yes, well when you're running the engine, it charges the batteries, as I'm sure you know. So you guys had basically unlimited electricity. That's not the case anymore."

"I see," Gable said, rubbing the bridge of his nose. "I suppose that is another thing we should have considered. The solar panels, the wind generator, how much power can that give us?"

"I'm not sure yet," Peter said. "There's been a steady drop in voltage in the primary house bank…that's the set of batteries dedicated to running the lights, the pumps, all that sort of stuff. I've got the wind generator and panels charging the bank that's in use, but demand is exceeding supply. There is a diesel generator, and we could use it, but it's important to save our fuel for emergencies."

Gable nodded. "What can we do?"

"Cut down use. Minimal lighting, less water, and no hot water. Absolutely no microwave or laundry machines, and no refrigeration. Whatever fish we don't eat we're going to have to dry. I have a few buckets of salt that I brought over, feel free to use them."

"Very well. I'll inform the others, but…" Gable stopped and frowned. "I suppose it's rather childish, now that I think of it."

"What is?"

"Well, it's just that we used to watch a movie every Friday night, together. It helped us keep our sanity, let us hear something other than the constant rain…we were in the southern hemisphere, until recently. You got snow, we got rain. I don't suppose…"

"You have movies?" Peter asked. "On disk?" There had been a few at the house, but after the first month he had decided it wasn't worth the propane to run the generator. He had snuck in the occasional movie anyway, but quickly got bored with the few titles he had on hand. To watch a movie again, one he hadn't seen, that would be something.

"A substantial library, actually."

"Every Friday night," Peter said. "I think that's a wonderful idea. I'm sure we can make it work."

"Thank you," Gable said. "So tell me, Peter, if you don't mind an old man's curiosity, what did you do, before the event? A ship's captain perhaps? Or a captain of industry?" Peter searched his eyes for signs of sarcasm, but was surprised to find that he was serious.

"No," he said, shaking his head. "Nothing quite so interesting. I taught English at Brooklyn College. Adjunct professor."

"Oh?" Gable said. "PhD?"

"MFA. What about you? Penny mentioned you were a physicist."

"Yes," Gable said, looking strangely conflicted. For a moment, it seemed as though he didn't want to say any more. "My work led to the isolation of the Higgs boson."

"The what?"

"That's the particle associated with the Higgs Field," Gable explained. "It's responsible for generating elementary particle masses. It had been proposed as a solution to the hierarchy problem in the standard model, but until we actually isolated it, it was purely theoretical."

"Right…" Peter said, smiling. "You'll have to explain what that all means one of these days."

"I would love nothing more captain, believe me, but being up here is making me queasy."

"That's a bit backwards, doc," Peter said. "You're supposed to be queasy down below and come up here for relief."

Gable grinned broadly. "I have never been one to follow convention, Peter. I apologize for not being able to speak to you further about my work. Perhaps when you are taking a rest below?"

"Sure, that would be great, but don't worry if we don't get around to it. Penny will probably know what you're talking about, she'll explain it to me."

"She is a remarkable young woman, that one," Gable said. "If I were twenty years younger you would have some competition."

Peter smiled. "I'm glad you're not, sir, no offense. I don't think I could stack up."

"You're damned right!" Gable clapped him on the back affectionately. "Well, captain, if you don't mind, I'm going to go lie down for a bit. It was a pleasure speaking with you." He turned to go.

"Actually," Peter said. "There's another thing I wanted to ask you about before you go."

"Oh?"

"New York," Peter said, frowning. He had tried to convince himself to risk an overland route that would take them out of visual range, but he couldn't get around the danger.

"What about…" Gable started to say, then nodded. "Oh, my."

"Yeah. Do you think it will be a problem…you know, for the others?"

Gable sighed. "Honestly, Peter, I don't know. But I suppose we'll find out, won't we?"

"I guess we will."

* * *

Penny was the first among the others to spot them. She was working the jib sheet on the winch, watching the tells on the sail to set the optimal line tension. She had them pressed perfectly flat against the sailcloth when she stood up suddenly and pointed.

"Peter look!"

The air was thick and visibility was poor, but he could just make them out up ahead, past the rocky islands of New Jersey's palisades. They stood like ominous sentinels, guarding the way to the old Atlantic. Their glassy corpses were made all the more eerie by the orange glow of the low hanging sun.

"Good lord," Burgoyne said as he reeled in his fishing pole. Once the line was retrieved, he set the pole on the deck and went forward, his eyes fixed straight ahead.

"I'm going to get Brad and the others," Penny said. "They need to see this."

"I'm not sure that's such a…" he started to say, but she had already disappeared down the hatch. *Brad* and the others, she had said.

Within moments they were all on deck, staring somberly at the approaching apparitions. Peter loosened the sails slightly, just enough to reduce the heel to five degrees and make everyone more comfortable. Archangel slowed to just under seven knots and glided gracefully towards the world's largest graveyard.

The slapping of waves against the hull and the creaking of the rigging was accompanied by an almost otherworldly whistling as the wind cut its way through the forest of cadaverous skyscrapers. Only the tallest of New York's behemoths were spared the ignoble fate of complete submergence, though there were so many of these jutting from the water that the city still managed to look crowded. The density of smaller protrusions, buildings just big enough to break the surface, increased as they approached, until Peter could squint his eyes and pretend he was flying in a dirigible over a fog shrouded city. He felt something warm on his arm and realized it was Penny's hand. Reaching over, he pressed her to him and felt the subtle trembling of her body as she watched the looming nightmare.

As always, Peter's mind tried to find words with which to give meaning to what he was seeing, but the great poets and writers failed him. Perhaps words would come later, when the memory of this terrible place no longer burned so intensely.

Soon the towering mausoleums of Manhattan island were joined by the stark Jersey City skyline to their right. Only a few buildings broke the ocean's surface there, though those few were tall enough to compete for attention with their siblings on the other side of the passage.

Had this really been the center of the free world, just a few months ago? Had millions of people scurried around this glass and steel megalopolis, filling it with the sounds and smells of life? Peter had walked the streets of this city for the better part of his adult life, always filled with the inescapable conclusion that he did not belong. Would he have cherished those moments, had he known what was ahead? He wanted to believe that he would have.

"Do you know which one is the Goldman Sachs tower?" Dr. Foster asked dryly, snapping him back to reality. She was staring across the opposite side towards Jersey City.

"That one," Peter pointed. "It's the smaller of the two big ones over there. The taller one is part of the Harborside Financial Plaza. Why do you ask?"

"My brother..." she started to say, then buried her head in her hands. She didn't cry, she just sat still, not moving. Maybe it would have been better to risk an overland route. He knew he should probably tighten the sails and get past this place as quickly as he could, but he was overcome with a grim fascination. He allowed the boat to drift closer, until they were just on the edge of what would have been the Hudson River, approaching Battery Park and the World Financial Center.

"I don't see the statue of Liberty," Penny said softly. "I never got the chance…"

"You wouldn't," Peter explained. "It's less than four hundred feet tall, even with the pedestal."

"Captain!" Brad shouted, pointing towards the Manhattan side.

"What is it?" The note of alarm in Brad's voice brought Peter to a state of alertness. He scanned the buildings to their left, but couldn't see anything.

"I saw someone!" Brad shouted excitedly. "On the roof of that building!"

Peter looked where he pointed, but couldn't see any movement.

"Are we going to stop?" Penny asked, pushing away so she could look up at him. "If someone survived…" He knew what she was thinking. He should have taken a different route.

"No."

"Why not?" Brad asked.

"Peter," Penny said sternly. "If there are survivors we have to stop."

"No."

"Peter!" she shouted, glaring up at him. "My—"

In a single smooth motion he switched on the autopilot and grabbed her by her upper arms. He stared at her, hard. He had moved so fast that he had shocked her, and her lower lip was trembling as she looked at him with wide eyes.

"Don't. Don't hope. If there were people still alive here, they would be shouting from the roof tops, doing whatever they could to get our attention. If someone was there, if it wasn't a bird Brad saw, then they aren't trying to be found. Don't you get it?"

"Get what?" she said weakly.

"Thousands of people must have survived the tsunami in these buildings. Thousands! They had no supplies, nothing to fish with, no way to get around from building to building even. They couldn't swim, the water was freezing."

"But some could still be alive!"

"Yes."

She tried to break free of his grip. "I don't understand! We have to—"

"Penny!" he barked, startling her again. "Remember Major Sullivan's story. No food, no supplies. Only one thing to eat. Whatever is alive here…we want nothing to do with it."

Her mouth dropped open. She shook her head. "No."

"Oh man," Brad said. "I didn't even think of that."

"Penny I'm so sorry," he said softly, and let her go. He expected her to run from him, but she did the opposite. He held her tightly while she cried, his shirt soaked where her face pressed into his chest. The others stood quietly, looking away. Brad continued to scan the roof tops, but they didn't see anything else.

Slowly, steadily, the spectral monoliths of the once great city of New York faded into the mist.

Chapter 20 – Exploration

The poor waters spill
The stars, waters broken, forsaken.
—The heavens are not shaken, you say, love,
Its stars stand still.
- D. H. Lawrence

He found Penny on the bed, lying on her stomach with her hands under her chin. She was wearing the same clothes from before and her eyes were red and swollen. Peter closed the hatch behind him, then went over to the nav station to double check the proximity alert. The stateroom was opulent. Queen bed, private bathroom with shower and tub, all trimmed with the same lacquered wood and creamy leather as he had admired in the saloon. It also had a full array of controls and instruments. He could sail the boat almost entirely from this room, if he had to.

"Shouldn't you be at the helm?" she murmured without looking up.

"I can leave if you want," he said, preparing to go. He was exhausted, both physically and emotionally, but he would go if she wanted to be alone. He had already hurt her enough, hurt all of them. He could always sleep on one of the settees in the main saloon, since it had its own nav station with a radar interface.

"No," she said. "I didn't mean it like that. I'm sorry."

"I'm the one who's sorry," he said as he shrugged out of his safety harness. "I should never have taken us through that place." He sat down on the bed next to her and stroked her hair. She rolled over, laying her head on his lap.

"Talk to me," she said. "About anything."

"Okay," he said, trying to think of something to distract her, then remembered his conversation with Dr. Gable.

"What's a Higgs boson?"

She turned her head and regarded him with a quizzical expression. "Are you serious?"

"Not everyone on this tub is a genius, Pen. Some of us drive boats for a living."

"Right," she said, the hint of a smile forming in the corners of her mouth. "But seriously, why would you want to know about Higgs bosons?"

"I was talking to Dr. Gable…"

"Really? I couldn't get much out of him. What did he tell you?"

"That he discovered the Higgs boson and proved some theoretical model."

"That was *him*?" Penny said, her eyes flaring with excitement. She sat up. "He's *that* Dr. Gable? Dr. Emmet Gable? I should have realized…I'm such an idiot!"

"Yeah, he said his name was Emmet."

"No wonder he didn't want to tell me. He probably thought I'd be all over him with questions and stuff."

"Was he right?"

"You're god damned right he was right! He made one of the greatest discoveries of our time!"

Peter stared at her, charmed by her enthusiasm and thankful that he had managed to distract her. She was so beautiful when she was animated, even with the redness around her eyes.

"So he's pretty smart, this guy, eh?"

"Yeah, just a little." She nudged him. "He's a freakin' rock star. Most physicists are either experimental or theoretical, but Gable was both, and he kicked ass at everything he did. In school we spend a lot of time with his papers, his theoretical stuff, but few people actually understood them, and his experimental work was real cutting edge stuff too. He believed that people had created but failed to observe the Higgs boson. He didn't make a lot of friends, but I guess he was right."

"So explain it to me," he said. "What's the big deal?"

"Okay," she said excitedly, holding up her hands. "You have to keep in mind that I was a grad student, and only first year. I don't have my head around all this stuff yet, but I think I can explain the elementary aspects so that you can get it at least as much as I do, okay?"

"Alright, I'm listening."

"Okay, so there's this theory of how subatomic particles interact and it's called the 'standard model.' The interactions that it describes are responsible for all matter in the universe....visible matter, anyway. There's also dark matter, but that's neither here nor there."

"I'm with you so far."

"Alright, so this theory governs the rules of particle interaction...it defines the behavior of the twelve fundamental matter particles, the quarks and leptons, as well as the force carriers—the photons, gluons and W and Z bosons. Don't worry about the names, I'm just spitting them out for my own sake. What's important is that the theory isn't complete. There's a hierarchy problem... gravity. Gravity is very, very weak compared to the other forces like electromagnetism and strong and weak nuclear interaction, in fact it's so weak that it doesn't factor into the standard model. The math doesn't add up, if you'll pardon my pun."

"It doesn't seem weak," he said. "I mean, things fall pretty hard, don't they?"

"No it doesn't seem weak at all, but that's because we're dealing with such massive objects. The planet, us. If you look at gravity between, say, two electrons, it's something like forty orders of magnitude weaker than the other forces...that's like billions and billions and billions of times weaker... and that doesn't fit. If you follow the rules and the math of the model, all forces should be the same."

"I'm not following, Penny, I'm sorry. I get what you're saying, but there are too many side concepts I'm missing, like what all the particles do, what are these nuclear interactions, how do force carriers work, or why it even matters that gravity is weaker."

"You're asking all the right questions, but they're not important right now. I mean I'd love to explain it all someday, if you want to learn, but it will take a long time. To understand the Higgs boson, though, you just have to understand that the standard model doesn't add up, mathematically speaking. It only makes sense—mathematically—if all the fundamental particles are massless, or more accurately, get their mass through an external mechanism."

"Okay," he said, glad to finally be able to understand something. "So you can't get the numbers to crunch unless mass is controlled by some external force."

"Yes. So, a guy named…hey!" She laughed and poked him playfully. "I never even realized the connection."

"What is it? What connection?"

"The guy's name was Peter, Peter Higgs!"

"What guy?"

"They guy who proposed the Higgs mechanism."

"Oh," he said, grinning. "That guy."

She shook her head. "Yeah, that guy. Anyway, he proposed a very simple and elegant solution. All of space is permeated by a field, like the electromagnetic field, and as particles move through this field, they acquire mass. He called it the Higgs field. And because we know from quantum mechanics that fields have particles associated with them—the electromagnetic field, for instance, has the photon—we know that the Higgs field must also have a particle. The Higgs boson."

"So it's like an ether? It's everywhere, this Higgs field?"

"Sort of, yes."

"Didn't the Michelson Morley experiment prove there was no ether?"

"Who's the smartass now?" she said.

"Still you."

"Anyway, yes it did. But they were looking for something different, a medium for light to travel through. There is no such medium. The only connection in fact is your choice of the word 'ether.'"

"Sorry," he said.

Her smile broadened. "You're forgiven, this time."

"Okay so it's a field, like the electromagnetic field, and it's everywhere, giving things mass, and it's made up of Higgs bosons. So what then is a boson? I mean I may not need to know what all the other particles do, but this one seems pertinent."

"And you are *im*pertinent." She giggled. "Sorry, I'm just being silly. Bosons are force carrier particles, as opposed to matter particles. To get any more in depth I'd have to start speaking Klingon again."

"Please don't," Peter said. "You're already enough of a giant nerd."

Her mouth opened, eyes widening. "Peter!"

He smiled. "I'm just teasing! Besides, I think nerd chicks are hot."

"Peter!"

He laughed. "Sorry, sorry." He was caught up in her sudden enthusiasm, and playful teasing had always been one of the ways he expressed his affection. She seemed happy to play along.

"So where were we?"

"The Higgs field gives particles masses. How does it do that?"

"Well it's not easy to explain, but I can give you an analogy if you want."

"Shoot."

"It's not my analogy, just something I picked up on the internet, but it's very handy. Imagine a Hollywood party, lots of normal people, hanging out, evenly spaced, waiting for the big star. She shows up, entering the room from one side and headed to the other. As soon as she enters the room, people start clustering around her because they are strongly attracted to her. As she moves, she gathers people around her, while those she leaves behind space out evenly again. Because of this cluster of people, she has greater momentum as she moves. She's harder to stop while moving because you have to stop all those people too, and harder to get going again if stopped, for the same reason. That, in a nutshell, is how the Higgs field works. The crowd is the field, the people are the Higgs bosons and the star is a matter particle."

"That I can get," he said. "So what did Gable discover? It sounds like you people had all this stuff figured out already."

"It was purely theoretical," she explained. "No one had ever actually observed a Higgs boson until Dr. Gable did it. The implications are astonishing."

"Astonishing? How? I mean I get why it's very important, to understand the universe and all, but why astonishing?"

"It's like fire," she said, and he could see her start to look past him as her imagination took flight. "You start out with some burning sticks and you can get warm and cook on them, but before you know it you have internal combustion and jet airplanes. Isolating the Higgs boson means that one day, maybe very soon, we will be able to control the Higgs field."

"Hey!" he said, realizing what she was talking about. "If the

Higgs field gives particles their mass, and you can manipulate that field…you can do anything. Floating cities, hover cars, and who knows what else!"

She nodded. "Yes, Peter. Amazing, isn't it? Just like in Mass Effect."

"Is that another video game?"

"Yes! You're starting to understand me. Though they never linked it to the Higgs field in that game, it was just mysterious alien tech."

"Such a nerd."

"Hey!"

"You're right though, it is astonishing. It's just too bad we'll never get the chance to realize any of it." And just like that, her enthusiasm came crashing down.

"Yeah," she said, clearly bummed. "Too bad."

"Oh, shit, Pen, I'm sorry," he said, feeling like an idiot. "I didn't mean to screw up your mood."

"No," she said, managing a weak smile. "It's okay." She was silent for a moment, then said, "Peter, do you think…my mom and dad…"

"You shouldn't…"

"Please, just answer. Do you think my mom and dad survived the tsunami and…" She couldn't bring herself to finish.

"What were they doing in the city?" He wanted to reassure her, but she was too smart for an empty answer. It had to be something substantial.

"They were tourists. They wanted to see the stupid Christmas tree and stuff like that."

"Were they staying in a hotel?"

"Yeah."

"Then no, not a chance."

"Are you sure?"

"There are no hotels tall enough."

She looked down at her hands for a while, then said, "Thank you." She looked like she wanted to say more, but changed her mind. "I'm really tired. Are you coming to bed? I mean, with the helm and all?"

"Yeah, it's all good. We're out on the open sea and I have that proximity alarm."

"I'm glad," she said. "I really need you right now."

After they made love, he fell asleep holding her tightly. He had always hated sleeping next to someone else. He couldn't stand the contact, the heat or the constant movements. With her it was different—he couldn't stand to let her go. She woke up several times during the night, whimpering, panting. He calmed her, soothed her back to sleep, but every time he closed his own eyes he saw them, the empty shells of New York. They were all around him, an endless forest of glass and steel, and inside each one things moved in the darkness. Hungry, savage things that had once been people. Some of them knew his name and called out to him.

"Peter…" they whispered with their raspy voices. "Peter…"

* * *

"Peter!" It was Penny's voice. "Peter wake up. Something's wrong."

He was alert in an instant, and he didn't need her to tell him what was going on. The bed was open on both sides, but he would have had to climb up to get off on the far right.

"What's happening?" Penny cried, her eyes darting around, terrified. The boat was heeling at least forty five degrees, with occasional dips beyond that.

Peter smiled to reassure her. "Nothing to worry about, just weather. If you're up to it, get your raingear and harness on and join me up on deck. *Do not* leave the hatchway without clipping into the jack lines."

She nodded, but didn't budge, still scared.

Tossing on his rain jacket and harness, Peter left the stateroom through the cabin door and made his way across the salon to the central hatch. The others were coming out of their rooms, barely able to stand. The boat was so severely tilted things were falling off of surfaces and rolling back and forth on the cabin sole with every wave.

Seeing them all peering through their doors, he finally had a complete picture of the living arrangements. Archangel had three aft staterooms, including the owner's cabin that he and Penny were sharing. There were two smaller but equally opulent guest rooms, each with two beds. Gable occupied one, while Dr. Foster was in the second. Burgoyne and Brad each stood in the doorway of one of the forward staterooms intended for the crew. Peter wondered why Burgoyne didn't just live in the guest cabin with Foster, he had picked up enough hints throughout the day to know that they were sleeping together.

"What's going on?" Foster demanded, visibly terrified.

"Weather," Peter said. "Nothing to worry about. No one up on deck without jacking in. Do it at the hatch, don't go out there unless you're tethered. Hatch stays closed at all times, got it?"

There were assorted nods.

"Captain, do you need help?" Brad asked as he pulled a shirt over his head.

"Where's Burgoyne? One of you was supposed to be up there."

"He was," Brad explained. "I mean he is..." His eyes widened. "Do you think…"

"Come on up. Don't forget to jack in. Help Penny if she's coming."

He opened the central hatch and looked outside, spotting Burgoyne at the wheel. A spray of water hit Peter in the face as a black rolling mass swept over the side. Flashes of lighting brightened the turbulent sky while rain pounded into his head with enough force to sting. He clipped his tether to the jack line and stepped out on deck, shutting the hatch behind him.

He could hear the strain of the rigging as the gale force wind smashed into the sails, burying Archangel's port gunwale under the water. He felt his stomach lighten as the deck fell out from under him. The boat collapsed over the crest of a massive swell as a wave crashed over the side and into the cockpit, burying Peter knee deep in frothy sea water before disappearing into the cockpit drains.

"Go below," he told Burgoyne. "I'll take it from here. Next time wake me before it gets this crazy."

Burgoyne nodded, clearly exhausted and terrified, and carefully made his way to the hatch.

It wasn't easy to do, but he managed to let out the jib and mainsheets. The electric winches had no problem under normal loads, but under this level of strain they needed some cajoling. The lines were so taut that they looked like they would snap, but any one of them was strong enough to haul a thirty foot sailboat out of the water and dangle it in the air, and some even looked thick enough to handle Archangel. The sails loosened and started to flap violently as the mast sprang up straight. The powerless boat started to bob uncontrollably as it was subject to the whims of the storm. Peter reefed the sails, enjoying the ease with which the electric furler turned the oversized monsters into storm sails in seconds. Once the boat was back under control, he fully furled the jib and let out the third and smallest of the head sails.

Archangel heeled to just over fifteen degrees and slammed through the waves at ten knots, stabilizing as soon as the sails caught the wind. Peter had managed twelve knots before going to bed, but that was in much less wind. The storm made it difficult to balance the rig and speed had to be sacrificed for safety. The lines wouldn't fail, but a sail could rip and he refused to take that chance. Archangel was the last of her kind, and there would be no replacement parts.

The hatch opened and Penny's head popped out, obscured by the hood of her red rain jacket. She clipped her tether to the line and stepped onto the deck, clutching whatever she could reach. Brad followed.

"I need you to hold the wheel," Peter shouted to Penny, trying to be heard above the rain and crashing waves. "Keep the boat at a hundred and ten degrees." He pointed to the compass as she stumbled to the wheel and grabbed onto it. Peter waited until she was steady before letting go.

"You're going to help me with the sails," Peter said to Brad. "We're going to see how much speed we can squeeze out of this bad boy."

"Isn't this dangerous?" Brad yelled. "This looks like a really bad storm!"

Peter shook his head. "Are you kidding? A boat like this? Day in the park, as long as you don't get sick."

"Good to know," Brad said, smiling. "I thought we were going to die!"

"I still might," Penny shouted. "Die that is."

Peter turned to her, concerned. "Are you getting sick?"

"I was, down below, but I'm a bit better now."

"Just look out over the horizon. Remember it's all in your head."

"It doesn't feel like it's in my head!"

The radar display on the instrument cluster began to buzz. The proximity alert, which he had readjusted for one nautical mile, was going off. He had previously set it much further out, but with the height of the waves he had a choice between fidelity and range.

"Captain!" Brad shouted. "Look!" He pointed out towards the port bow, where a dark shape was just barely visible past the sails.

"That's not good," Peter said. "What the hell is that thing?"

"I think it's an iceberg," Brad said. "A pretty big one!"

Peter studied the relative position between the boat and the object, and saw that the wind and waves were slowly pushing Archangel towards a collision course.

Chapter 21 – Maelstrom

'And now the STORM-BLAST Came, and he
Was tyrannous and strong;
He struck with his o'ertaking wings,
And chased us south along.
- Samuel Taylor Coleridge

It wasn't an iceberg, that much became clear almost immediately. It was much too big and too symmetrical.

"Start the diesel," Peter ordered. "Once it's idling, kill it." He didn't want to waste fuel, but inches from collision was not the best time to discover that the engine wouldn't start.

Penny hit the ignition button and he could feel it turning over, but it wouldn't catch.

"Check the fuel cutoff." A diesel engine did not use spark plugs, it relied on compression to ignite the air fuel mixture. The only way to shut it down was to cut off the fuel.

"That was it," she shouted, pushed in the knob then cranked the engine again. It caught almost immediately and was idling steadily in seconds.

"Kill it," Peter said, running his hand across his throat for emphasis. "Don't forget to push the cutoff back in." He was surprised that a boat as fancy as Archangel didn't have an automatic cutoff. Or perhaps it did, with a manual as backup. He would have to look into it.

Checking the instruments, Peter noticed that their speed over land was almost thirteen knots, as opposed to a speed over water of ten knots. That meant that they were riding a current. The object, whatever the hell it was, was also riding the same current, but it would be a lot slower than they were. It was possible that they would pass it, but it was also possible that they wouldn't. The engine wouldn't help them much, unless they needed to sail into the wind or had to make some quick maneuvers.

"I think it's an oil tanker!" Penny shouted. "I can almost make out the bridge." Peter strained to see, but couldn't quite make it out before a flash of lightning in the distance illuminated the night long enough to see that Penny was right. It's rust streaked hull glistened with rain and sea water as it pitched and rolled in the angry sea.

"It's very low in the water," Brad pointed out. "No lights."

"A tsunami survivor," Peter said. "At least the ship is. Get ready guys, we're about to jibe, then run. Penny, when I tell you, steer hard to port to three hundred and thirty degrees."

"Run?" Brad asked. "What does that mean?"

"It means we're going to sail with the wind and get behind that thing, then come around to the leeward side. It's going to get nasty. Brad, furl the storm jib, we're going to fly something bigger."

When Brad had the small headsail stowed, Peter raised the mainsail almost all the way up.

"Hard to port!" he shouted, and the boat started to swing towards the looming tanker as Penny worked the wheel. "Compensate early or you'll over steer." The boom snapped out hard to the right as Peter let out the mainsheet and the wind caught the sail, pushing the boat from behind. The bow came to rest pretty close to where he wanted it and the boat began to pitch and roll violently, completely at the mercy of the waves and wind while it ran northwest towards what was once the southern coast of Long Island.

"I'm gonna be sick," Penny said, looking pale. Archangel's bow disappeared under the water as a large swell pushed them from behind. He saw her eyes widen in terror. He realized that to her it must appear as though the boat were going under. Before he could say anything the bow popped free, dumping a mass of water over the pilothouse and into the cockpit.

"Holy shit!" Penny swore, staring down at her clothes which were soaked past her waist.

"Not much longer," Peter assured her. "Hold it steady. Brad, forget the jib, we're doing fine with just the mainsail."

Within minutes they were behind the tanker, getting dangerously close. They heard the groaning and creaking of its steel hull as the sea tossed it about like a hunk of driftwood.

"Towards thee I roll," Peter said, quoting Melville. "Thou all-destroying but unconquering whale; to the last I grapple with thee;

from hell's heart I stab at thee; for hate's sake I spit my last breath at thee." Had it been a coincidence that that was one of the few books in which he had sought solace?

"Are you quoting Moby dick?" Penny said, shouting to be heard over the wind. "Tell me you're not quoting Moby Dick when we're about to be killed by an ocean going behemoth, you giant book nerd!"

"I am!" Peter shouted back. "It's glorious!"

"Maniac!" But she saw the glee in his eyes and her smile mirrored his own as they sailed past the tanker's monstrous hull.

"Penny, on my mark, hard to starboard, back to a hundred and ten. Remember to compensate early. Brad… as soon as the boom starts moving, we're going to haul in that mainsheet like there's no tomorrow. Mark!"

Penny spun the wheel and the boat turned to the right. The mainsail flapped violently until the wind caught it, then the boom started to swing hard around.

"Now! Haul!" Peter shouted. "Haul!" The electric winch could have handled the job, but Peter was becoming wary of pushing them too hard. If one of them failed, he wouldn't be able to repair it.

They hauled, hand over hand, managing to catch the boom before it snapped all the way to the other side. The wind caught the sail, the boat heeled and they coasted forward, picking up more and more speed as Peter unfurled and set the storm jib.

"Yeah!" he shouted, invigorated by the struggle. There was nothing, nothing at all like matching a good boat against a violent sea, and Archangel was the best boat he had ever set foot on.

"Are we out of the woods?" Penny shouted.

"Yes," Peter said. "We're good now. But we were never in the woods. Piece of cake." He had put the tanker far enough off the starboard side that it did not noticeably cut into their wind, but he could still make out some of the details of its deck. Not a single light shone anywhere. It was a ghost ship, drifting dead in the water and fading into the night as the wind pushed them north. If he ever ran in to Colonel Hamilton again, he would tell him about this ship. There might be enough oil in there to run his tanks and trucks for decades, provided he could figure out how to get to it and refine it.

Thinking of the ship made him realize what else it was likely to have on board. Diesel fuel. Perhaps it would be worth investigating after the storm.

"Good," Penny said. "Take the helm please." Brad rushed over to grab the wheel as she stumbled over to the side of the cockpit and vomited all over the teak deck, not realizing how much boat was left after the raised cockpit boundary.

"Oh crap," she swore. "I'm sorry. I'll clean up whatever the rain doesn't get."

"No need," Peter said, grinning. "Hold on tight!" He winched in the mainsheet until the force of the wind buried the port side of the boat under the water, then let it out to return the heel to normal. "All done." He laughed as he saw her wry smile, unable to contain his joy. He couldn't remember a time when he felt more in control, more alive.

"Show off!" Penny said.

"That's a hell of a way to swab the deck," Brad said.

They sailed steadily onwards through the storm until the sun peeked above the horizon and the sea began to calm. A steady westerly wind blew them along at Archangel's top speed of twelve knots. As the golden orb rose into the sky, the clouds caught fire, rippling with hues of orange and red. The scene was mirrored in the surface of the sea so that it looked like the whole world was nothing but sky.

"It's the most beautiful thing I've ever seen," Penny said, pressing up against him.

"Nah," Peter said. "I've seen better."

She looked up at him. "Oh really? Where?"

"Right here," he said, staring into her eyes.

Only the slightest sound betrayed her intake of breath. Her eyes sparkled in the morning light as she stood on her tiptoes to kiss him.

Chapter 22 – Bounty

At length did cross an Albatross,
Thorough the fog it came;
As if it had been a Christian soul,
We hailed it in God's name.
It ate the food it ne'er had eat,
And round and round it flew.
The ice did split with a thunder-fit;
The helmsman steered us through!
- Samuel Taylor Coleridge

The tender raced over the now calm surface of the ocean, bouncing slightly over gentle swells. Peter sat at the bow, holding his rifle and staring ahead at the distant shape of the tanker as the occasional spray misted his face and neck. It was strange knowing that this was the sort of mission he would have been sent on had fate allowed him to compete his training. Though the goal was not likely to have been retrieval of waterlogged diesel fuel.

Penny sat just behind him, similarly armed, and Brad manned the outboard. A small anchor intended for the tender, attached to a length of knotted rope, occupied the center of the boat.

"It makes me feel so small," Penny said, staring out at the horizon. "It's different on Archangel. You know?" She had to speak loudly to be heard over the roaring motor. The sun glared from a sky almost completely devoid of clouds. Their speed made it pleasantly cool, but the heat and humidity was waiting for them to slow down.

"Yeah," Peter said. "I know. It can be overwhelming."

She cocked her head and grinned. "What, no poetry, Prof? Losing your touch?"

Peter narrowed his eyes at her and grinned.

"Oh for the breath of the briny deep, and the tug of a bellying sail. With the sea-gull's cry across the sky, and a passing boatman's hail. For, be she fierce or be she gay, the sea is a famous friend alway.

"It's called 'A Sailor's Song,' by Paul Lawrence Dunbar, born in 1872 in Ohio, the son of freed slaves from Kentucky. Died of tuberculosis in1906 at the age of thirty three. Still think I'm losing my touch?"

She shook her head and laughed, then said, "Okay, okay, you've still got it."

"How about you?" Peter said. "When you look out onto the ocean, what do you think of? What comes to mind?"

"Sushi."

"I'm going to find a piece of driftwood, carve a paddle, and put you over my knee. In a gentle and loving manner, of course."

"I'm kidding!" she said, still laughing. "Besides, who says I won't like that? Fine, fine, I have a quote for you too, but it's not poetry, it's from my favorite book. 'The sea is only the embodiment of a supernatural and wonderful existence. It is nothing but love and emotion, it is the living infinite.'"

"Jules Verne!" he said. "I thought you only liked video games."

"I told you, Captain Smartass, I love submarines. But I never told you why. Now you know. My dad used to read it to me." Her smile left her and she slumped as she exhaled a long and slow breath.

"I'm sorry," he said, and put a hand on her shoulder.

She smiled faintly and shrugged. "We need to cherish the good memories."

"Indeed."

The tanker was coming up fast, and Peter turned his attention to finding a good place to gain entry. The ship was massive, over a thousand feet long, with raised sections at the bow and stern. The deck was mostly flat except for the superstructure and a dizzying array of deck fixtures presumably related to the loading and unloading of crude oil. Orange and brown rust streaked the pale blue hull and obstructed any markings it may have once displayed. Other than the rust and signs of general neglect, the ship appeared to be sound. Its hull was very low in the water, but the top of the gunwale was still a good thirty feet above the water line. Peter had studied the design of such ships in Seal training but it had been too long ago and he had never had a chance to put what he'd learned into practice. He did remember that it being as low in the water as it was meant it was either severely waterlogged, filled to the brim with oil, or both.

"There," he said, pointing to the vessel's port beam. "That's as good a place as any."

Brad lowered the throttle and the tender dropped off of plane and idled its way towards the center of the behemoth. Peter watched for signs of movement but saw nothing. The ship loomed over them, a truly imposing sight. The sheer size of it was incredible. It was like a floating city.

Peter took the dinghy anchor and grabbed it by the knotted rope. "Get down," he said and waited until the others hugged the deck before he swung it around and around and around. Once it had built up enough momentum, he tossed it up and over the tanker's railing. It hit with a loud clang that made Peter cringe. If there were anyone alive on that ship, they would know that someone was coming aboard. He should have realized that when he'd made his plan, but failing to do so was part of what being an "almost Seal" entailed. He pulled on the rope until the anchor caught on something, gave it a few violent tugs to make sure it was firmly seated, then tied the other end to a cleat on the dinghy's bow.

"Alrighty then," he said. "Let's go."

He had tied knots into the rope every couple of feet and used them to climb up to the railing, then swung himself over. He brought up his rifle and surveyed the deck while the others followed. It was streaked with rust but otherwise spotless, washed clean of any and all signs of habitation. That was a good sign, at least for them. Not so much for whoever had survived the event on board.

The deck had been painted a flat maroon color, and much of that remained, though unrelenting sun, wind and spray had turned much of it into a chalky brown that blended with the rust and gave it a mottled orange aspect. It spread out all around them, impossibly big, its farthest edges hazy in the humid ocean air.

"How do I look?" Penny asked, brandishing her carbine as she looked around the desolate tanker. "I feel like Arnold Schwarzenegger." She did look good in the camouflage tactical vest and leg-strapped pistol holster, but then she looked good in anything.

"Before or after he became a politician?" Peter teased.

"I'm not sure. What's the difference?" They all shared a laugh.

"Hey Brad," Peter said. "Are you ready for this?" Brad wielded one of Peter's shotguns, a bullpup design that held fourteen rounds of buckshot in twin user selectable magazine tubes. It was only twenty six inches long—the pistol grip and trigger were located forward of the receiver. In close quarters, it was incredibly deadly and superior to a carbine, though it required more skill to use effectively. Brad didn't really have that skill, but he did tend to hit what he shot at with it. Peter had wanted to use it himself, but Brad was a terrible shot and wouldn't be able to hit anything with a rifle.

The younger man shrugged. "Ready as I'll ever be, I guess. Let's do this!"

"Alright," Peter said. "Just like we practiced."

"Got it," Penny said, sweeping the area to the right of them with her muzzle as she surveyed her surroundings. Brad covered the rear, and Peter focused his attention on the front left. They made their way to the superstructure, navigating their way around pipes, drums and other deck fixtures as the deck gently rocked underneath them in the calm seas.

The superstructure, which had been painted white, looked a lot more worn than the deck. The deck's orange brown rust had blended into the maroon paint, whereas on the superstructure the blemishes stood out like oozing sores on pale skin. They found a hatchway right away. Peter approached and tried to open it, but the lever was stuck. A few taps with the butt of his rifle freed it, and they stepped into the dark hallway.

"Lights on," Peter said as he led the way inside. The corridor bloomed painfully bright as they activated their weapon lights. The shadows danced and jumped as the beams swept back and forth across the walls.

"So where to now?" Penny said. "This thing is a maze." True to her description, the long corridor was beset with hatches, doorways and offshoots.

"Down," Peter said. "We're already most of the way aft. That's where the engine's gonna be, and, I assume, the fuel lines, if not the tanks."

"Wouldn't the tank fill be above deck?" Brad asked.

"Yes," Peter said. "But we have no idea what it looks like, nor would we have any way to siphon the fuel. Our best bet is to find the fuel line to the engines, find a value or otherwise tap it, and draw it from there."

"That's going to be a lot of trips with five gallon containers," Brad said.

Peter nodded, though Brad was behind him and couldn't see the gesture. "Yeah. But we don't have a lot of choice."

"This place is spooky," Penny said as they slowly made their way down the corridor. "I feel like someone is watching me." Their lights danced across walls and shone into rooms. Peter had expected to find a mess, but everything appeared orderly. Most of the rooms they were passing were crew quarters. The bunks were neatly made, the cabinets were closed and there were few items scattered about. Inside the superstructure there was minimal rust, though some had crept in from around portholes and wall seams.

"I wonder if anyone survived," Brad said.

"I'm sure most of them did," Peter said. "At first."

"Dammit Peter," Penny said. "I wish you hadn't said that."

"Sorry, but there's no other alternative. I doubt any are still alive. If they could get the engines working, they would have made landfall, such as it would have been." He paused, noticing something ahead. "There." Just ahead, a rusty steel stairway descended into the darkness.

"Did you hear that?" Brad said suddenly, and Peter froze.

He listened and heard nothing.

"I could have sworn—" Brad said.

"Shh!" Peter said, raising his hand in a gesture of silence.

From the depths of the behemoth, he heard a shuffling sound. Barely audible. So faint that he could almost will it to be a figment of his imagination. But after a few seconds, it became louder.

"Something's coming," Peter said. "Back off, assume defensive positions!"

"Shit," Penny said as she backed away and pointed her rifle at the stairway. "Shit, shit, shit. This better not be some apocalyptic zombie shit, Peter, or I'm going to be very pissed off!"

They waited for several minutes. The shuffling grew louder, but then stopped. Nothing came up the stairs.

"Peter," Penny said.

"Yes?"

"This is some fucked up bullshit."

"What is?"

"Abandoned ship? Shuffling sounds? Come on, it's like we're in a cliché survival horror game."

"I never played those. But we've gotta go down there. Whatever it is, it most likely can't hurt us. And by whatever, I mean whoever."

"Most likely?" she said.

"I don't like that, man," Brad said. "Most likely doesn't mean definitely."

"Look you two," Peter said. "This isn't a video game, and whoever is down there, if it is indeed someone and not some shit rolling around as the boat rocks, they aren't going to be in a very healthy state. So let's cut the crap and do what we came here to do. Okay?"

"Okay," Penny and Brad said at the same time.

"Good. Let's go." He started down the stairs before they could protest. When the staircase turned a hundred and eighty degrees, the smell became stronger, and he realized that he had been smelling it all along but hadn't noticed. It was familiar, but he couldn't place it.

"What the hell is that?" Penny said. "Rotting food?" Peter pictured her wrinkling her nose, but he couldn't see her as she was behind him and shining her light in his direction. Their lights were glaringly bright against the mostly white walls that the rust hadn't reached yet.

The stairs took them directly into the engine room. They emerged onto a catwalk that ran along all four walls. They could see the engines in the shadowy space below as the beams from their lights darted about. Pipes and ductwork ran along the ceiling and parts of the walls, and a particularly large duct, painted white, obscured the catwalk directly in front of them. A shape shambled around the duct and into view.

Penny gasped, Brad screamed. Peter brought up his rifle.

It shuffled towards them with a lumbering gait. It was short, squat, and as their lights danced over it they saw that it was covered in dried gore. It was mostly dark red with patches of white and black. Its eyes were yellow and dead as it glared at them.

Peter heard Brad's rifle click off of safe.

"Hold your fire!" Peter shouted. "Don't shoot! Hold your fire."

The gore crusted pelican continued to walk towards them, its pace slowing as it approached. The dried blood on its plumage told Peter a story he didn't want to know, and he shone his light down into the lower section of the engine room to confirm it. What was left of the bodies lay in the open space just below the ladder that descended from the catwalk. There were eight or nine in the pile. One body was apart from the others. A pistol lay at its side. Peter's light glinted off of spent shell casings that littered the maroon painted floor. The color hid the dried blood. Judging by the state of the bodies, they couldn't have been dead more than a few days, perhaps a week.

"My god," Penny said, shining her own light down below.

The pelican chirped and honked and walked closer. It was in a sad state. It's breastbone was prominent in its chest.

"It must have gotten trapped down here," Peter said. "And…scavenged."

"Do we…" Brad said, hesitating. "Do we have to kill it? I mean, it ate people…"

"Don't be retarded," Penny said. "It's coming to us for help." She seemed all too happy to focus on something besides the grizzly scene below.

"Alright," Peter said. "We have work to do. Penny, let's find somewhere we can tap the diesel fuel and start ferrying operations. Brad, go back to Archangel and sail it here, keep at least two hundred meters away from the tanker."

"What about the bird?" Penny asked. The pelican, as though sensing it was being discussed, honked at them, then chirped three times and ambled closer.

"We'll take him back with us when we're done," Peter said. "Feed him, clean him, and send him on his way."

"I think it's an Australian pelican," Penny said. "As far as I know, they are the only ones who scavenge meat."

"Why is that significant?" Brad said.

"Because," Penny said. "It's an *Australian* pelican, Brad. It's from Australia. We are not in Australia. Another piece of the puzzle, I suppose. Whatever happened caused birds from as far away as Australia to end up in North America. Unless it escaped from a zoo or something."

"Interesting," Peter said. He didn't mind stalling. Going down into the lower level was something he was all too eager to avoid for as long as possible. "Australia is almost as far south as it gets, so would they have gotten rain or snow? Don't the seasons reverse that far south?"

"Yes," Penny said. "It's in the temperate zone, so their summer is December through February. But Australia's climate is mostly governed by the subtropical high pressure belt. I have no idea what happened there once the global climate patterns were disrupted."

"It's also shielded by the Southern Ocean," Brad said, reminding Peter that he too was a highly educated genius. Or, as he preferred to think of him, an over-educated smartass. "But I don't think climate would be their biggest problem."

"What do you mean?" Peter said.

"Oh shit," Penny said. "That's right. It's the lowest of the continents in terms of elevation."

The pelican edged closer and pecked Peter's leg with its beak. The peck was gentle, an attention grabber rather than any sort of attack. Peter absentmindedly patted the bird's head before he realized what he was doing. He didn't know anything about pelicans, and the bird could be dangerous. But neither Brad nor Penny seemed alarmed, so he figured it was okay. A few flakes of dried blood stuck to his palm, and he wiped it on his pants.

Brad nodded. "Yep. Australia is gone, it's just a few chains of tiny islands now."

"So would that explain what this bird is doing here?" Peter said.

Brad shook his head. "I don't think so, they mostly hang out on the water. There would be more than enough land for them, and an abundance of food. Something happened that caused them—because I'm guessing this isn't the only one—to fly the fuck out of there."

"It's probably linked to the event itself," Penny said. "Rather than what happened after."

"Yeah," Brad said. "Pelicans aren't migratory birds. So if they ended up here, something bad caused them to leave."

"Alright," Peter said. "We can chit chat once we're back on Archangel. We have work to do, let's get it done."

Chapter 23 – Remembrance

So, too, the buck that trimmed my terraces,
Our whilom gardener, called the garden his;
Who now, deposed, surveys my plain abode
And his late kingdom, only from the road.
- Robert Louis Stevenson

They sailed without incident for the next five days, averaging a speed of just over ten knots. The pelican took off on the morning of the fifth day. It had allowed them to transport it to Archangel, where it partook of fresh water and fish with unabashed glee. Peter had hosed it off with the boat's seawater deck pump and watched it fill out and return to health as it preened itself and shambled about the boat, sticking its beak into everyone's business. He enjoyed having it around and missed it after it left, but he didn't miss dealing with the jumbo sized bird crap it had deposited all over the deck. He thought Penny would probably miss it more than anyone else. She had named it "Walter" and it had seemed to like her the most.

They had found a diesel line on the tanker and managed to ferry almost three hundred gallons of fuel before the line ran dry. The main tank wasn't empty, but they couldn't find any other way to get at it, so that had been it for fuel. Though three hundred gallons in a sailboat, even one as big as Archangel, was nothing to shake a stick at. They had also found a partially stocked sick bay with some valuable medical supplies. That and a couple of weapons and associated ammunition had been the extent of their bounty, and it was well worth the effort.

With the autopilot doing most of the steering, Peter had time for some long overdue maintenance tasks. He swapped out the desalination filter in the watermaker, lubricated all of the seacocks and bled the water out of the fuel filter. He found the maintenance log and cringed when he saw the last time the engine oil was changed. That was one of the first things he remedied, saving the old oil in the empty bottles of the new. Archangel carried an impressive quantity of spare parts and fluids, but he would need to stretch them out for as long as possible. There weren't likely to be any replacements. The tanker had been full of crude oil, but he doubted he could just pour that into the engine without refining it.

When the weather was calm, he spent time teaching some of the others how to sail, and how to shoot. Dr. Foster refused to participate in the shooting at first, but after some goading from Penny she reluctantly agreed to some basic lessons. Burgoyne was a pretty good shot, but Brad was hopeless with anything other than Peter's bullpup shotgun, with which he proved surprisingly adept. By the end of the third day, all of them knew how to load and reload most of the weapons and operate the safeties, where present. Peter gave each of them a gun, leaving it as their individual responsibility. Even Foster consented to keeping a small pistol in her stateroom.

When Penny wasn't spending time with Peter, she was with one of the two Dr. Gables. The senior Gable had taken to lecturing her in front of a whiteboard, and she spent hours scribbling incomprehensible notes into an unused logbook. The time she spent with Brad was difficult for Peter, though he decided not to obsess over it. She showed no signs of any romantic interest in the younger Gable, nor he in her, and her attitude towards Peter never changed except that they grew closer and more comfortable with one another. She proved quite adventurous in finding new ways to express her affections, which resulted in more time on watch for the others while Peter slept off his exertions both at and off the helm.

On the evening of the fifth day after their passage through New York, the elder Dr. Gable announced that it was Friday. At first, Peter wasn't sure of the significance, but then he remembered their conversation—it was movie night. Thanks to a steady wind and calm seas, he was able to join the others in the lower salon lounge as they watched one of the Daniel Craig James Bond movies on the giant in-wall LCD monitor. He sat there, transfixed by the sights and sounds as Penny pressed close, holding tightly onto his arm. The story was compelling, a tale of vengeance and romance with over the top action and violence that was somehow made believable by competent directing.

Momentarily distracted out of his immersion, he was struck by how similar this was to how life used to be. Here he was, inside an elegant lounge with a group of friends and a beautiful young woman on his arm. They were sitting on a couch, watching a movie, munching on crackers and sipping water from cups. It was a different reality than the one he was used to. The elder Gable had been right, movie night was important.

The people on the screen wore clean, stylish clothes, walked around in spectacular places and did the most ordinary, the most wonderful things, like crossing a busy street or making a phone call. When it was over, Peter was momentarily confused, unsure of where he was. It all came flooding back suddenly: the snow, the isolation, Penny. He remembered the men he had killed, the things he had seen and heard. It was too much, too quickly, and he excused himself and went topside into a world painted in shades of purple by the setting sun.

Once up on deck, he made his way to the bow, where he sat leaning on the stainless steel rails with his legs dangling out over the side. No longer able to contain himself, he wept as silently as he could. He didn't hear Penny walking up behind him.

"Do you want to be alone?" she asked.

"No."

She sat down and held him, stroking his hair softly. The bow rose and fell gently as Archangel cut through the waves. They sat in silence, watching the water rush by. This far forward, Peter couldn't see any part of the boat and could pretend he was flying over the water like a sea bird searching for fish below the dark green surface. He could almost make out shapes moving beneath the waves.

"Penny!" he shouted suddenly, pointing down at the water. The first of the dolphins broke the surface as its graceful form leapt into the air, showing them a brief glimpse of its perpetually grinning face before it disappeared beneath the sea. He could make out several more riding Archangel's bow wave.

"They're beautiful," she said softly. Somehow seeing the dolphins made everything all right. If there were dolphins happy and healthy enough to ride bow waves, then the planet wasn't dead, the ecological cycle had not been broken. Things had changed, but there was still hope.

With the proximity alert set out to three nautical miles and relatively tranquil seas, Peter was able to sleep soundly through the night.

The next morning, he found himself alone with Dr. Gable, who was cheerfully manning a fishing pole. They had been catching fish steadily since they first set out. Back in the house, Peter had worried that no deer would survive the snow and that there would be nothing to eat after the thaw, but of course he hadn't known that he had been just a few miles from the ocean. At least one major fishing season had been skipped thus far, and all the fish that would have made it onto someone's dinner plate in the last four months were swimming free and breeding.

"We're going to make landfall in a few hours," Peter said.

"Hmm? What?" Dr. Gable asked, turning to face him. "Sorry, I was daydreaming."

"Landfall, doc," Peter repeated. "We're going to make landfall in two, maybe three hours."

"Oh. Already? That's wonderful."

"How far inland is this place?"

"Well, if the contour lines can be trusted, it's about five and a half kilometers, or just under three and a half miles. Of course the terrain will be mountainous and difficult."

"Who do you need with you?" Peter asked, calculating potential risks and how to nullify them. He had always been particularly adept at coming up with problems, reasons why something wouldn't work, and solutions. His academic colleagues had considered him negative, a bad influence on their forward thinking, positive outlooks.

"No one, I suppose," Gable said, rubbing his chin. "Though Miss Penelope could be a great help to me. Shame about her, really."

"How so?" Peter asked, instantly defensive.

"She would have made a first class physicist. I would have been honored to accept her as a post doc fellow. Stellar head on her shoulders, that one."

"Oh." Gable was right, it was a shame. "But you're teaching her, right? She can still learn from the best."

"Yes, and it has been my sincere pleasure to do so, but honestly Peter, to what end? What use are calculations and particle dynamics in a world like this? No, Peter, you are the future, we're just relics of a bygone age. Better to teach her to be a warrior, a huntress." Gable's lips were pursed and he looked like he was about to start weeping. He had practically talked himself into depression.

"Don't be ridiculous," Peter said quickly, hoping to pull him up before he fell too far. "Civilization was set back, but it's not dead. I told you about Colonel Hamilton, and there are probably dozens more like him scattered all around the world. According to the topo maps, practically half of the US survived intact, so all we need is for someone to get out there and start using all those machines again, and to make new ones. We're going to need people like you and Penny to show us how."

Gable looked up and smiled appreciatively. "You're a good man, Peter. Penelope is lucky to have you."

"Yes I am," Penny said from behind him. "And I'm going to scream if you call me Penelope one more time."

Peter turned to face her, face flushing from embarrassment. "How much did you hear?"

"All of it," she said, then kissed him. "Your spooky captain sense is failing you, honey bun."

"So, um," Peter said to Gable, eager to change the subject. "Tell me again about this place we're going to."

For a moment, Peter saw the same hesitation in the scientist's face that he'd noticed when he first brought up their destination, but then the old man relaxed.

"It's a high altitude magnetometer observatory."

"A what?" Peter said.

"A magnetometer observatory," Gable repeated. "One of five built to study the altitude dependence of the geomagnetic field. They're officially a part of MEASURE…Magnetometers along the Eastern Atlantic Seaboard for Undergraduate Research and Education. But that's just a grant distribution issue. They were each built as independent facilities to pursue a very specific line of research."

"There's an extra 'a' in there somewhere," Peter muttered, but no one paid attention.

"Does that have anything to do with geomagnetic reversal?"

Penny asked.

Gable gave her a warm smile. "Indeed. There was a growing concern about it among some, not the least cause of which was the weakening magnetic field. This is not my area of expertise, but from what I understand these stations relied on altitude dependence data to support the polarity flip study."

"Wait a sec," Peter said. "Magnetic pole flip? Wasn't that supposed to cause some sort of disaster? Could that be…"

"Not at all," Gable said. "That's popular media drivel. Our planet has survived hundreds if not thousands of reversals. Fifteen million years ago the poles reversed fifty one times in a twelve million year period. Our hominid ancestors survived many such shifts without any noticeable increase in solar radiation. No, the only detrimental effects would be to certain species that rely on the Earth's magnetic field to navigate, and of course our own dependence on the field for communication would result in technological disruptions. Hardly the sort of disaster that has befallen us at present."

"Oh," Peter said, feeling stupid. "I guess it's a good thing there's no more television to delude the masses."

"Every cloud…" Gable began with a toothy grin.

"Yeah, okay, so why go there? What do you hope to learn?"

Gable hesitated. "I don't want to lie to you anymore, either of you, but I don't want to tell you, either. Not yet. Can you wait until I get the data I need?"

Peter was about to speak, then closed his mouth, not sure what to say.

"Professor," Penny said. "You're scaring me a little. What's going on?"

"I'm sorry, Penelope," Gable said, his face a mask of stern determination. "I would really prefer not to say anything until I have my data. Please understand."

"I trust you, doc," Peter said. "As long as you promise to tell me afterwards, I'm okay with it. Pen?"

"Me too, I guess," Penny said, though she didn't sound convinced. Peter wondered what she was so concerned about. He failed to see how readings on the Earth's magnetic field could have any relevance to anything but Gable's theories.

The old man smiled, relieved. "Thank you both. If you will excuse me, the fish aren't biting. I think I'll go have a nap. Please wake me when we're in sight of land."

"Will do."

Gable stowed the fishing pole and disappeared down the hatch.

"So what do you think he's up to?" Peter asked Penny.

She shrugged. "I don't know, Peter, but considering how determined he is to get there, it's a little unnerving. Maybe you shouldn't have let him off the hook so easily."

"I don't understand how magnetic field readings could be cause for concern."

"I don't either," she said, shaking her head. "That's what scares me."

Chapter 24 – Revelation

No one can conceive the variety of feelings which bore me
onwards, like a hurricane, in the first enthusiasm of success.
Life and death appeared to me ideal bounds,
which I should first break through,
and pour a torrent of light into our dark world.
- Mary Shelly

Peter watched the islands of Newfoundland creep out of the mist as the dinghy idled slowly towards landfall. What little he could see was like something from another world. Craggy mountain tops towered over the water, creating channels that disappeared into the mist like the entrances to a colossal maze. Some were a familiar mix of tree covered green and stone gray like the Catskills back home, others were brown and bare. Most of the mountains were flat like the Arizona mesas, yet some towered to conical peaks. The totality of the scene seemed almost artificial, as though a graphic artist had meshed together discrepant images to create a bizarre tableau.

"Spooky," Brad said, voicing Peter's thoughts. "I feel like I'm landing on an alien planet."

Of course it *was* alien. This was not the coast of Newfoundland as anyone had ever known it, as Peter had known it when he had sailed there years before. All that was left of that coast was hundreds of feet below the dinghy's fiberglass hull.

Glancing over his shoulder, Peter saw a brief glimpse of Archangel's stern before she disappeared into the fog. He wasn't too keen on leaving Burgoyne and Foster alone with the boat, but Brad would be returning shortly with the tender. With him sailing and Burgoyne shooting, they would probably be okay if anything happened to the landing party.

"Through that passage there," Gable pointed as he looked over his map. "That will take us closer to the observatory. Hopefully we will find a place to land."

"I'm sure we will," Peter said. "The problem will be finding a way to get up there. Some of those cliffs are quite steep."

"At least we haven't seen anyone alive out here yet," Penny said. "As odd a thing as that is to hope for, considering."

"I get it," Brad agreed. "Believe me I get it."

"We're getting close to the coast," Peter said quietly. "Let's cut the motor and get the oars out."

They drifted in silence towards the rocky bank, alert for any sign of movement. A few birds flew low over the scattered tree tops, circling aimlessly as though confused by the weak updrafts at this once great altitude, and Peter wondered if Walter the pelican was one of them. A gentle slope cut up through a patch of forest, steepening towards the top.

"Careful," Peter said to Brad as the boat approached the shore. "Let me look over the side and see how deep it is. We don't want to damage the boat."

They were able to guide the tender to land without scraping the hull, though Brad had to hold onto some coarse grass to keep the inflated tube pressed to the rocky landing as the others disembarked. Penny had a little trouble, unused to weight of her vest, but adjusted quickly and managed a graceful egress.

"Radio check in twenty minutes," Peter said as Brad prepared to push off. "We should be high enough by then." They had taken two hand-held marine VHF radios from Archangel, leaving a fixed unit on board. The radios were not optimal for land based communications as they operated on line of sight, which meant they could not be used from inside buildings or any place where physical objects interfered with the signal's path. Hardly the best choice, but it was all they had to work with.

"Gotcha," Brad said as he picked up the oars and started to row away from shore.

They watched him disappear into the mist.

"And I thought the tanker was spooky," Penny said.

Peter smiled and poked her playfully in the shoulder. "No more video game references, sailor."

"Aye aye skipper," she said.

The radio came alive. "Captain," It was Brad's voice, barely above a whisper. "There's another boat here, headed your way. It's small, they're rowing it. There's a guy with a gun."

Peter grabbed the radio and pressed the transmit button. "Did they see you?"

"No. I killed the motor and got out of there before they spotted me, but they may have heard me. Before I shut the motor off I mean."

"Stay off the radio until I call you." Peter had cursed the mist when they had first set out, but he was grateful for it now.

"Roger."

"Okay," Peter said, turning to the others. "We need to hide. See that ridge over there in the trees?"

"Yeah," Penny said. Gable nodded.

"Let's go."

As they moved, Peter looked around for signs of a path and found one, just the faintest hint of a trail heading up into the trees about thirty meters south of their position along the coast. Why hadn't he spotted it before? Or perhaps he had, and not realized its significance. The other boat came into view just as they crouched down behind the outcrop, their movements silenced by a bed of damp moss. As it glided closer to shore, Peter could see several people, including the one with the weapon. He felt his gut tighten as a feeling of dread started to form in its pit.

The man was heavily armed—military carbine, tactical vest and a holstered side arm. He wore assorted gear in pouches and clipped on to the vest, including a flashlight, radio and a pair of elaborate goggles with what looked like a heads up display projector. His weapon, an FN-P90, was equipped with a holographic sight and a tactical camera for shooting around corners. More to the point, everything he had fit correctly and he wore it with a casual elegance. A well trained and experienced soldier with a fully modern kit.

"That's not good," Peter muttered.

The others on the boat were a stark contrast. Where the soldier appeared clean and in good health, the people with him were bedraggled and haggard, their soiled clothes a match for their bleak expressions. There were four of them, three men and a young woman. She looked particularly rough. Her face was badly discolored and swollen around one eye. Their vessel was a large wooden rowboat covered in peeling green and white paint. Brackets on the gunwales as well as an external rudder suggested it may have had a mast at one time.

The civilians rowed the boat to shore, then all four climbed out while one tied it to a post that had been obscured from view by tall grass. The soldier motioned to the others and they stood back while he exited the craft and stood off to the side. While he watched, the four hauled several canvas sacks out of the boat. The woman tripped and dropped one, spilling several fish.

The soldier was on her in an instant. He kicked her hard into the water, where she collapsed on all fours, soaking her dirty dress. Peter's red dot reticle was on his head before he realized what he was doing, but he lowered it quickly. It was not the time for action—there wasn't enough information.

"Stupid bitch!" the soldier cursed with what sounded like a French accent. "You better get them all." The woman fumbled in the water and managed to recover the fish, which fortunately for her were either dead or too weak to swim away.

"French Canadian," Gable whispered.

When the fish were back in the sacks, the four civilians each grabbed one and slung them over their shoulders. The soldier motioned for them to move, and they set off up the path and disappeared into the woods.

"What the hell was that?" Penny said. "Did you see the way he kicked her?"

"I don't know," Peter said. "But I don't like it. That soldier was very well armed. If there are more like him, we should get the hell out of here."

"Peter," Gable said sternly. "I need that data."

"We'll check it out," Peter said. "Go see what's up there. But doc, I'm gonna tell you right now, there's no way I'm going to fight someone as well armed as he was, not if there's more of them. With that gun camera he could hide behind a rock or a wall and shoot us all without exposing himself. That's some serious gear." Peter was reminded of the advantage he had held over the skinheads because of his night vision goggles and red dot sight. "If we can get to that station unobserved, great, if not, we'll see what we're up against and I'll make my decision."

Gable looked like he was going to say something, then nodded.

"What about those people? That woman?" Penny demanded.

"I don't know," Peter admitted. "We'll see." She didn't seem satisfied by that answer, but didn't press either. "Let's go. We're going after that group, see where they go."

Following behind Peter, they made their way up the trail, moving slowly, cautiously. Peter held his rifle at the low ready position with the stock on his shoulder and the muzzle pointed down at an angle, ready to snap up at any time. Penny mimicked him.

He was putting her life in danger yet again, he realized. He almost ordered them all back, but managed to shrug off the impulse. They were just going to do a little reconnaissance. The soldier had not seemed particularly alert to anything but the civilians he was escorting. He hadn't even bothered to look around. Like Peter in the last few weeks of his solitude, the soldier had grown complacent. No one understood better than he how easy it was to believe there was no one else left in the world.

After about twenty minutes of walking they were high enough to see the water beyond the edge of the mountain. The sun had burned off most of the fog, though patches of mist still clung to the cliff sides. Peter took out the radio.

"Archangel, this is away team, come in," he said. "Come in Archangel."

"Away team," Penny said, rolling her eyes. "One to beam up."

Peter smiled. "What, video games are less nerdy than Star Trek?"

"Um…yes? Where have you been?"

"Well you understood the reference, *and* you play video games. That makes you twice the nerd I am!" Humor was good, it broke the tension, and they all needed that, particularly Gable. Peter had never seen the old man more edgy. Penny was tense as well, seeing that woman being abused had hit her hard. She might have needed the distraction more than Gable.

She opened her mouth to retort.

"Away team, this is Archangel, we read you." It was Foster's voice.

"Is Brad back?" Peter asked the radio.

"Roger, he's just pulling up now."

"Good, maintain radio silence. I want you to head further from the coast, another mile or so should do it."

"Trouble?"

"Maybe. Brad will explain."

"Understood."

They continued through the forest, occasionally emerging into open terrain. Peter used the binoculars he had taken from Archangel's helm to track the soldier and his group. The people carrying the bags moved slowly, so Peter had to order a halt every time the trees thinned out to allow the fishermen to keep far enough ahead. Eventually, they crested a ridge and saw a chain link fence surrounding a small concrete building. Its roof was covered in satellite dishes and two pickup trucks stood in a small parking lot around back.

"That's it," Gable said. "That's the observatory." They crouched down near a clump of boulders shielded from view by low hanging foliage and thick bushes. The fence was about a hundred and fifty yards from their position.

Peter watched as the soldier and his party approached the facility. Two more men, armed with full sized rifles, opened the gate to let them pass. They had the same advanced optics and gun camera as the first soldier.

"I'm sorry doc," Peter said, shaking his head. "If that's the observatory, this is the end of the line. We're going back."

"Peter," Gable said. "I…"

"I know you need the data, doc, but we're not getting in there without a fight."

"You don't understand, we have to!" Gable looked strangely intense.

"No, Dr. Gable, *you* don't understand. This isn't a movie, and I'm not James Bond. Those people are soldiers, if I start shooting, I might get one of them before they take cover and return fire, and they're not going to miss. Even if it's just those three, at least one of us is going to die, and that's just not acceptable."

Gable's face was growing red. He look like he was about to start shouting.

"Listen to him, professor," Penny said, trying to calm him. "He has a gift for these things. He can measure a situation and know exactly what will happen, I've seen him do it before, and so have you. If he says at least one of us going to die, then at least one of us is going to die."

Peter looked at her, almost overcome by a sudden burst of gratitude. Such a simple thing it was, to have someone support him, to believe in him. Yet what a profound impact it had.

Gable slumped, defeated. "You don't understand. We have to know. We're so close!"

"Have to know what?" Penny demanded. "I think it's time you were up front with us, Emmet."

Gable nodded as he lowered himself to a sitting position, his back against a tree trunk. He rubbed his eyes, and looked very tired. For the first time since they'd met him, the scientist was showing his age. His usual exuberance was gone.

"If we're all going to die," he said.

"All of us?" Peter asked. "Our group?"

Gable shook his head. "All of us. Everyone, everything."

"I don't get it. How can a magnetic field observatory tell us if we're all going to die?"

"Oh my god," Penny whispered, looking pale. "It can't be. I've been trying to figure out what you were up to, trying so hard to get to this observatory, and how that relates to the event. I could only come up with one thing, though the details are beyond me. Please tell me I'm wrong."

"What?" Peter demanded. "What can't be? What the hell is going on here?"

"Let him tell it," she said. "I...I hope to god I'm wrong."

"You're not," Gable said. "I know you well enough by now to know what you're thinking."

"Enough of this," Peter snapped. "Tell me what you know. Now."

"Do you want the short answer or do you want me to explain?" Gable didn't flinch from his anger, in fact he seemed to embrace it.

"Explain," Peter said. Part of him wanted to shake Gable and demand he get to the point, but he knew that he would probably not understand unless it was spelled out for him. They were far enough from the facility, and out of sight, so there was no danger in lingering.

"I isolated the Higgs boson after I was brought on board at the

LHC."

"The Large Hadron Collider," Penny cut in for Peter's benefit. "It was the largest and most powerful particle accelerator ever built." She shivered and wrapped her arms around herself. "Holy fuck please make me wrong."

"Largest, yes," Gable corrected. "But not the most powerful, not by a long shot."

Penny wrinkled her brow. "I thought…"

"After my work at the LHC, I was hired by the US Department of Energy to head up a team in a new facility in Antarctica. A smaller, more compact version of the LHC, with a much larger collision chamber."

"How do you build something like that in Antarctica?" Penny asked. "And how do you keep it from sinking into the ice?"

"You don't," Gable said. "You build it in pieces and airlift it. As for sinking, that's what they wanted. They built it with a modular access point above the living quarters. As it sank lower, they added another rung, so to speak. Each section had hydraulic alignment points that kept the beam pipes perfectly straight, compensating for uneven sinking. They wanted it in the ice, it served as a heat exchanger for the liquid helium."

"How much smaller was it?" Penny asked.

"Eleven kilometers," Gable said. "Conventional accelerators rely on multiple orbits around a circular path, but this one used two straight beam pipes, each just over five kilometers long. At the LHC, there were over a thousand dipole magnets keeping the particle beams on their circular course. At the Antarctic collider, those magnets were all used to accelerate the particles in a linear path. There was a lot of new technology involved, and the more efficient cooling system allowed for a greater energy delivery as well. I don't know the rest, I'm afraid, I'm not an engineer. What I do know is that the accelerator was powerful enough to achieve ninety-nine point nine, nine, nine and more nines times the speed of light, just like the LHC, but it could do it almost instantly, and repetitively."

"What was it used for?" Peter asked. "And why didn't I ever hear about it?"

"It was kept secret," he explained. "After the controversy surrounding CERN's accelerator, certain experiments had to be taken off the table in light of public scrutiny. The need for something that could operate outside the media spotlight was recognized. Very foolish in retrospect, I suppose, though it could have done a lot of good, in the proper hands."

"Are you saying this had something to do with what happened?" Peter asked, shocked. He had become content with the idea that he would never know, never learn the truth. He wasn't sure he didn't want to keep it that way.

"Undoubtedly," Gable admitted. "Considering that the event seems to have happened somewhere in the extreme southern hemisphere. But I wasn't there, I don't know anything for certain."

"But you must suspect…"

"Oh yes! I suspect alright. That's why we're here, and why we can't stop now."

"Go on."

"My work at the facility centered around the manipulation of the Higgs field," Gable explained. "I figured out a way to amplify the field in the collision chamber, increasing the mass in an area proportionate to the frequency of particle production, accounting, of course, for antiparticle annihilation."

"The what?"

"Multiple collisions!" Penny said, excitedly. "One after the other, each producing a Higgs boson…increasing the density of Higgs particles!"

Gable smiled faintly. "Essentially, though I'm afraid I'm simplifying things quite a bit. No offense, Penelope, but not even you can understand the full picture, not yet, anyway. But, yes, essentially, that's what I did."

"No offense taken, professor," she said. "And you're right of course, though I do hope to change that."

"You will," he said. "Assuming any of us are around to do anything at all."

"I don't understand…" Peter protested.

"Yes you do," Penny said. "You just forgot. We talked about this…about increasing the density of the Higgs field to increase the mass of objects in that field."

Peter nodded, remembering. "Sorry, you're right, you guys are just talking too fast for me to keep up." He wasn't used to being the dumb one in the group, but he was glad for Penny, and proud of her.

"So what were you working on?" Peter asked. "What use is increasing mass?"

Gable frowned. "What use? The potential for research was incredible! Imagine being able to test equations by manipulating particle masses! Despite that, however, I was much more interested in *reducing* the density of the Higgs field."

"How would you do that?" Penny asked. "Antiparticles?"

"Not exactly. A Higgs boson is neutral, and is therefore its own antiparticle. I can't even being to explain that part, I apologize. In all honesty I hadn't actually worked it out, though I had some pretty good ideas. The implications of being able to reduce mass…"

"Yeah," Peter said. "Penny and I talked about this, but we were just speculating. Antigravity?"

"Technically that is not correct," Gable explained patiently. "Gravity would not be affected, only the mass of the objects over which it has influence. To reduce gravity itself I would have to manipulate the mass of the entire planet…but I digress. The practical effects are similar to what you are picturing. Efficient transportation, cheap space flight, even faster than light travel would potentially have been possible. Decades down the road, of course, but possible."

"Just knowing that such a thing could be done would have changed everything," Penny said, clearly awestruck. Peter couldn't blame her. This was some heady stuff.

"But…" Peter started to say, unsure of how to phrase it. "You're saying that your research somehow caused the event? Destroyed human civilization?"

"No!" Gable said sternly. "Not my work! *Theirs*." He practically hissed the last word, his tone venomous.

"Theirs?"

"The Department of Defense. They took over the project as soon as I was able to demonstrate a successful increase in the density of the Higgs field. When I wouldn't go along, I was relieved of my position and threatened with prison if I violated their nondisclosure agreement."

"I was right," Penny said somberly. "Those sons of bitches."

"Right about what?" Peter asked. "Would someone just tell me?"

"Black holes," Gable said. "They wanted to create stable black holes."

Chapter 25 – Doom

I beheld the wretch —
the miserable monster whom I had created.
- Mary Shelly

"Wait a minute," Penny said. "Microscopic black holes are supposed to dissipate as soon as they form."

"They do, yes," Gable said. "Certain collisions produce particle antiparticle pairs, protons and antiprotons. They form, then annihilate each other, creating a microscopic black hole that instantly dissipates. It can't stick around because it is not massive enough to survive, and there is actually an escape of matter…the outer edge of the event horizon is…well…fuzzy. However, there is some wiggle room in the conservation of mass. Because of Heisenberg's uncertainty principle, you can't be certain that something isn't being created or destroyed. If you increase the vacuum energy outside the black hole, you would provide a mass reservoir. Couple that with an increase in frequency…"

"Whoa there, doc," Peter said, holding up his hands. "You're losing me."

"Sorry, I'm just thinking out loud. The simplest way to explain it is that you can create a stable black hole by cheating. You repeat the collisions that created the first one over and over, at such a high frequency that the forming and dissipating black holes might as well be one single entity. In fact they may very well coalesce into a single black hole. Such a thing wasn't possible in a conventional collider, but…"

"But why would they want to do that?" Penny asked. "Such microscopic black holes wouldn't be very powerful. The second you stop the collisions they would just dissipate."

"Yes, unless you were to increase their mass."

"By feeding them? Isn't that dangerous? What if it became stable?"

"I don't know about feeding them," Gable said. "But that's not what they were up to, not exactly. Think."

"I don't…" she started to say, then her face lit up. "The Higgs field! You pump up the density of the Higgs field. Then you can increase the mass of the black hole and make it stable!"

"Yes. But only so long as the increased Higgs field density is maintained. Take that away, and the black hole becomes unstable…it no longer has enough mass to hold itself together."

"Okay," Peter said. "I actually understand that, which is weird enough. But what's the point?"

"Energy?" Penny asked.

"Not exactly," Gable said. "I'm speculating, but I'd wager they were trying to make a black hole bomb. Drop it over a city, it sucks in everything, or drop the Higgs field suddenly and it becomes unstable and explodes. Such an explosion…"

"Jesus," Penny said. She looked away for a moment, her eyes darting back and forth as her fingertips carved patterns out of the air. "If the black hole were massive enough, such an explosion could…it could…."

"Vaporize, or launch into the atmosphere, all of the ice in Antarctica," Gable said.

"Oh my god! You think that's what happened?"

The old man nodded. "You could get the black hole to dissipate by gradually lowering the Higgs field intensity. But if something went wrong, say the radiation emitted by the black hole interfered with the control circuitry…"

"Holy fuck," Peter said, shaking his head. He didn't want to believe it. He couldn't believe it. "*We* did this? We did this to ourselves? Trying to make a *weapon*?"

Gable nodded grimly. "I'm afraid so. Without knowing exactly what they were doing I can only use rough estimates in my calculations, but I have managed to predict a range of possibilities from a small inconsequential release of energy to an explosion powerful enough to do what Penelope has described. Considering that such an explosion did in fact take place…"

"But what about all the extra water?" Penny protested. "All the ice in Antarctica would only account for a two hundred foot rise in sea level, and that's not accounting for whatever percentage was launched out into space."

"That does explain all the snow though," Peter muttered. "All that time, it was Antarctic ice I was shoveling away. I don't know whether to laugh or cry."

"I can't explain it," Gable admitted. "But if there is an answer, it's going to be there, at ground zero, and that answer can have terrifying implications."

"How so?" she asked. "I mean I know it's scary as hell, but do you have anything specific in mind?"

"You've been looking for a hydrological solution to explain a discrepancy in displacement of about twenty five million cubic kilometers."

"Yes."

"I think you should be looking for a geological solution instead."

"Geological…oh…you mean…"

"All of the evidence I have been able to gather," Gable explained. "Points to an explosion many orders of magnitude above that of a Teller-Ulam design thermonuclear weapon." He turned to Peter. "The so called hydrogen bomb."

"Order of magnitude?" Peter asked.

"Multiples of ten," Penny explained. "One order of magnitude higher is ten times more, two orders of magnitude is one hundred times more. And so on."

"Holy shit!"

"Yeah."

"Such an explosion," Gable continued. "Could have vaporized more than the ice. Perhaps the crust."

"You mean the *crust* crust?" Peter said, gaping. "As in the Earth's crust?"

"I am not a geologist, but I believe so, yes. Especially considering the ongoing seismic events. The result of the explosion could have caused one of a number of geological events that may have devastating effects on our planet, but it's useless to speculate until we know what's actually there."

"I'll say it again," Peter said. "Holy shit. Those fucking idiots!"

"Yes," Gable agreed. "Those fucking idiots."

"Is that why you want to take geomagnetic readings?" Penny asked. "To explain the rise in sea level?"

"No. I'm afraid I have distracted you from your initial concerns."

"Then why…oh shit." Her face darkened.

"Because some of my calculations suggest the black hole may have survived the explosion."

Peter stared at him for a moment. Neither he nor Penny were able to speak.

"To answer the questions you are about to ask me," Gable said. "Such a black hole would slowly sink to the center of the Earth, where it would suck up the planet, from within, and gradually destroy not only the Earth, but also its moon, and eventually our solar system."

"Will you be able to tell?" Penny asked. "If it's still there…"

"Not right away, but yes," Gable said. "If we can get into the observatory, and if those men did not damage the equipment."

"I guess we're going into that station after all," Peter said grimly. He picked up the radio. "Archangel, this is away team. Come in."

"Archangel here."

"Send Brad back to the pickup point."

"Roger."

"I thought we were going to the station," Penny said, confused.

"Have him bring six MREs, four canteens of water and a roll of duct tape," Peter said into the radio. "You can find the canteens with the rest of my stuff in the central port storage locker."

"Understood."

He turned to Penny. "We are. You're not. I will not put your life in danger, not again. You're going back to the boat."

"The hell I am!" she said. "I'm coming with you and that's that. Whatever you're planning, you're going to need fire support, like the last time."

"No, you're not." There was no need to correct her terminology—fire support actually meant indirect fire, like artillery, but he felt her use of it was more fitting in their new reality.

"Try and stop me."

Peter reached into the folds of his vest and produced a large zip tie. "Don't make me do it, because I will if I have to. This time is different. I don't think there's a very good chance we're getting out of this alive, and I'm not gonna throw your life away when I don't have to. Gable has to do this, and I have to get him there. No one else has to die."

She glared at him with such anger he almost flinched away, but then picked up her rifle and started down the hill towards the landing. He sighed, relieved. No matter what happened here, she would live. At least as long as anyone would, if Gable was right.

For a brief instant, he asked himself why he wasn't involving all of the others to increase their odds. He dismissed it as a foolish idea. They weren't trained for this and they had no experience. They would just get in the way. Only Penny would be an asset, but she was too valuable to risk.

Even as his mind moved on to other matters, doubt lingered. There was something wrong with his logic—a flaw in his thinking—but he had no time to figure out what it was. There was work to do.

Chapter 26 – Desperation

They ask me where I've been,
And what I've done and seen.
But what can I reply
Who know it wasn't I,
But someone just like me,
Who went across the sea
And with my head and hands
Killed men in foreign lands...
Though I must bear the blame
Because he bore my name.
- Wilfrid Wilson Gibson

As Peter watched the boat pull up to the landing, he realized that if he did not get his fear under control he was going to die. He was starting to shake, and if nothing else, that alone would get him killed. This was different from anything he had ever done before, he had no way to prepare himself, no experience to draw on for comfort.

"What the hell am I even doing here?" he muttered to himself. Since leaving the cabin, his life had taken a bizarre turn. Before the event, he had been a nobody, a small man in a big world, living a comfortable life in an all too typical relationship that was a balancing act between convenience and tolerance. Instead of chasing money like nearly everyone he knew, he indulged his passion for his hobbies, leaving his uninteresting career as a minor inconvenience he had to endure to get to what he really wanted to do. The most someone like him could hope for was a well funded retirement and continuing distraction from his sad reality by television and other forms of modern entertainment. The dreams of his childhood had fallen one by one, crushed by the weight of seven billion people scrambling for the same trivial rewards. He had bought rations and assault rifles not because he had believed anything was going to happen, but because deep down in some subconscious part of his brain he had known that the only chance for him to make anything of his life was for civilization to end, for the resource hoarding game to reset.

It turned out, however grimly, that he had been right. He had somehow found the only man that really knew what was going on, and he would be the one to get that man to where he needed to go. He was the captain of a boat that was grand even before the event, with the respect and trust of its crew. Most importantly he had Penny, a brilliant, beautiful young woman who, for the time being at least, wanted to be with him. He hadn't wanted the event, would do anything, give anything, to bring all those people back—his family, his friends, everyone. Yet he could not argue with the fact that his life post event, at least after meeting Penny, was the sort of thing he could only have dreamt about when the world was normal.

Shaking off his musings, he reminded himself that his new life would only last if he could survive the next few minutes. Otherwise, he would be lying face down on a gravel trail, bleeding out into the Newfoundland soil. Not for the first time, he wondered if he shouldn't just abandon the plan and get the hell out of there. One way or another, they would find out about the black hole eventually.

"Get a grip, Peter," he whispered through clenched teeth. It was too late to change his mind. He was committed.

Just as it had the day before, the boat bumped against the rocky shore and the four civilians—different people this time—got out. The soldier, still the same man, climbed out of the boat last and turned his back to Peter, who was crouching behind a large bush at the edge of the woods bordering the shore. He and Gable had spent the night up on the mountain, taking turns watching the observatory. Towards evening, some of the civilians had come out with buckets and hung some fish to dry on clotheslines. Peter realized then that the observatory residents would most likely fish again the following day and had come up with his plan.

The soldier looked bored, even from behind. He was shifting his weight from foot to foot, looking around idly and humming an unfamiliar tune. Peter knew that now was the time to act. He had Gable's jacket wrapped around his left hand, secured with duct tape. In that hand he held a nine millimeter pistol, which he dared not discharge unless absolutely necessary, at least not more than once. Once the first shot tore a hole in the jacket, it was possible for the sound of subsequent shots to reach the observatory five miles away. He could not afford to risk it, his plan required that they be caught by surprise.

Whoever these soldiers were, their guard was down, they were sloppy. No radio checks, no hand signals, no identification codes. These men were like him on that day he had been chopping wood, and like him they would be caught off guard, only what would be waiting for them was death, not a wonderful new life. Had that only been a few weeks ago? It felt like years.

Taking a last deep breath, he started to move. He did not sneak, he did not run. He walked casually around the tree and towards the soldier, following the path he had cleared of leaves and twigs. Determination and certainty of purpose—that was the difference between the victor and the vanquished. He had been taught that in BUDs and SQT, but hadn't fully understood it until this moment. In his right hand, he held a knife in an ice pick grip, point down, and he would have to use that knife to end the life of another human being. Any hesitation, any deviation from that simple action would result in his death. The one who started a fight usually finished it, as long as he stayed the course. He knew what he had to do, and he did it. The one who was caught by surprise only reacted, and was not in control.

The soldier heard him and turned around. Had Peter been sneaking, or running, the man would have recognized the danger, but as it was his eyes registered confusion as he fumbled for his gun. Peter ran the last few steps, but the soldier managed to bring up the P90 almost in time. His left hand held straight out in front of him, Peter squeezed the pistol's trigger. The blast was loud, but not nearly what he had expected. He saw the man flinch back, saw the ripples of his vest as the bullet smashed into his chest. The soldier did not fall, and there was no blood, but Peter got the time he needed.

He stabbed down with the knife, but not with the intent to kill. He put the blade between the soldier's arms, where he still held the submachine gun, put his left foot in front of the man's right, yanked forward with his knife hand to unbalance him and threw him over his hip with his pistol hand wrapped around the man's back. The soldier hit the ground with a hard thump and went limp. Peter was on him in an instant, ready to plunge the knife down into his throat, but it wasn't necessary. The soldier's head had hit a sharp rock. A hip throw was a very dangerous technique, even on a safety mat. The person being thrown usually grabbed onto his assailant to ease his fall, but the soldier hadn't wanted to let go of his weapon. He lay there, twitching, his quivering eyes rolled back to expose the whites as blood welled from the grisly wound on his head. Peter felt the spot where the bullet had struck the man and his fingers found the slug flattened between a rigid ballistic plate and layers of anti-spalling kevlar. The soldier's radio had not been damaged, and it was silent. The others had not heard the gun shot.

Peter stared at the man as he died and started to feel sick. He breathed deeply, trying to quell the rising nausea. Maybe he should have tried talking to him, maybe the soldiers would have just let Gable into the observatory to take his readings. After all, what did they have to lose? Maybe they would have been just as interested to learn the truth as he was. Why had he just gone straight to murder? What sort of man had he become?

"Peter!" It was Gable's voice, full of alarm. He looked up and saw the civilians, the fishermen, walking towards him. There were four men of varying ages wearing worn and patched clothing that ranged from blue jeans to mismatched track suits. Peter tore the jacket off his left hand, transferred the pistol to his right and pointed it at them. They stopped.

"Are you going to kill us too?" one them asked, a young man with an unkempt beard. His tone was reserved, almost apathetic.

"I don't want to," Peter said calmly. "Will I need to?"

"Who are you?" another asked. He was older, almost as old as Gable, though he had no beard. Both spoke with a peculiar accent, a bit heavier than typical Canadian. The other two were as young as the one with the beard.

"I'll ask the questions for now," Peter said. "I take it that you are not exactly friends with these men?" He indicated the soldier, who had finally stopped moving.

The older man spat in the direction of the dead soldier. "No."

"Good. If I were to tell you that I intended to kill them all, what would you say?"

"We'd say thank you," the younger one said. Each of the four was now staring at the dead soldier.

"What happened to the girl?" Peter asked, lowering his pistol. "The one from yesterday?"

The four exchanged glances. "The women don't usually go fishing," the young one with the beard explained. "They're for... other things. Amanda pissed them off, so they punished her."

"I see. I'm Peter. My friend over there is Emmet." Upon hearing his name, Gable came out from behind the outcropping, awkwardly clutching Peter's rifle.

"Ethan," the young one with the beard said, then pointed to the oldest one. "This is Liam, my dad. You're Americans?"

"Yeah."

The other two introduced themselves as Aidan and Logan. Peter noticed that Logan was crying as he stared at the dead soldier.

"You alright?" he asked.

Logan nodded. "I can't believe he's finally dead. You'll kill all of them?"

"Yes, but I think we need to talk first. I'd like to find out all I can about what's going on up there."

"We'll tell you everything you need to know," Liam said. "You have to know what these animals have done."

"Good," Peter said. "I'm also hoping you'll help me. I have a plan."

"Anything."

"First," Peter said. "Help me strip this guy before he bleeds all over his clothes. We're going to need those, and we don't have much time."

Chapter 27 – War

They buried me in Flanders
Upon the field of blood,
And long I've lain forgotten
Deep in the Flemmish mud.
But now you march in Flanders,
The very spit of me;
To the ending of the day's march
I'll bear you company.
- Wilfrid Wilson Gibson

Half an hour later, Peter marched up the mountain trail behind the four sack-bearing fishermen. He carried the soldier's gun and wore the man's uniform and armored vest. Gable kept pace for now, holding Peter's rifle, but he would fall back to their original observation point when they neared the facility. He was supposed to provide cover fire, but Peter didn't really expect him to be very effective, certainly not nearly as effective as Penny would have been. The physicist carried the rifle as though it were a poisonous viper. He had shown no hesitation learning to shoot back on the boat, but seeing Peter kill the soldier had apparently brought a new dimension to the weapon, an aspect that had not manifested when shooting paper coffee cups tossed overboard for target practice.

As they had prepared to carry out Peter's plan, the four fishermen answered more questions than Peter asked in their eagerness to tell their story. The telling had the beneficial effect of dispelling the doubts he had felt after killing the soldier. The man deserved far worse than a quick death.

What was coming up was the most difficult part of Peter's plan, and he was afraid, though not as much as he had been down by the landing. He was back in familiar territory, doing the sort of things he had done before. The P90 was a strangle little weapon, but he had familiarized himself with it as much as he could without firing it. It was a bullpup design, like the shotgun he had given Brad. The trigger and pistol grip were offset from the firing chamber, moved almost all the way forward. The little Belgian subma-chine gun was less than twenty inches long, yet had a ten and a half inch barrel and a full length stock. This gave it reasonable ac-curacy and the ability to carry a fifty round magazine. Unlike Pe-ter's own carbine, this weapon was fully automatic. That would help offset its smaller and less powerful cartridge, but he would have to be careful not to waste too much ammunition. He didn't have enough training with it to be able to change magazines quick-ly while under stress.

The observatory came into view, a lot sooner than Peter would have liked. On cue, Gable left the group and disappeared into the trees. Soon there would be no turning back. Peter wasn't sure if he was ready for what he had to do, but he had little choice. His hands were shaky and uncertain, and every step he took felt like he was plowing though molasses. But he kept moving forward.

According to the prisoners, the soldiers were Canadian army regulars, and there had been an entire platoon of them in the moun-tains after the tsunami hit. There was a disagreement among the men as to what they should do. The vast majority wanted to gather up as many survivors as they could and start rebuilding what they could. Eleven of them felt differently, and so they had murdered the rest while they slept. Three had been killed in the ensuing fire-fight, leaving eight.

"Okay people," Peter said. "Keep calm. Look down at the ground, just do what you always do. When I start shooting…"

"Hit the dirt," Liam said.

"Just like we drilled." Peter didn't know if four quick practice runs counted as a drill, but it would have to do.

The remaining eight soldiers had in fact looked for survivors, but they had something else in mind. They gathered up thirty two people, eleven women and twenty one men. All of the women young and pretty, all the men able to work. The rest they just left behind to starve or freeze to death—the elderly, the infirm, the children. They made their home in the observatory, which was sit-uated much like Peter's cabin in a place where wind and elevation combined to keep it from being buried under the snow.

As they approached the two sentries by the gate, Peter was thankful for the goggles and for the fact that the dead soldier's hair color and length more or less matched his own. Dark brown hair was not exactly rare, but he suspected that short hair was. Peter had learned to cut his own, and Penny had taken over the job after they met. If the man's hair had been long, Peter would have had to engage from much farther away.

"Stay calm," he whispered as they got within fifty yards. His hands were sweating and he could feel his heart pounding. He walked behind the prisoners, which protected him from undue scrutiny yet also prevented him from firing until he left the safety of that position.

Forty yards. The sentries were looking at him, but didn't show any signs of excessive curiosity.

The months during the constant snowfall had been the worst for the observatory prisoners. The women were raped repeatedly, the men were worked hard, sometimes to death. They searched for and carried back supplies, food, anything they could find. Eight died from starvation or exposure, two were killed as examples. One of the women committed suicide, another injured one of the soldiers. She was executed, her throat cut, but not before she was tortured while the other prisoners were forced to watch.

Thirty yards. Peter started to drift sideways.

When the snow stopped, the fishing had started, and life became a little more bearable, but no one forgot what had happened. Some of the dead were friends or relatives of those left alive. Tallying the survivors, Peter was left with seven soldiers and nineteen prisoners. The odds were not in his favor.

Twenty five yards. One of the sentries craned his neck for a better look.

Peter picked up his pace and raised his hand, as though calling for the guards' attention. Once he was past the prisoners he crouched, raised the P90 and placed the reticle on the first man's head. The sentries stared, dumbfounded. He squeezed the trigger, worrying that somehow the strange little design wouldn't work, that something would go wrong. The weapon barked in his hands as the sonic booms thundered across the mountain tops. The sentry's head twisted as a spray of blood showered the man next to him. The other sentry was already moving, aiming, but it was too late. Another bark and he was down, a stream of red flowing from a hole in his throat. The four prisoners stood frozen.

"Get down!" Peter shouted. "Move your asses!" They jumped into action at the sound of his voice and got down on the ground, just as they had practiced. Peter got up and raced towards the gate, swung it open and ran inside. As soon as he was in, he turned around, ducked behind one of the short concrete pillars, set his weapon to semi-automatic and began shooting into the tree line, in the direction from which he had come, being careful not to shoot anywhere near Gable's position.

Within seconds the door was slammed open and there was shouting from inside. He heard the blast of fully automatic rifle fire and prayed to a god he didn't believe in that it wasn't aimed at him.

"Tabarnaque! Qu'est-ce qui ce passe?" someone shouted as Peter saw movement in the periphery of his vision. Soldiers took cover behind similar pillars on both sides of him and fired into the trees, the same place Peter was shooting. They had done exactly what he expected. Hearing gunfire, they ran out and saw two of their men down and a third taking cover and firing into the trees. Naturally, they joined him.

Another burst of automatic fire roared from the doorway, then another man ran out and took cover next to Peter.

"Rapport!" he shouted, then his eyes widened in surprise. Peter pointed the stubby little submachine gun at his face and pulled the trigger.

There was so much noise, so much gunfire, he could hardly think straight, but he remembered his plan. He fell back to the wall, set his weapon to full auto, aimed at each of the three remaining soldiers in turn and squeezed off a burst into each one's back. The last one was wearing an armored vest, and Peter had to empty the weapon into him before he dropped. Some were still twitching.

Reaching into a vest pocket, Peter pulled out a spare magazine. He fumbled with the P90's mag release, finally getting it, and inserted the new one. Just as he released the slide, he realized there were only four soldiers in front of him, not counting the two dead sentries. There should have been five.

He felt the bullets hit him before he heard them. The impact left him unable to breathe, it was like being kicked by a horse. He collapsed on his knees as he felt something warm spreading on his back.

"Damn you Gable," he cursed, wishing the scientist were actually capable of providing cover fire. He turned around, knowing he was already dead, when the wall next to the fifth soldier erupted in a puff of dust. Another puff gushed out before he heard the shots. The soldier ducked back inside the doorway.

Gable had done it. Somehow he had not only started shooting, but was doing so with remarkable accuracy.

His back on fire, Peter crept along the wall to the doorway and switched on his goggle's display, then turned on the gun camera. As he got to the edge, the puffs of dust from the concrete wall moved higher. Gable had seen him and adjusted his aim. Peter could hardly believe how effective the old man was proving to be. If not for his supporting fire, the remaining soldier would have been free to deploy his own weapon camera.

It took Peter a second to adjust to the view in his goggles. It was very strange, like playing a video game in the middle of a firefight. He stuck the P90 around the edge of the door and saw the crouching man on the display. He squeezed the trigger and didn't release it until the submachine gun was empty.

Turning in Gable's direction, he dropped the gun and motioned frantically with the arm he could still move towards the other soldiers, some of whom were still moving. One was crawling. Within seconds, the incoming fire was directed at them. Each was hit several times, starting with the crawling one, then the shooting stopped. Nothing moved.

Peter collapsed, leaning against the wall, breathing heavily. His back was numb, the pain was largely gone, but his vision was blurry and he couldn't seem to catch his breath. After a minute or so, the prisoners started to pick their heads up and look around. None of them had been hit. They started to get to their feet, and Liam ran over to Peter.

"He's been shot!" he screamed.

Peter saw Gable running along the trail, still holding the rifle. The other prisoners clustered around Peter, who was starting to feel faint, and strangely thirsty.

"Water," he said. "I need water."

"Get him some water!" Liam screamed, and Ethan, his son, ran inside the observatory. He came out, accompanied by several others. They were looking around, dumbfounded.

Gable pressed his way through the crowd. "Oh my god, Peter, you've been shot!"

"Give me my rifle," Peter said, reaching out for his carbine, wanting to hold something familiar. His hand brushed the barrel as he took it. It was cold.

"I don't understand..."

"Make way!" a voice boomed through the din. A woman's voice. Penny's voice. "Out of my way!" she screamed again, and before Peter knew what was happening, she was kneeling over him, her tears falling on his face. "Oh Peter!"

"What...what are you doing here? How did you get here?"

"Not now, Peter, here." She took the bottle of water Ethan had brought and put it to Peter's lips. He drank. The numbness in his shoulder was spreading to his arm.

"Get that vest off!" Penny ordered. "Turn him over!"

"How did you get here?" Peter demanded as several hands reached out to move him. He was placed onto his stomach and couldn't see what was going on around him.

"I never left," Penny said. "I made Brad take me back after you left the landing. I told you, you idiot, you need fire support."

"I'm going to kill him," Peter mumbled. He felt his vest slide off of him, every tug and jerk brought a flash of pain.

"Don't blame Brad. He can't say no to me." In that moment he wasn't sure what hurt more, the bullet or those words.

"It doesn't look bad," Gable said as he ripped open Peter's shirt. "The armor stopped the first one. This one looks like it's lodged in his shoulder blade. We'll have to get him back to Archangel.

"What's Archangel?" someone asked.

"Penny," Peter said.

"Yes?"

"Thank you."

"We have a doctor," someone shouted. "Get Olivia!"

"You're going to be okay, Peter," Penny said. "You hear me? You're going to be okay."

"Thanks to you."

"That was a crazy fucked up thing you did," Penny said, still crying. "What were you thinking? Taking on so many of them. They were soldiers, Peter, not thugs!"

"I'm sorry, I know it was stupid."

"It was brilliant," she said, surprising him. "It was goddamned brilliant."

"I'll second that." It was Liam's voice. "Can't believe how simple you made it look."

"I messed it up," Peter said.

"Yeah you did," Penny said. "When you tried to send me back."

"Because I need fire support." He managed a laugh, though it sent lances of fire through his back.

"Yeah," she said, laughing through her tears. "Because you need fire support."

"Make a hole!" a woman shouted. "Everyone step back." Everyone moved away, except Penny. Someone knelt over him and started touching his back. He felt more of his shirt being cut away.

"I think I can see the bullet," the woman, presumably Olivia, said. He heard her fishing around in some sort of bag. Metallic things clanged together. He felt something very cold and wet splash onto his wound and felt searing pain. He gasped, but didn't cry out.

"That's the best disinfectant I have," Olivia said apologetically. "But it'll do the trick… the wound is not deep at all." It smelled like some sort of alcohol. She reached into her bag and pulled something out, then touched it to Peter's back, and cut. More pain, worse than before. Taking something else out of the bag, she started to dig around inside his wound. Now the pain was unbearable, and this time he did cry out. The instrument she was holding felt like a pair of pliers that had grabbed a hold of one of his bones and was twisting and jerking it.

"Hold still!" Olivia ordered.

"Will he be alright?" It was Penny.

"He'll be fine, as soon as I get this out and close him up. We have some antibiotics."

"We have plenty on our ship, too." Gable's voice.

The pliers finally popped free as they tore something out of him.

"There it is," Olivia said. "Now to close him up." She splashed some more alcohol on him, but he was already fading. Everything fell away into blackness, including the pain.

Chapter 28 – Frustration

This day, time travails with a mighty birth,
This day, Truth stoops from heaven and visits earth,
Ere night descends, I shall more surely know
What guide to follow, in what path to go;
I wait in hope–I wait in solemn fear,
The oracle of God–the sole–true God–to hear.
- Charlotte Brontë

He awoke to a faint background hum and the sounds of a keyboard clicking slowly. A yellow lamp hung above his head. It wasn't very bright, but it still hurt his eyes to look at it.

"He's awake," someone said. "Get Penny." It sounded like Gable. The clicking stopped.

He tried to sit up, but his left shoulder exploded. Grunting, he fell back onto the pillow. A pillow? Where was he? His vision cleared, but not completely. He felt strange, almost drunk.

He was lying on a cot in a room with gray walls. A maze of pipes and unlit fluorescent fixtures hung from a tall ceiling and several computer desks flanked a large concrete pedestal in the room's center. An aluminum cylinder protruded from the top of the platform, connected to a wire harness that disappeared from view behind the contraption.

Trying to lift himself using his good arm, he managed to sit up without too much pain.

"You need to lie down, Peter." It was Gable after all. As his vision cleared more he recognized the scientist's face. The old man was sitting at one of the computer desks.

"There's electricity?" Peter asked, confused. "Where are we?"

"They were kind enough to let us use the generator," Gable explained. "We're inside the station."

Suddenly, Peter remembered why they were here. "Is it…are we going to…"

"I don't know yet," Gable said, and Peter could hear the tension in his voice. "I'm just trying to figure out how to use the software. I'll let you know as soon I know anything, but it may be a while."

"Peter!" Penny ran into the room and was kneeling by his side before his brain could process her arrival. "You need to lie down. I'll get the doctor." She started to get up.

"No," he protested. "I'm fine. Don't go. Why do I feel like I just drank a bottle of whisky?"

She smiled, reached over and kissed him on the forehead. "Dr. Carpenter, Olivia, she gave you some Oxycodone. It's an opiate pain killer. I'm so glad you're alright." Her eyes were red and surrounded by dark circles, but the sight of her still quickened his pulse. Would he ever get tired of looking at her?

"Is it bad?" Peter asked, trying to remember what had happened. It was like a dream, the harder he tried to focus on an individual detail the more elusive it became.

"No," Penny said. "You were very lucky. It didn't penetrate your shoulder blade. Olivia says removing the bullet did a lot more damage than the bullet itself. You'll be on your feet in a day, and you'll have full use of your arm in a week or two, at least that's what she thinks."

He nodded, relieved.

"Oh Peter, it's so awful, what these people have been through…"

"These people?" He remembered as soon as he asked the question. "Oh, the prisoners. Are they okay?" It was a stupid question, but he couldn't think clearly enough to phrase a better one.

She shook her head. "Some of the girls…they haven't left the room where they used to keep them. It's like they can't believe they're free."

He nodded, but he was too groggy to really understand what she was saying. "They'll get better."

"I hope they get the chance." She turned to Gable, who was busy clicking away with mouse and keyboard.

"I hope we all do."

"Yeah," she said, shaking her head grimly. "Hey!" She was suddenly excited. "I have something for you. Maybe it will cheer you up." She sprang up to her feet and sprinted out of the room. Only seconds later, she was back, holding Peter's rifle. She knelt down by his cot and put the weapon on his lap.

"Take it off safety," she said.

Confused, Peter looked down at the rifle and flicked the safety knob with his good hand, enjoying the familiar click as the mechanism engaged.

"Again."

"Huh?"

"Flick it again."

He clicked it back on safety, then disengaged it once more. "Why?"

"No, don't flick it back, just do it again, from where it is now."

Still confused, he pushed the lever again and it clicked over once more. He stared at it, wrinkling his brow. It shouldn't do that, not unless…

"It's select fire!" he said, excited. "Is this my rifle?" It looked like his, in every detail. "How did you do that? Is it full auto or burst?"

"Full auto," she said proudly. "I did it to mine too, and I have the parts to do more. As to how, I almost chose robotics instead of physics. This was a piece of cake, once I had the parts."

He cocked his head sideways, not understanding. He hated this feeling, it would have been better to take the pain. He would not have felt that way before, in his old life, but things had changed. He could not afford too much idle time. There were people who counted on him. She looked at him, smiling patiently, and waited.

"Oh," he said, suddenly getting it. "You're talking about college. Building robots…it must have been a breeze for you to figure out how to swap the auto sear."

"Exactly. It's more than the auto sear, though. Hammer, bolt carrier, an extra hole…anyway, the soldiers had M16s, so all the parts matched."

"They're actually C7s, there are some differences in the specs, but most of the parts are the same."

"Army nerd!"

"Navy."

"Whatever," Penny said, smiling. "There's other stuff too. Tons of ammunition…I hope the cartridges are the same?"

"They are."

"There are also grenades, machine guns, even some rocket launchers. The prisoners…the people said we can take everything, but I think we should leave at least half for them. What do you think? Assuming we still need it …" She looked at Gable.

He rubbed his eyes with his right hand. Too much, too soon. "Whatever you think is best. I think I'll lie down now."

"Okay, you get some rest. Should I take this?" She reached for his rifle.

"No, leave it. Penny, thank you so much, for everything. For saving my ass, for the rifle. I don't know what I'd do without you."

"Say you were an idiot for trying to send me away."

"I was."

"Say it."

"I was an idiot for trying to send you away."

She kissed him. "Other than the aforementioned idiocy, you were incredible, Peter. Absolutely incredible."

He smiled. "Almost a Seal."

"Fuck that. Seals were almost you."

He chuckled. "Let's not get carried away."

"No," she said. "I mean it. You're incredible. Maybe you never knew it before, but then…stars are only visible in darkness."

"Is that from a poem?"

She smiled. "Imagine Dragons."

"Why?"

She giggled and put her hand over her mouth. "You're hopeless. Now lie down now, get some sleep."

"No more oxy-condoms, okay?" he said. "I need a clear head."

She nodded, biting her lip to hold back laughter, then lowered him to the pillow. He closed his eyes and was almost instantly asleep.

* * *

"Blast it!" Gable shouted. "I can't make sense of this!"

Peter opened his eyes. The same dim light and a dull pain in his shoulder greeted him.

"I've been going through the damned data for hours," Gable complained. "I'll need a damned computer program to plot it all so that I can see the patterns."

"So what do we do?" Penny asked. "The suspense is killing me."

"I'm going to have to take one of these laptops," Gable said. "And try to write a program that can do what I need, or make the charts by hand. Either way, it's going to take days. Maybe longer."

"Can I help?" she asked.

"Can you do any coding?"

"Some. Java, mostly."

"That should do," Gable said, then let out a long sigh and rubbed his eyes. "I need a break. It's been a long day."

"So what are we going to do in the mean time?" Penny asked. "Where do we go? Do you still want us along?"

"Us? You mean you and Peter?"

"Yeah."

"Of course! We can't get along without the two of you. Besides, you still have your education to finish."

"You wouldn't mind?" she asked, and Peter heard the excitement in her voice. She really wanted this, and he was glad for her.

"Young lady you have a doctorate to finish, and I won't take the end of civilization as an excuse. Your friend saw to that."

"Thank you so much, Emmet, you don't know what that would mean to me."

Peter felt like a voyeur, listening in to what they thought was a private conversation. He stirred in the cot, making sure they heard him.

"Peter!" Penny moved to the side of the cot. "Still no answers," she explained apologetically. "Dr. Gable will need a few days with a computer to figure it out."

"Meh," Peter grumbled. "I think if there were a black hole in the center of the Earth it wouldn't be that hard to see."

"I wish it were that simple," Gable muttered without taking his eyes off the data. "I can only guess at its rate of expansion."

"How are you feeling?" Penny asked.

"Much better," Peter said, swallowing to try to get some saliva in his painfully dry throat. "Help me up, please. I remember something about machine guns and rocket launchers."

"You would."

She helped him out of bed and took him into a corridor, past a series of doors and into what looked like a storage room. It was piled high with green crates, some of which were open. Penny had spoken truly. There were two belt fed machine guns... Canadian M60 variants... a stack of C7 rifles and P90s. There were also boxes of hand grenades, AT4 anti-tank rockets and a ton of ammunition, assuming the labels on the closed crates could be trusted. That was just the stuff he could see.

"Am I dead?" Peter asked, mouth hanging open. If the soldiers had brought some of this stuff to bear against him, he wouldn't have had a chance.

"Let me guess," she said, grinning wryly. "You're in heaven."

"Well there *is* an angel," he said, and kissed her. His shoulder throbbed and stung with every movement, but it wasn't too bad. A lot better than not being able to think clearly.

The next few days were spent loading weapons and supplies onto Archangel. Liam, who had taken charge of the former prisoners, assigned several of the men to help, including his son Ethan. They seemed eager to lend a hand, and kept trying to get Peter to take more than he had decided on. He tried to explain that they would need to defend themselves, but none of them seemed to have a clue what to do with the stuff.

Despite having only one useable arm, Peter decided to try to train some of them as best he could with the weapons. They were willing, but a bit leery of handling the very things that had been used to oppress them. He thought to offer them some provisions, but they were doing quite well in that regard. The soldiers had been ruthless and thorough, and the supplies they had managed to horde were impressive. The Newfoundlanders could live in comfort for many months while they learned to rebuild what they could no longer scavenge. The one thing that Liam agreed to accept were a few DVDs that the crew of Archangel had already seen. It seemed these relics of a lost age would be quite valuable in the new world, perhaps even more so than food.

Gable hardly left the magnetometer room, alternating between plugging the old data into one of the station's laptops and monitoring the new data as it was collected. Penny tried to help him by writing a program to plot the results, but after a day of struggling with it, she gave up.

"I just can't remember enough Java to do this," she said apologetically. "And without the Internet…"

"It's fine, Penelope," Gable said. "I can do this manually, it will just take longer. Besides, some of what you've already written will speed my work up considerably." He was obsessed, hardly able to take his eyes off the computer screen.

While he walked around the station, Peter caught glimpses of some of the women that had suffered at the hands of the soldiers. Most stayed out of sight, quiet and alone. He was glad that he had been able to save them, but he wished he hadn't needed to. How could people be such bastards?

A few of the women recovered very quickly, at least on the outside, and interacted freely with Peter and his group. Amanda, the girl they had seen on the boat, was one of these. She was particularly interested in what was taking place in the rest of the world. Peter told her about Colonel Hamilton, and how he was going to try to rebuild. She seemed hesitant to believe that soldiers could be doing something good, but Peter couldn't really blame her after what she had been through.

As friendly and helpful as some of the people seemed, Peter sensed the darkness that lay just under the surface. He had heard only the barest details of what they had endured, and despite a morbid curiosity he decided not to press for more information. Part of that darkness showed in what they had done with the bodies. They had not buried the soldiers, but had dragged them away from the station and left them there to rot. Some of the men went to the site every now and then to watch as animals came to scavenge the corpses. They reported some arctic foxes, a large cat and one of them swore he spotted a polar bear, though no one believed him. Regardless, the very fact that some animals survived the snow was invigorating. Perhaps not surprisingly, Peter was not the only one who felt that way. There was no talk of hunting, the sea would provide all of their food, and they seemed to agree that the creatures of the land needed just as much time to recuperate as they did.

On the fourth day, they bid farewell to the Newfoundlanders and tendered back to Archangel for the last time. Liam, Ethan and

Amanda stood on the shore as the dinghy sped away. Peter waved farewell, wondering if they would make it. They had everything they needed to survive, to thrive even, but sometimes that wasn't enough.

Chapter 29 – Disaster

O never give the heart outright,
For they, for all smooth lips can say,
Have given their hearts up to the play.
And who could play it well enough
If deaf and dumb and blind with love?
He that made this knows all the cost,
For he gave all his heart and lost.
-William Butler Yeats

Archangel sailed southwest towards Montreal, pushed along by a warm and steady breeze. Everyone was busy with their various chores, but all thoughts were of Gable and his magnetometer data. It was difficult to go about day to day business not knowing if the entire planet was about to explode.

Planning for the best while preparing for the worst, they had decided to head to Antarctica to investigate the cause of the massive seal level rise, but not before taking a quick look at the western part of the United States. According to topographic maps, more than half of the US was high enough to be well above sea level, and it was possible that most of it could have been subject to months of rain instead of snow. Flooding would have caused massive damage, but it was likely that a substantial number of people had survived—at least by post-apocalyptic standards.

Peter charted a course that took them around the submerged northeastern tip of the US and down along the St. Lawrence River to Lake Ontario. He had been tempted to take a chance and sail straight over what used to be land, but in the end he decided against it. They weren't in any sort of hurry, and this course was a lot more complicated and would keep him busy, which was a handy distraction from thoughts of black holes and imminent death. It would be difficult to sail over Lake Ontario without thinking of the nearby Catskills island and the old cabin, but he would get over it. Archangel was his home now, and it was a better home than he had ever had.

Five days after being shot, his shoulder was much better. He could use his arm normally as long as he didn't try to lift anything heavy. Penny and Brad had to help him with some of the winch work at first, but he was starting to be able to do everything on his own. This was a tremendous relief, as he had worried that there would be lasting complications despite Olivia's assurances to the contrary.

Long hours at the helm also gave him time to think, something he hadn't had much of a chance to do since Gable's revelation about the cause of the event and the black hole. He was surprised to find himself thinking most often of simple things—everyday events, the unseasonably warm temperatures, his relationship with Penny. The one thing he had trouble thinking about was the disaster itself.

"Some say the world will end in fire," he said, quoting Robert Frost as he watched a band of gold appear on the horizon, heralding the coming sunrise. "Some say in ice. From what I've tasted of desire, I hold with those who favor fire." The world had in fact ended in fire, an explosion such as he could not even imagine had vaporized Antarctica.

"But if it had to perish twice," he continued. "I think I know enough of hate, to know that for destruction ice, is also great, and would suffice." A poem, or a prophecy? The world had perished twice, in a manner of speaking, and the second death had been the ceaseless precipitation of Antarctic ice that killed most of those who survived the first calamity.

Despite being moved by Frost's words, he felt very little about the event itself. It was so long ago, and so overwhelming in scope that it had become little more than an intellectual curiosity. The black hole was the same way, it was so beyond him that he couldn't get himself to take it seriously. The only genuine feelings of sympathy he had left, if he were to be truly honest with himself, were for the penguins. Poor little bastards must have never known what hit them.

He was alone on deck when Archangel passed twenty miles south of Montreal just as the sun broke the eastern horizon. It was his one deviation from a safe course over former waterways. There was no reason to put people through another New York.

"You're up early," Penny said, coming up behind him. "Where are we?"

"Montreal, more or less," he said. "How's Gable?" Peter could only imagine the pressure the man was under, he was almost literally carrying the weight of the world.

"He's still at it," Penny said. "He's been up all night."

"He should take a break. World's not going anywhere today. At least I hope not."

"Can I ask you a favor?" She leaned against him, cocking her head seductively. She knew how to get what she wanted, though it wasn't necessary.

"Of course."

"Stop glaring at Brad. He feels bad enough as it is. Besides, if he hadn't done it…"

He frowned. "I'd be dead, I know. Was I glaring?"

"A bit."

"Okay, okay. You can tell your boyfriend I'm okay with what he did."

She pulled away from him, her expression turning dark.

"That's not funny, Peter."

He instantly regretted his words, wanted to take them back. "Pen, I'm sorry…" He had no idea why he said that.

"I'll see you later," she said in a measured tone, and walked down the hatch.

"Shit," he cursed. "Way to go, asshole." He knew they were bound to fight sooner or later, and if it had to be over Brad, then this was a lot better than the alternatives he had imagined. Still, he had been unfair, and he knew he should do something about it.

Setting the autopilot, he made his way down to the main salon and went to the nav table, where he had left a stack of marine maps. After staring at the maps long enough to admit to himself that they had nothing to do with why he came down there, he decided to head to the galley and have some breakfast—another pretext, though he actually was hungry. He found Burgoyne there, cutting up a fish.

"Good morning Peter," he said. "Want some breakfast?"

"Yeah, I guess. What are we having?" This part of the boat was not like the rest. There was no fancy wood, no leather settees.

It was plain, white, utilitarian. Archangel had been built as a pleasure cruiser and designed around a four person staff. This galley was where meals were supposed to be prepared for the passengers, not by them. There was also a small but comfortable crew mess across from the working area. The management of space in the boat's design was astounding. There was so much more packed inside than Archangel's size suggested. The people who had designed those tiny model apartments at IKEA could have learned a lot from the vessel's architects.

"Fish pancakes," Burgoyne said with a smile. "I'm using some of the sugar the Newfoundlanders gave us."

"They were too generous," Peter said, leaning against the dormant refrigerator. "They should have kept a lot more than they did." He had shut down the refrigerator and freezer, both of which were being used as storage for nonperishable foodstuffs.

"Perhaps. Listen, Peter, I wanted to talk to you for a bit."

"Oh?" Burgoyne had hardly spoken two words to him that were not related to carrying out his duties since they'd met.

"I wanted to apologize. I've treated you poorly, and you didn't deserve it."

Peter raised an eyebrow. "Thank you, Burgoyne, I appreciate that. But you weren't so bad."

"Please, call me David."

"Okay, David. You don't need to apologize, I understand completely. I was some stranger and you resented me taking over. I would have felt the same way."

Burgoyne nodded. "I'm glad you understand, but I don't feel that way anymore." He extended his hand, and Peter shook it. "In fact I'm glad you're here."

"Thank you, David," Peter said, smiling. "In that case maybe you won't mind a bunkmate for a night or two, I think I might be in the doghouse."

Burgoyne looked uncomfortable. "I'm sorry to hear that, Peter, but that room is free now. I… I moved in with Dr. Foster. She and I are…"

"I know, Burgoyne, we all know. Congratulations." Peter clapped him on the back, and the marine biologist smiled warmly. "Speaking of Penny, have you seen her?" The two forward cabins just past the galley were both empty.

"No, but I think she's up on deck. I heard people moving around up there and the only people besides you and I that are awake are Penny and Brad. Except for Gable, of course, but he's…well, you know."

"Be right back, then, I have an apology to make. Save me a pancake."

He went back through the lounge up to the upper salon and through the hatch. He didn't see anyone in either the center or aft cockpits, so he went up on deck and looked towards the bow.

Penny was there, her arms wrapped around Brad.

Peter froze, stared, not comprehending.

She was holding him tightly, swaying slightly back and forth, perhaps to accommodate the boat's gentle rolling. His head rested on her shoulder. She pulled away and put both hands on Brad's cheeks, looking up at him intently.

Then she turned and saw Peter. Her eyes widened, and she let go of Brad and started towards him.

Peter turned away and walked towards the aft access hatch, trying not to stumble.

"No," he whispered, shaking his head. "Not now, not like this." He had known, prepared, but he wasn't ready.

"Peter!" she cried out, moving quickly to catch up. He hastened his steps, desperate to enter the sanctuary of their cabin. His cabin. There was too much pain. He had to get away from it, from her.

"Peter wait!"

He stumbled down the stairs and went straight to the lacquered closet door. He slammed into it hard, hitting his head against the wood. The physical pain brought relief.

"No." How could he have deluded himself all this time?

"Peter where the hell are you going?" She was behind him, in the hatch, then she was down, pulling on his arm. "It's not what you think, Peter."

"No," he repeated.

"Peter look at me!"

"No!" Why couldn't she leave him alone?

"Stop being an idiot!" she shouted. "I told you it's not what you think!"

He whirled on her and she momentarily recoiled, seeing the rage in his eyes.

"What is it then?" he snarled, trying his best to control himself. "You tell me something that will make it right. Tell me one of your lies!"

Her eyes flared, she stepped back. "You bastard."

He glared at her, but the anger was slowly fading, giving way to doubt. What had he done? *Don't believe any of her lies*, Brown Mustache had said.

"You absolute bastard," she said coldly. She remembered.

He opened his mouth, but nothing came out. Part of him wanted to scream at her, part of him wanted to hold her.

He tried again. "Tell me what that was."

She narrowed her eyes. "What's the point? It would just be one of my lies." Her tone was hard, cold.

"Penny…"

"No," she said, shaking her head. "I don't want to hear it. You come find me when I don't hate you anymore. And don't ask me how long that will take." She turned on her heel and stormed up the hatch. He almost went after her, but then he saw them in his mind, holding each other. The anger returned.

"Go to hell!" he screamed, but he wasn't sure she could hear him.

He paced. Back and forth, his mind telling him a thousand different stories. She had tricked him from the start, been with Brad since they'd met. She was just using him for his…no, that made no sense. What could she possibly need to use him for?

She didn't love either of them, but used both to get what she wanted. That sounded more like it. Hadn't she lied to him with the first words out of her mouth? She said she wanted food, shelter, but that wasn't the truth. She wanted someone to murder the men that were chasing her, trying to bring her to justice. How did Peter know the story she had told him was the truth? He had buried his guilt, forgotten about it, but was it *his* guilt? Was she not really to blame?

No, that wasn't right. He had learned to judge people by what they did, not what they said or what they thought. People could justify anything, but actions didn't lie. She was brave, she had risked her life to save him. She stood by his side, no matter what crazy thing he decided to do, even when he tried to send her away. It had to be something else.

She had fallen in love with Brad slowly, tried to deny it, then when Peter had referred to him as her boyfriend, she had seen the truth, went to him, confessed her love. That little bastard didn't need much encouragement, he had wanted her from the start.

"Keep an eye on your daughter," Peter growled. "You miserable son of a bitch, I'll fucking kill you." He pulled his pistol out of its holster, his hands trembling, eager for blood.

He shook his head, clearing it.

"What the hell," he said, more than a little disturbed by how much he wanted to shoot away his pain. "Get a hold of yourself, you goddamned lunatic." He put the gun back.

That last one made no sense either. She had tried to tell him it wasn't what he thought, gotten angry when he accused her of lying. If she had been deceiving him, she would have reacted with guilt.

There had to be something he didn't know, something that would explain it. A part of him screamed for him to abandon that line of thinking. Whatever else he could come up with to explain it, she had been embracing Brad, whom he damned well knew she was supposed to be with. He had known that from the start, no matter what fairy tales he had told himself about a new world, new rules. She was at the prime of her life, she needed someone like her, someone full of vigor, not a used up old man like him.

He put his hands over his face. "Get a grip, for god's sake, get a fucking grip."

He stopped pacing, turned to the bed and collapsed on top of it, still clutching his head in his hands.

"Peter?" Dr. Foster's voice, from behind the cabin door. He had probably woken her with the commotion. "Peter are you alright?"

"No," he said, trying his best to keep his voice calm. "I'm not feeling well. Could you please ask Burgoyne... David... to take the helm? All he has to do is trim the sails when the boat changes course, I've programmed our route into the autopilot. It will steer by waypoints."

"Sure, no problem," she said, and he heard the concern in her voice. "You just rest, okay?"

"Thank you. Please make sure he understands that someone either has to keep watch or he needs to set the proximity alarm and stay near one of the interfaces."

"I will Peter, you just lie down and don't worry."

"Thank you, Diana, I appreciate it."

He heard her walk away, and wished he could call her back. He didn't want to be alone. Suddenly finding lying down unbearable, he got up to pace again. He needed to calm down, organize his thoughts. Most importantly, he needed to resist his newest and most powerful impulse, to run to Penny and beg for forgiveness. He had made that mistake with Jennifer, always giving in to her tantrums, consoling her, trying to put things back to normal, even when he was the one that should have been angry. Resentment had grown quickly and spread until there was nothing else left. No, that was not a path he would take again. He had seen what he had seen, and it had to be explained before he could do anything else.

"Oh great," he said. "Now you're comparing Penny to *her*." He loved Penny. Desperately, urgently, loved her. He wasn't sure he had ever loved Jennifer, and if he had, she had bled it out of him over many years until even the memory of it was gone.

He couldn't stay in his quarters, not like this. He went up on deck and to the helm, where he was greeted by a surprised Burgoyne.

"Diana just said you were ill," he said, confused.

Peter did his best to smile reassuringly. "It was just a passing thing. I feel great now. Go relax, I'll take it from here."

Burgoyne seemed uncertain. "Are you sure? I don't mind it."

Peter shook his head, still smiling. "Positive. I need to be here right now."

"If you say so."

When he was alone, he attacked the sail controls with a vengeance, trimming, re-trimming, checking the wind tells, trimming again. He increased the boat's speed by half a knot, then a full knot, then one and a half knots.

He checked the course, checked it again. He studied the electronic maps in the chartplotter, compared them to the land maps in his GPS. He watched the wind speed and direction, watched their effect on speed over water, on speed over land. Every time the wind shifted or the autopilot turned the wheel to change course, he trimmed the sails again, and again.

They were well into Lake Ontario by the time the sun set and the darkness of a moonless night dropped an impenetrable veil over Archangel. He was exhausted, could barely keep his eyes open, but he stayed at the helm, checking the instruments, watching the radar. Eventually, he sat down, just for a minute, and fell asleep.

* * *

Starting awake, he opened his eyes to an orange sky. He was confused, cold and hungry. The fight with Penny came back to him quickly, as did the image of her holding Brad. A brief panic overtook him, but he quickly calmed himself. Checking the instruments to make sure they were still on course, he walked to the aft cockpit and through the hatch into his stateroom, expecting to find Penny asleep in their bed.

She wasn't there. She hadn't been there. The sheets were in exactly the same state he had left them.

He went through the cabin door, heading to the pilothouse. No one else was about, though he did hear running water from Burgoyne and Foster's room. Crossing the empty salon, he descended the steps to the lounge. He could see the galley and the crew quarters up ahead. The cabin on the right had been Burgoyne's and was now vacant. If Penny had wanted to spend the night away from him, that's where he would find her. He didn't know what he would say to her, not exactly, but he knew he had to make it right. There was a perfectly reasonable explanation for what he had seen, he was sure of it, and he had reacted like a petulant child instead of the rational older adult he was supposed to be. He had to make amends.

The door opened, and Penny stepped out into the hallway. From the door on the left.

Brad's door.

She didn't see him. She crossed the hall to the other cabin and closed the door behind her.

Peter couldn't move. He stood still, staring at the door she had come from. There was no ambiguity in what he had just seen. No mistake, no explanation. Where before he had acted like a child, at odds with the rational part of his mind, now even that part was in step with his conclusion: Penny had spent the night in Brad's room.

Slowly, he turned around and walked back to his stateroom. A simple matter of left or right. The lady or the tiger.

He smiled sadly as a single tear escaped his restraint. It had been a beautiful dream.

Chapter 30 – Despair

He would not stay for me, and who can wonder?
He would not stay for me to stand and gaze.
I shook his hand, and tore my heart in sunder,
And went with half my life about my ways.
- Alfred Edward Housman

He watched Archangel as it disappeared behind the edge of the mountain, sailing back to its original course on autopilot. It would be the last time he would ever see it. The tender sped over the tranquil water, bouncing gently in the morning swells. Burgoyne steered expertly, watching the approaching shoreline as he guided the boat around floating logs and the tops of trees that occasionally peeked above the water's surface.

"Remember to give her my note," Peter said, every word an effort of will.

"I won't forget Peter," Burgoyne said without taking his eyes off the coastline.

"Wait," he said. "Don't give it to her right away. Wait until she's happy again."

"I know, you told me. I wish you wouldn't go. I don't understand why. I know it has something to do with her, but…"

"I know, David, and I appreciate what you're doing for me, despite not knowing."

Burgoyne cut the throttle and the boat fell off plane and quickly slowed. Peter looked ahead and saw the shore, coming up quickly. Too quickly. Was it time already? Was it really over?

"What will you do?" Burgoyne asked. "You hardly took any food."

"I'm going to see a man about a job," he said, knowing it wasn't much of an answer.

"They're not going to be happy with me," Burgoyne said. "They're going to want answers."

"Penny will know. She can tell them, when she's ready." Saying that name, seeing her face behind his closed eyelids, it was worse than any pain he had ever felt, even the crushing solitude that had nearly killed him. But he had to let her go. To fight for her would be selfish, and he loved her too much for that.

"We still need you."

"No," he said, shaking his head. "You don't. Penny and…" He found it hard to say his name without snarling. "And Brad, they're really good with the boat, and you're not that bad yourself, though you could stand to put more time in. You all know what to do, you've all done it." He pictured Brad touching her, kissing her. He saw the two of them together, in his bed, he saw her looking into his eyes as he made love to her, and he wanted to crawl into a deep hole and die.

"With you around to tell us," Burgoyne said, and Peter was momentarily confused, but then remembered their conversation. It was too hard, to talk, to be with people. He needed to be alone.

"You don't need me anymore. I've taught you all I can."

"Somehow," Burgoyne said, extending his hand. "I doubt that very much. It was an honor to know you, captain." The boat brushed bottom and came to a stop near the shore. Peter took Burgoyne's hand and shook it firmly. For a moment, he could almost imagine it was possible to stay.

"And you, Dr. Burgoyne." Peter picked up his pack, struggling with the weight, and tossed it over the side onto the grassy shore. Picking up his rifle, he walked over the side and stepped onto land, then pushed the boat while Burgoyne reversed the motor.

Peter watched silently as the tender idled away from shore. The little boat turned about and leapt forward, rising up on plane as Burgoyne gunned the motor. It sped away noisily, until all that was left was its wake, and that too gradually faded away.

He stood there for as long as he could stand it, then struggled to put on the heavy pack, turned around and started walking southeast, looking for a road.

The pain and the loss were unbearable. The suddenness of it was the worst part. Just yesterday morning, everything had been perfect, or so it had seemed. All gone now, in the blink of an eye—a simple matter of two doors, left or right.

The pack pressed into his shoulder, crushing it. Peter focused on the physical pain, relished in it. Every flare, every jolt a relief from his true agony. He walked without paying attention to where he was going. It was the same featureless forest, the same muddy soil. Where he had once seen beauty, there was only bleakness, only despair. Upturned trees got in his way, but he walked around them without caring how much of his progress such obstacles eroded.

For once, he was glad for his age, for without the benefit of experience, without knowing that one day this pain would pass, he would have been unable to go on, would have put a bullet in his head as soon as Burgoyne and the tender got out of earshot. Even knowing what he knew, every step was a struggle. Relief was so close, so easy, it was hard not to reach for that weapon.

After about an hour of walking, he stumbled onto a cracked and pitted road. There were no signs, but it didn't matter. He turned south and picked up his pace, ignoring the protests of his body under the heavy pack. The sun was well past its apex when he came to the remains of a village or hamlet. Expecting to run into survivors, he readied his rifle and approached cautiously, but he didn't see any movement. There were cars, several of them, but none were salvageable. They had been hit hard by the tsunami—bent axles and bent frames to start with, rending all the other damage moot. Even if the gas tanks were not waterlogged, none of them would be able to start, let alone move. He continued walking.

Toward dusk he came across another village, this one above the tsunami line, and it was not deserted.

Two men with hunting rifles came out to greet him. He could see others moving amongst the standing houses—some women, even a few children. He held his rifle low as the men approached him, weapons ready, but not pointing at him.

"What do you want?" one of them said, and Peter sensed the fear in his voice. They were both older men, probably in their fifties or sixties. Typical upstate New Yorkers, though a bit more ragged than he was used to seeing them.

"I need a truck," he said flatly. "Or a car. Nothing fancy, it just has to get me a little past Delhi."

They looked at his rifle, his armored vest and the four hand grenades that were clipped to it, then exchanged nervous glances.

"What do you have to trade?" one of them asked.

"How about a couple of hand grenades? Maybe some ammunition?"

"You're serious?"

Peter nodded. "Why not? You can still find cars that work, but where can you get grenades?"

"How about a ride instead?" the other asked. "I can take you. For just the grenades. What do you say?"

"Deal." Peter said. The two men relaxed and lowered their weapons.

"Let's go then."

They took him further into the village, past the curious eyes of the denizens. A woman held tightly onto a little girl, looking at Peter as though he were a dangerous animal. Was it his weaponry, or his face? He had never experienced being the object of such fear, not only from the women, but everyone, including the man who had offered to drive him. He knew what they saw when they looked at him, a man who had nothing to lose. A walking corpse.

"This'll get us there," the driver said, pointing to a blue pickup truck. Another Dodge. Why did it have to be a Dodge? He looked over to the side of the road, where he expected Penny to come out and call him a Country Joe, her hazel eyes alive with mirth.

"Thank you." He unclipped two hand grenades and handed them to him. The driver took them nervously, carefully, and passed them to the other one.

"You want to wait 'till morning?" the other man asked.

"No, I need to go now."

"It'll be hard at night…"

"Now, please."

"Okay, I guess." He turned to the other man. "Tell Sandra I'll be back by the afternoon."

"Maybe I should come with you?" the other one asked.

The driver looked at Peter, then back at his friend. "Might not be a bad idea. I mean I don't want to be alone on the way back. I guess you'll have to ride in back, though. Doesn't seem fair to make our new friend sit back there."

"That's okay," Peter said. "I'll ride in back."

"Suit yourself." The man was visibly relieved.

Peter tossed his gear into the bed, then climbed inside after it.

The man cranked the engine and put the truck in gear. Peter watched the faces of the townsfolk as the vehicle pulled away. They were fearful, cautious, but they were clean, and well fed. He wondered if they had been fishing or just living off some stored supplies somewhere.

The road was rough in places, but the truck pushed on with few problems. The villagers knew how to drive a four wheeler, and all Peter had to do was sit in the back and watch the miles between him and his old life pile on. Was it his old life? Or was his old life what he was coming back to? Such archaic labels didn't seem fitting anymore. Life was a lot more fluid now than it once had been.

The truck drove through several villages, most of which were completely destroyed. They saw people in a few, but no one came out to bother them. There were signs of rebuilding. Some of the damaged sections of road had been filled in with gravel, sometimes dirt. He saw repairs in progress in some of the towns, and even some activity on a few of the farms they passed. Peter would have found it fascinating, before, but now he just watched it roll by without paying much attention.

Towards daybreak they came to an impassible section of road, just before Delhi. Peter's jeep might have made it, but not this truck. It was route 28, where his journey had started, though this section was far north of Peter's cabin.

"I'm sorry, sir," the driver said through the open back window. "We can't take you any further."

"You mean farther," he corrected, and smiled, remembering his *old* old life.

"What?"

"That's okay," Peter said. "I can walk the rest of the way. Thank you."

"You take care now," one of them said. Peter didn't bother to notice which one.

As the truck pulled away, he struggled into his pack and carefully descended the rocky face of the broken road. He was top heavy and had to take care not to trip. A broken leg would mean his death, and the greatest danger he faced was that he didn't care.

After scrambling up the other side, he walked along the road to the outskirts of Delhi. He saw a group of deer sprinting off in the distance and felt a small tingle of hope somewhere deep under his grief, but couldn't quite manage to hold onto it.

Delhi, once the seat of the county government, was a ghost town. Many of the buildings had survived, mostly those that were larger and made of brick or concrete, but there were no signs of life. There had been a university there, but that wasn't on his way and he had no interest in deviating from his course to investigate. Or did he?

For a moment he hesitated, staring wistfully in its direction. Perhaps some of the students had survived, perhaps there was someone there, a girl, who was beautiful and smart, with dyed blond hair and expressive eyes. Maybe she was in trouble and needed his help, needed him to kill someone and save her.

He shook his head as he felt the tears flow down his face. That was the way to madness. He turned back and kept walking, forcing one foot in front of the other. Just shy of noon he walked past the empty remains of the beef farm next to his property, crested the hill and saw his driveway. The road by his house had been repaired. Where there used to be a pile of debris, there was now a smooth gravel surface. They had been busy, these people.

He couldn't help feel a little bit apprehensive as he approached, but it was a muted, surface emotion that distracted him long enough from his true feelings that their return burned all the more fiercely.

Two soldiers stood guard at the base of the long driveway. He saw a humvee parked on the hill just past the entrance. From what little he could see of his house from the road, it was surrounded by large tents and military vehicles. The colonel had been serious about his intentions.

The soldiers saw him approach and raised their weapons.

"Halt!" one of them shouted. "This is a restricted military area."

"Not for me it isn't," Peter yelled back. "This is my house."

The soldiers looked confused. They had not expected that answer.

"I'm a friend of the colonel's," he continued. "I'd be happy to wait while you let him know I'm here."

"The colonel?" Was there more than one?

"Colonel Hamilton," Peter said, coming closer. He had his hands out in front of him and his rifle swung freely in its sling as he walked.

"Another one?" the first soldier asked. Peter wondered what he meant. What other colonel?

"General Hamilton," the other corrected. "How did you know he used to be a colonel?"

"Weren't they all?" Peter asked.

"What?" the first one asked, confused.

"I told you, I'm a friend of his." He got within twenty yards of the soldiers and stopped walking. "Please tell him I'm here. This is my house, I allowed him to use it for his base of operations when we met by the coast a couple of weeks ago."

The soldiers exchanged glances. "The general isn't here."

"How about Major Sullivan?"

Upon hearing that name, they relaxed a bit. "Colonel Sullivan is here, hold on while we radio him. What's your name?"

"Peter Anderson."

One of them walked to the humvee and spoke into a radio. The one that remained never took his rifle off of Peter. Less than a minute later, the soldier who had used the radio came back.

"You're okay to go up to the house," he said. "Sorry about the cold greet, but we don't see too many people with that much fire-power."

Peter nodded. "Thank you. I'm glad to see you guys are taking good care of my house."

They frowned, but didn't say anything.

The walk up his driveway was a strange experience. It was his property, familiar, welcoming, yet also strange, almost alien. There were tents all over, and where there weren't tents there were parked trucks, humvees and other pieces of equipment he remembered from their first camp. Bright green grass grew on unmolested patches of his fields, and what trees remained were mottled with budding leaves. Everywhere he looked there were soldiers. They were walking, sitting, talking, laughing. Up by the house was the familiar mess tent, behind which stood several Abrams tanks. Three helicopters sat on the open field above his pond, the same three he had seen flying overhead just before he and Penny had first run into Brad.

He stopped, struggling to get a hold of himself. It was best not to think about either of them. But what else could he think about? He and Penny had been here, together. This was the same road she had used to get to his house, cold, hungry and alone. This was the same road they had driven down together, when he had explained how she would do just fine as a spotter. Where he stood was just yards away from where he had snapped at her for not wanting to take her rifle out of the jeep.

He had come here to get away, to forget, but she was here, waiting for him. She would be everywhere he went, until he could forget.

Steeling himself, he resumed his walk up to the house. Soon he would be busy with work, with responsibilities. He doubted the colonel—the general—would make him a regular soldier. He had more to offer than that. Perhaps he would be made a noncom, given a squad, or even an officer with his own platoon. The more responsibility, the better. The more he could keep busy.

Doubts surfaced. What if Hamilton did make him a rankless private? Could he stand the tedium of guard duty, or other mindless work, while his demons devoured him from the inside? The general didn't know what he was capable of, only what he had seen at the skinhead camp. It would be better to ask what Hamilton had in mind before accepting any offers. Though if it did not work out, what would he do? Where could he go?

"Captain!" someone shouted. The voice was familiar. Maybe it was someone he had met when he dined with the officers. In his periphery he saw someone headed in his direction, moving urgently. Was he talking to Peter? Why would the man call him "captain"? Had Hamilton already set aside a position for him?

"Captain!" Closer this time. He could almost place the voice, it was almost too familiar. He was suddenly certain the voice was addressing him. He spun to face it.

Brad.

The young scientist was running towards him. Peter's hands itched for his rifle. The embodiment of his pain, within sight, within reach.

Reason overcame emotion. Confusion followed. What was

Brad doing here? He wasn't supposed to be here.

"Captain!" Brad cried as he ran up to him and stopped just short of a collision. "Holy shit am I glad to see you. We have to go, there's no time!"

Peter couldn't stop himself. He grabbed Brad by his collar and slammed him into the side of a nearby truck. Some soldiers started towards him, but Brad put up his hands, smiled and said, "It's okay guys, we're just talking."

"What the fuck are you doing here?" Peter growled, trembling with fury. "How did you get here?"

"We took your jeep," he explained. "I'll tell you everything on the way, we have to go now!"

"We?" Peter demanded. "Who the fuck is we?"

"Penny, Penny and me. She knew we would never catch up to you on foot, so she made us take Archangel to the place where we met, where we grounded…"

"Penny?"

He let him go. Suddenly he was so dizzy he could hardly stand. Penny was here? *Here*?

"Why?" Was all he could manage to say.

"Why?" Brad cried, shaking his head. "*You* are asking *me* why? Why the hell did you leave, man? She came here to find you!"

Peter stumbled back, his mind reeling.

"I don't…" He moved towards the truck and leaned against it. "I don't understand."

"Look, I'd love to tell you whatever the hell you want to know, but we have to go now! They're going to kill her!"

His mind snapped to attention. "Who is going to kill her?"

"The people in that town, man. They took her. They took her just before we got to the house. They had some stupid checkpoint with the soldiers. I thought I'd get help here, but the colonel…I mean the general…he's not here. I didn't know who else to talk to, then I saw you. You've got to help her!"

At first, it didn't sink in. He concentrated, and it seeped its way into his awareness. Penny had come looking for him. He didn't understand why, only that he had a second chance, and nothing else mattered. And then the rest of it hit him. Something else did matter.

He heard her voice. *She begged them. She begged them to let her go. She told them she hadn't done anything. She was only seventeen.*

They had her, and they were going to hang her, if they hadn't already.

"Where is the jeep?"

"Just over there!" He pointed, and Peter saw it. He wondered how he had missed it before.

"Let's go."

"What are you going to do?" Brad asked as he followed Peter to the vehicle.

"I'm going to go get her, and they better pray to their god that I'm not too late."

Chapter 31 – Wrath

In the fell clutch of circumstance
I have not winced nor cried aloud.
Under the bludgeonings of chance
My head is bloody, but unbow'd.

Beyond this place of wrath and tears
Looms but the Horror of the shade,
And yet the menace of the years
Finds and shall find me unafraid.
- William Ernest Henley

They pulled onto the road just as a humvee approached the driveway from the east.

"Did you talk to anyone?" Peter demanded. "Did you tell anyone why you're here?" His heart beat a cadence in double time, but there were things he had to know.

"Yeah," Brad said. "I talked to some officer, he said there was nothing they could do, that local justice was out of their jurisdiction. I wanted to see the col…the general, but they said I had to wait."

Peter watched the humvee nervously as it hesitated before entering the driveway. He was sure that someone inside had recognized the jeep and would try to stop him. He drove as fast as he dared, both because of the rough road, and because he didn't want to draw too much attention.

"Give me one good reason why I shouldn't shoot you right now," he said to Brad without looking at him. His mind was a jumble of emotions, at the forefront of which was urgency. He wanted to tune everything out, to focus only on Penny, on the fact that they had her, but he couldn't afford to lose himself in fear. If he allowed himself to dwell on the images his mind conjured, he would floor the gas and wreck the jeep before they got there. Images of her, dangling from a noose…

"What?" Brad cried, pulling back. "Shoot me? Why the hell

would you shoot me?"

"Don't play dumb. You fucking know why. I saw your little hug, and I saw her leave your room the next morning."

"What? *That's* what this is about? She wouldn't talk to me, but I guess I should have known!"

Peter turned to him, glaring. "You don't think that's *enough*?" he roared the last word, and Brad cringed away from him.

"No, man, you don't know what you're talking about!"

Peter opened his mouth to shout, but looked back towards the road, confused once again.

"Tell me you're not in love with her. Tell me she's not in love with you. Tell me something that will make me not want to kill you."

"You don't understand, captain…"

"Stop calling me that!" They crested the peak of the hill, half-way to the village.

Brad continued, undaunted. "I love Penny, I do, she's like my best friend. But I would never…could never do that, even if I wanted to. Even if she wanted to."

"Then what do you call—"

"There's things about me you don't know, man. About my life, before. It hasn't been easy for me. I told her, told her about Karen. I was a wreck, she was just there for me, the way a friend would be, that's what you saw."

"Who the hell is Karen?"

"She was my fiancé, before…" He looked away, tears in his eyes. "She used to live in Montreal. I wanted to see, but you…you took the boat away. I guess it was for the best, but…"

Montreal. He had thought to spare them. "You should have told me."

"Yeah, for a lot of reasons."

"But your room…"

"She just came to check up on me in the morning. I was a wreck, man, talking about killing myself. You two had a fight, I guess, she was in the room next door, must have heard me crying. I feel like such an idiot."

Peter was numb, but Brad wasn't finished.

"Even if that wasn't true, I could never do that. She loves you, man. She hardly left your side, when you were out, after being shot, except to work on your gun. She made me take her back after you ordered her to the boat. She had no food, no water but she didn't care. The way she talks about you…"

What had he done? He had been such a fool. Such a complete and utter fool. He had betrayed her love, and maybe her life.

"But even if it wasn't for Karen," Brad continued. "Even if I could be that way with someone so soon after, I would never do that to you. You're my captain. You saved my life, you gave us all purpose. No fucking way, man. How could you even think that?"

Delaware County, Land in the Sky. He had passed that sign so many times, but never with such purpose. The town was just around the bend.

"I'm sorry," he whispered. "I'm so sorry." Let it not be too late, he prayed. Please god, let it not be too late.

"Let's just get her back, okay, captain?"

He nodded. "How long ago did they take her?"

"I'm not sure, a few hours, three, maybe four?"

He processed the information. Just a few hours. Odds were she was still alive.

"Do you have a plan?" Brad said.

"Yes," Peter said. "We're going to get her out, and we're going to kill everyone who gets in our way."

Brad swallowed. "I know where they're keeping her, or where they were keeping her. They had me there too, for a little bit, then they let me go. I'm surprised they gave me back your jeep. She swore up and down that she didn't know me, that I had just given her a ride, but…"

"They're all about being fair," Peter hissed venomously.

Just around the corner from the town there was a small wooden booth. A man with a shotgun came out and put up his hand, indicating that they should stop.

Peter did, and lowered his window, putting on his best smile.

"Howdy," he said through clenched teeth, trying to keep his panic buried as deep inside as he could manage.

"Hi," the man said. He was tall, thin, big nose, bad skin. "You can't come into to town armed like that. Especially with…holy shit are those grenades? This area is protected by the US Military! One call from me on the radio and they'll be here to haul your ass away. You better turn around, buddy!"

"But I'm here for the hanging," Peter said. "Am I too late?"

The man hesitated, caught off guard. "No, that's tomorrow morning, so you best come back without all that hardware if you want to see it."

Peter's relief was palpable despite his best efforts to hide it. "No problem, sir, I'll just turn right around and come back tomorrow morning, without all this."

The man nodded, satisfied that his petty authority was being respected. "You have a nice day."

He drove a little past the man, who stood aside, then made a K turn. He fished in his vest and pulled out a zip tie. "Go in my pack," he said to Brad. "Get the big drum magazine."

He started back and waved to the guard, who waved back. Then Peter hit the gas, turned the wheel and ran him down. The man slammed into the jeep's steel bumper, his head smashing into the plastic fender. He crumpled like a rag doll without so much as a whimper.

Peter put the jeep in park and jumped out, drawing his pistol. Kneeling over the dazed guard, he shoved the weapon in his mouth, forcing it between his bloodstained teeth. The man was bleeding from several scrapes in his head, and one of his legs was splayed at an unnatural angle.

"Make a sound," Peter said. "Give me a fucking reason." The man's eyes were wide with fear. Peter smelled urine.

Rolling him over, he bound his hands behind his back with the zip tie. Going to the back of his jeep, he opened the trunk and got a roll of duct tape, which he used to cover the man's mouth. He zip tied his feet, then picked him up and tossed him into the ditch on the side of the road.

"Give me that drum," he said, taking it from Brad. He removed the magazine from his rifle and put it back into a pouch on his armored vest. He slammed the drum into position, then checked the chamber. He would have one hundred and one shots before he had to change magazines. He remembered the day Penny had first arrived, when he had stood at his window with this very rifle, deciding if it would be better to put a bullet in the approaching figure just to be safe.

"Holy shit, man, you're for real," Brad said, swallowing hard. "You're out for blood."

"Only if they stand in my way. Do you have a problem with that?"

Brad shook his head. "Give me a gun."

Peter looked at him for a moment, taking his measure, then picked up the guard's shotgun from where it had fallen near the jeep. "I believe this is your weapon of choice?" It was a gas operated Benelli with an adjustable stock, an excellent weapon.

Brad smiled grimly and took the gun. "We get her out, or we die."

Peter nodded. "Or we die."

Brad checked the chamber, then went to the ditch and took a belt full of shells from the guard. "I'm ready."

"I'm sorry, Brad," Peter said, suddenly overcome with shame. "I'm sorry I believed what I did, that I hated you. You never deserved it." Try as he might, even with hindsight, he couldn't understand why. He wasn't flighty or unbalanced, not usually, but his actions had been those of a slighted teenager. How could he have allowed this to happen?

"Forget about it man, I understand. Let's just do this."

They got back in the jeep and drove slowly, steadily into town. Peter's urgency had been relieved, replaced by determination.

There were people in the streets, but not many. This did not surprise him. Most would be busy rebuilding farms and planting crops. Those few they saw stared at them, but did not seem overly alarmed. They assumed they were safe behind their checkpoints, which was not unreasonable, considering that the general's camp was three miles away.

"There!" Brad said, pointing to a large Victorian. "See that smaller house behind the big one? That's where she is, around back. I'll show you."

"No need, I know it. You get behind the wheel and turn the jeep around, keep the motor running." He checked the gas—the gauge read a little less than half. He should have done that to begin with, but he had not been thinking clearly. "I'm going to do this as quietly as possible. We'll get her in the jeep and then we'll go straight to Archangel and get the hell out of here." The feeling of wrongness he had felt before returned. There was something off about his plan, but he didn't know what it was, and he didn't have time to figure it out.

"Sounds like a plan."

"Good." Peter waited until most of the pedestrians were out of sight, or at least far enough away not to pay too much attention, then got out of the jeep, rifle in hand, and headed for the house.

Once past the Victorian, both the house itself and its surrounding trees and outbuildings gave him some degree of concealment. The closer he got to the small house where they were keeping Penny, the less visible he would be to people in the street. When he was almost there, he brought up the rifle, crouched and started to move quietly. He advanced almost to the corner, then moved sideways, walking in a circle, exposing more and more of the back of the house while keeping the corner between him and whatever was on the other side.

There was one man with a hunting rifle. He stood near a door with a padlock on it. Peter had expected more than one, but it made more sense this way. She was just one girl, and these people had no reason to expect a rescue operation.

He advanced past the corner, startling the guard. "Drop it!" Peter ordered. "Give me a fucking reason and you're dead."

The man slipped out from under the rifle sling like it was a poisonous snake and backed away from the weapon, trembling with fear. "Don't shoot me!"

"On the ground," Peter said. "Now!"

The man dropped to his knees, then fell forward.

"Hands behind your back."

Peter walked up to him, never taking the red dot off his head, then crouched with his knee on the man's back, took one hand off of the rifle, grabbed a zip tie from his vest and secured his hands behind his back.

He stood up, grabbed the guard by his hair and pulled him up to his feet. The man cringed, but didn't cry out.

"Where's the key?"

"It's in my pocket, the front one, in my jacket!"

Peter reached inside and found it. He shoved the man up to the wall, opened the lock with his left hand and stood back. After a few seconds of waiting, he kicked the door open and swept what he could see with the red dot. Nothing. Grabbing his prisoner, he shoved him into the room, then entered behind him, sweeping the hidden corner with his rifle. Penny was there, pressed up against the wall. She looked so scared. Then she saw his face.

"Oh my god, Peter!" she shouted and ran to embrace him. He took her in his arms and pressed her close. She was alive. The tide of emotion was almost too much. He was lightheaded, it was difficult to stand. She was alive, and he was holding her.

"Peter I'm so sorry," she said, pulling away to look at him. "I was so stupid to get mad at you. I should have explained, I should have told you…oh my god you still don't know! It was never like that, Brad was just…"

"Shh," he said, putting a finger to her lips. "Brad told me everything. I'm the idiot, Penny."

"I love you Peter," she said, crying intensely. "I love you so much." She reached up to kiss him. The touch of her lips, a touch he thought he would never feel again, threatened to overwhelm him, and he couldn't afford it. He pulled away.

"We have to get out of here," he said. "Brad is waiting in the jeep."

She nodded, and they started out the door.

He heard the screeching of tires. Then he heard it again.

"What the hell?" Peter turned to his prisoner. "What's going on?"

"It's not my fault!" the man pleaded. "Please don't kill me!"

"What?" Peter demanded as he shoved the rifle barrel against the man's nose.

"Stewart, the other guy, he went to take a leak…"

There had been two after all. Of all the lousy timings. He kicked the guard in the groin hard enough that he collapsed to the floor in agony, then slammed the door shut as he and Penny ran out.

"Get the lock," he said, sweeping the area, looking for any sign of pursuit.

He heard it click.

"Get behind me, take this." He reached into his holster and

handed her his sidearm.

"Got it," she said, her voice trembling. He felt her tugging at his vest.

They moved cautiously around the side of the house and continued towards the street.

He saw Brad, and saw the panic in his eyes.

As they got near the jeep, men with rifles ran into view in the distance. A pickup truck pulled up, then another. Several men stood up on the beds, pointing rifles and shotguns in Peter's direction.

"Stop!" someone shouted. "Drop your weapon!" A man walked into view, tall, balding. He held his hands up before him, as though demanding calm.

"There's no reason to die here, let's just put your weapons down and we can come to an understanding."

"Peter." It was Penny. Her voice sounded strange. "That's him, that's the mayor. Don't let him take me alive. I can't…I can't go through that, what they did to Sandy…I just can't. I'd rather just shoot myself. They'll let you go if I'm dead." It was all falling apart. They'd been so close. A little more patience, some reconnaissance, that's all it would have taken. He had gambled on speed, going in and out quickly, and it almost worked. If only that miserable guard hadn't had to take a leak just at that moment. Almost a Seal. Almost.

"No," Peter said. "They're not going to hang you. I won't let them." He pointed his rifle at the mayor, then began to move towards the jeep.

"I said stop!" the mayor demanded. There were more than ten of them, maybe more than twenty, Peter couldn't be sure. Several trucks had pulled in, but there were also armed men behind trees, on the porches of the village homes that flanked the street. He couldn't keep track of them, and it would have been suicide to stop and count.

"I'll make you a deal," Peter shouted as he moved. "Take me, let her go. I'll answer for her crimes."

"No!" Penny shouted. "I won't let you!"

"You have your own crimes to answer for, Mr. Anderson," the mayor said.

He knew his name? How?

"That's right," the mayor continued. "We know all about the men you gunned down. You weren't the only survivor on that mountain."

So that was how they had tracked Penny to his house. There would be no bargaining with these people.

He had made it to the street, and started to back up towards the jeep.

"We'll give you ten seconds," the mayor shouted. "Then we'll gun you down like dogs in the street. We might be able to spare your life, maybe you didn't know what she'd done. There's no reason to die for her. Did the little whore tell you how she escaped?"

Peter stopped moving.

"Peter," Penny said. "I'm sorry. I'm sorry you had to end up here with me."

"There's nowhere I'd rather be than with you, and I'm so sorry that I forgot that."

"Ten," the mayor shouted. "Get ready to shoot, boys."

Peter began to tremble, filled with rage and frustration. It wasn't fair. He had lost her once, and now he had her back, only to lose her again, forever. His whole life, so typical, so like that of everyone else, a series of failures and losses, culminating in this moment.

"Penny," he said calmly. "I want you to grab me around the neck and hop on my back. Wrap your legs around my waist."

"Why?"

"Nine."

"Just do it. Don't worry about my shoulder. Take a grenade, get ready to pull the pin. When I start shooting, you start throwing. The first one at that red truck."

"Eight."

He felt her arms around his neck, then felt her weight on his back as her legs tightened above his hips. She was lighter than his pack had been, or at least it felt that way. He could do this.

"Seven."

He pushed against the safety lever, which was set to "fire". It clicked over once more. It had been her gift to him.

"Six."

More trucks, this time pulling up behind him. They were surrounded. He didn't dare turn to look. He didn't think for a second that the mayor would keep his word about the count.

"What are you going to do?" she whispered in his ear.

"We're going to fight."

"Can we make it?"

Angles, movement patterns, probabilities—his mind raced to find a way. He *could* do this. The ones behind him couldn't shoot without hitting the ones in front. He would open fire, moving sideways, putting the jeep between Penny and the men at his back, then he would turn, lay down enough fire to force them to take cover, move to the woods. The grenades would give them something to think about besides shooting at him. It could work, it had to work, but Penny was so exposed! He should have thought to give her his vest.

"I don't know."

"Five. You're surrounded now, Mr. Anderson, I suggest you put your weapon down."

"Peter," Penny whispered. He felt her lips on his neck. "You were never almost anything to me."

He froze for a fraction of a second. What she said, it wasn't quite right. He was never almost anything *with* her.

"Four."

Suddenly there was something tugging at his awareness, something trying to bore its way out of the deepest recesses of his conscious mind. Despite everything happening, he turned his attention to it, trying to amplify it, but it eluded him. There was something wrong with him. Something that made him keep making the same mistakes over and over again. He was doing it at that very moment, he was sure of it, but he couldn't quite understand what it was. Couldn't quite see it.

Movement behind him, a lot of it, men moving into position. Surrounded. Too many. There was no hope, but he had to try.

"I'm sorry I failed you," he said to Penny, and raised his weapon. If only he could understand, if only that idea would move faster, form faster. Maybe it could help him. Maybe he had one decision left to make, and maybe this time he wouldn't screw it up. If only—

"Three."

"You never failed me."

Shouting from behind him. It wasn't the mayor. Something about that voice. It was familiar.

"Two!"

Movement in his periphery, rifle barrels all round him, moving, pointing. But how could he see the rifles barrels? If he were surrounded, then—

"Marines! Prepare to engage!"

None of the rifles were pointed at him.

"OOHRAH!"

Their boots thundered in unison as they moved past him, and the ground trembled at their passing. On both sides they came, closing the line between him and mayor's gunmen. Everywhere he looked, people were setting down their weapons as the marines advanced toward the townsmen. He felt Penny's tears on his neck, and in that moment, Peter saw everything clearly.

He finally understood: he couldn't ever be anything that mattered on his own.

Chapter 32 – Closure

Anger may in time change to gladness; vexation may be succeeded by content. But a kingdom that has once been destroyed can never come again into being; nor can the dead ever be brought back to life.
— Sun Tzu

"Down on the ground!" Lieutenant Goldstein shouted. "Anyone still standing when I'm done talking is dead!"

Peter was speechless. He couldn't move, all he could do was stand there, staring dumbly at Goldstein's wonderful face. He was awed, both by how close he had come to losing everything because of his own stupidity, and by his sudden epiphany.

The townspeople, both those that had been holding weapons and those just watching, dropped to the ground like bowling pins. The mayor hesitated, glared at the lieutenant, but finally dropped down onto his stomach.

"Hands on top of your heads!" Goldstein commanded. "Sergeant Smith, take a detail and police up those weapons."

"Yes sir!" one of the marines shouted. "Qasim, Feingold, you're with me." They moved through the prostrated crowd, collecting guns.

Goldstein's arrival had opened the floodgate, and Peter's dawning realization was blinding as it crested the horizon of his awareness. It all made sense now, all of his decisions, all of his failures, they all stood naked and exposed under the rising sun of understanding. He had blamed Jennifer for his marital problems, but he realized now that it had been his fault. He was always doing things on his own, not including her, and so she had withdrawn.

In Seal training, when he had injured himself, he had thought only of himself, only of graduating. He hadn't considered how his injury would have affected his fellow candidates, who counted on him to pull his weight. He hadn't functioned as part of a team. It was a wonder that he made it as far as he had.

In the midst of a bitter divorce, forced to sell the house he loved, he hadn't sought comfort in the company of friends or family. He had gone to that house, to be alone with his misery. When the disaster struck, he had survived, because he had prepared in a very specific way, not relying on others, but only on himself, by himself. Alone.

His isolation, so terrible, so unbearable, and yet, he had borne it, and perhaps more than that. When Penny had shown up, Peter had sworn off solitude, but he kept trying to return to it every chance he got. He had never even considered going to the village to live among others, and he knew that he probably wouldn't have even if it hadn't been for her. When Hamilton had offered him a position, he hadn't even considered it, he just turned him down reflexively. Joining something, being part of something, that was against his nature. He hadn't ever realized it before, but he knew it now. Even when he had done it, when he'd joined the navy, when he'd taken a job at the university, he fought against it without realizing, undermined himself without knowing.

"You're a sight for sore eyes, Anderson," Goldstein said. "You're lucky I saw your jeep pull away, or this could have gotten ugly."

"Thank you," Peter said, so softly that he wasn't sure if Goldstein heard him. He was always trying to escape from the commitments he made. He hadn't wanted to stay on Archangel, and had spent his entire relationship with Penny looking for an excuse to get out of it. He hadn't wanted that—the pain of losing her still burned so hot he couldn't focus on it without flinching—but the first chance he got, he ran away. To be alone. He had been such a fool. Even right before Goldstein's arrival, when he had been planning his escape, he hadn't factored in Brad, or even Penny, whom he had wanted to keep as protected as he could, thinking he could do it all by himself. Always alone, in word and deed.

"Don't just stand there, Anderson," Goldstein said. "Set that little lady down and shake my hand. You're making me look bad in front of my jarheads."

Penny climbed off his back, but she didn't let go. Still shaking, Peter held his hand out and the Lieutenant grabbed it firmly.

"I believe this makes us even," Goldstein said.

Peter shook his head. "No, not even close. What I owe you can never be repaid." His head was spinning.

"Glad to help. Now maybe you can explain to me what's going on here."

"I will," Peter said. "But, aren't you going to get in trouble for this?"

Goldstein smiled. "Maybe, but we won't have to wait long to find out." He motioned towards the road, where a humvee was pulling into sight, followed by a deuce and a half cargo truck. The vehicles came to a stop just past Goldstein's parked humvees. Soldiers spilled out of the truck as General Hamilton climbed out of the humvee and started walking towards them.

"Now we're in for it," Goldstein said.

"What's going on here, gentlemen?" the general asked, then noticed Peter. "Mr. Anderson? What are you doing with my officer?" The general's soldiers joined the marines, pointing their weapons at the prostrated townspeople.

"General!" someone shouted. It was the mayor. "General I demand to speak with you!"

Hamilton turned towards him. "Get that man up," he ordered. Two marines ran over to the mayor and helped him to his feet. Brushing dirt off his clothes, the balding man glared at Peter as he walked up to the general. Peter felt Penny's hands tighten their grip on his sleeves as she pressed close to him. He could feel her body shaking.

"I demand that you call off your men!" the mayor shouted. "You came here swearing that you would respect our jurisdiction. You talked about restoring the United States, and now this? This is an outrage!"

"I'll ask that you watch your tone," the general said coldly. "I believe I deserve a modicum of respect." The mayor opened his mouth, but then closed it, clearly cowed.

"Sorry, general, but…"

"You will calmly explain to me what has happened here."

"Gladly." He pointed to Penny. "This girl is a murderer! She escaped once before, thanks to him." He pointed to Peter. "And *he* killed four men that were trying to bring her to justice. And now that we captured her again, he came to break her out. They both deserve to hang, and justice must be done! You said yourself how important it was to maintain order."

Hamilton turned to Peter. "Is this true, son?"

Peter sighed, not sure what to say. He borrowed Penny's words. "It is, and it isn't."

"I think you'd better tell me the whole story, Mr. Anderson."

"It's not very complicated," Peter said, running through the details in his head. "She was with some friends, after the event. They went from house to house, looking for food…"

"Why would you let *him* tell you?" the mayor interrupted. "He's a murderer! He'll just twist the truth to his own ends—"

Hamilton turned to the mayor, who instantly stopped talking. "I will be the judge of that, sir." The mayor looked like he wanted to protest, but didn't.

"Continue," the general ordered.

"Yes, sir. They came to an occupied house, the couple there wouldn't let them in, wouldn't share their food. There were five of them, three girls and two guys. One of the guys shot the man, beat the woman to death. Some of the others, including Penny, tried to stop him, but they couldn't. Then these…" He motioned to the mayor. "These animals showed up. They grabbed them all, pronounced them all guilty on the spot, hung the boys, and one of the girls. A seventeen year old girl. She had done nothing." Peter's anger returned as he talked. The object of that anger was so close, but he could not strike out.

"Penny escaped, and killed two of them in the process. It was the only way she could get away. The last one, another teenage girl, was shot in the attempt. After that she found me, and then they came for her. I stopped them."

"You mean you murdered them," the mayor hissed.

"I killed them, yes. And I would do it again."

The general nodded. "Sounds like a big fucking mess, if you ask me. I think enough people died, don't you mayor?"

"No!" he shouted. "Not enough. These two… You heard what he said, he'd do it again! These were members of our community. Husbands, fathers…"

Hamilton nodded grimly, then turned to Peter. "I need a word with you, alone."

Peter nodded, and followed the general as he walked away from the others.

"General!" the mayor said, but Hamilton ignored him.

"I told you before," Hamilton said as soon as they were out of earshot. "I have to uphold the rule of law. I can't interfere. It's a damned shame, because I don't think that man is going to give you a fair trial. But if I step in now, interfere in a civilian matter, then everything—everything!—I'm trying to build here, it's going to fall apart. I can't do that, Anderson. I won't do that. As much as I want to."

Peter nodded. "I understand, sir." Every time he had acted since leaving his house, it had almost ended badly, and he had needed to be saved. Twice by Penny, and now by Goldstein. He had considered the previous incidents failures on his part, but the failure wasn't that he had needed saving. The best-laid schemes o' mice an' men gang aft agley, wrote the Scottish poet Robert Burns. Things always went wrong, and that was why not even Seals worked alone. His failure wasn't ending up in situations in which he needed help, it was failing to realize that he *would* need help. Thinking that he could act as an army—or navy—of one. He had created situations that led to that help manifesting—such as when he had saved Goldstein and thereby indebted him to help when the opportunity presented itself—but not intentionally or with any foresight.

"I'm sorry, son," Hamilton said. "You did right by one of my officers, and I think that you're a good man. I'll do what I can. I'll testify to your character. I don't know that it will help any, but I'll try. And I'll keep them from hanging you…both of you. I can do that much, at least."

"You can do more sir," Peter said, knowing what he had to do. All of his decisions had gone wrong, because they were based on his one greatest failure. He had never seen it before, but he saw it now, clearly, as well as what he had to do to fix it. He had one big decision left to make, and for the first time in his life, he was going to make the right one.

Hamilton frowned. "Anderson, I've already explained—"

"You can't interfere in civilian matters. I understand that. But after this conversation, I'm not going to be a civilian, and neither is

Penny. You offered me a job. I'm going to take it, and so is she, and you do want her too, because of what we have to offer."

Hamilton cocked his head at him, and betrayed the tiniest hint of a smile. Had he planned for this very thing?

"I'm listening," he said.

"We have a boat—a ship. It's a marine research vessel, sail powered. Comes with its own scientists. I can't guarantee that they will agree to this, but I have a very strong feeling that sailing with a purpose and with support is going to appeal to them very strongly. I'm its captain, Penny is its first mate. You're going to need this ship, because you're going to need to understand your new world if you're going to be rebuilding it, and most of the world is an ocean. I'm offering you this ship, under my captaincy, as part of your navy.

Hamilton's smile deepened. "I know all about your boat, son, and yes, you're right, I want it. And I like the idea of leaving you in charge of it."

Peter nodded. "I'm also offering you my special warfare training. I don't know if you have any real Seals left, but if you don't, I can pass the training along. The last two weeks…well, we're just going to have to live without that part."

"Your offer is a good one," Hamilton said. Then he pursed his lips, thinking. "It could work. It's irregular, particularly in the young lady's case, since she was never active duty before this moment. But this is one of the reasons the military has courts…there isn't exactly a fully functioning civilian authority at the moment. We could court martial the both of you. You would still have a trial, albeit a fair one, and if you were to be found guilty, you would both be shot. Once we get that ball rolling, I won't be able to stop it."

Peter nodded. "I'm willing to take that chance." His decision felt right. In fact, it felt amazing. Not just because he was confident that it would save them both, but because he had experienced an incredibly rare moment of clarity, and more importantly, he had been able to act on it in time. Most of the world didn't get a second chance, but he had just had his third.

Hamilton turned away and walked back to the others.

"General!" the mayor said. "You promised me that you

wouldn't interfere!"

"Commander Anderson is an officer in the United States Navy," Hamilton said, and Peter blinked, surprised. Commander? He had been a junior grade lieutenant in the reserves. He had not been expecting such a high rank, but he supposed it made sense. Commanding a ship required a command rank.

Hamilton turned to Penny and gave her a questioning look. She looked confused for a second, then her eyes widened with comprehension, and she nodded.

"They both are," the general continued. "And as such, they will be tried by a military tribunal."

"That's outrageous!" the mayor said. "You promised me that you wouldn't—"

"Yes," Hamilton said. "I promised you that I would uphold the rule of law, and I keep my promises. As military officers, they fall under my jurisdiction. But I am not pardoning them, mayor. There will be a trial, and you will aid my prosecutor and testify against them. I have a JAG officer on my staff. She can work out the legalities."

"Good," the mayor said. "Let's do that. Let's have a trial."

"I must ask you," Hamilton said with a cautionary tone. "As a personal favor to me, to just let this go. Please. A lot of grief can be avoided. People can move on with their lives. If there is a trial, I will want all the facts, mayor, *all of them*. Everything will be considered, and there could be consequences, even for you."

"There must be justice, general," the mayor said. "We can't rebuild if we abandon our principles."

"So be it," Hamilton said.

Chapter 33 – Hope

I must go down to the seas again,
to the lonely sea and the sky,
And all I ask is a tall ship and a star to steer her by,
And the wheel's kick and the wind's song
and the white sail's shaking,
And a gray mist on the sea's face,
and a gray dawn breaking.
- John Masefield

The boat cut through the choppy water at a hair over twelve knots, the fastest Peter had ever managed. Despite that, the conning tower of the USS Connecticut easily outpaced them as she disappeared beneath the waves, leaving Archangel to dance along her wake in solitude.

Now that the supplies had been unloaded, Peter was eager to put as much distance between them and the Catskills Island as he could. Too many painful, difficult memories.

After the trial, they had left the body hanging for two days before the townspeople had taken it down. Peter came to look at it each day, so that he would never forget what happened there, but now he wondered if that had been such a good idea. So much pain, so much anger, all connected to that place. All the poor bastard had to do was let it go. In a way, he had hanged himself, which Peter supposed was fitting.

"Commander Anderson," Penny said, coming up behind him. "What are you doing out of uniform?" She kissed him, and he set the autopilot so that he could hold her.

"You're one to talk, ensign," he said. How Hamilton had managed to get them uniforms that fit, complete with name plates, was a secret the general hadn't shared. He wasn't sure how he felt about the budweiser. Technically, he never earned it, but Hamilton was right. He was as close to a Seal as they had left.

"But I think uniforms are hot," she said. "You don't want me gawking at the jarheads, do you?" Three marines had been as-

signed to his command, two men and a woman, all ground pound-
ers who didn't know a boat from a bathtub. They were quick learn-
ers though, and Peter was comforted by their presence. No longer
would the group's safety rest squarely on his shoulders. No, he
corrected. It had never rested on his shoulders, not alone. Thinking
that was a failing he would work hard to leave behind.

He turned back to Penny and saw the truth behind her jovial
façade and his expression turned serious. "Penny, I'm so sorry. I
was so stupid. I almost...I almost—"

She silenced him with a finger on his lips.

"We both were," she said, and pressed her head into his shoulder. "Let's not talk about it anymore, okay?"

Long seconds ticked away as they as they held each other, until Peter said, "So how are you holding up?"

She pulled away and smiled up at him. "Not too bad. I just
don't know how to relax. Between what's happened and the black
hole..."

"He's still at it, eh?"

"That's almost all he does now. He's convinced he can still
find it, but...Peter, it's been so long!"

He shrugged. "I'm not too worried about it."

"How can you say that? How can you stand not knowing if all
of this is for nothing?" They left the helm and sat opposite each
other on the cockpit benches. The wind caught a few loose locks of
her hair and brushed them against her forehead.

"Well there's the fact that he's been at it *too* long," he said.
"Anyway, how is everyone adjusting? I've been busy with the lo-
gistics and all."

"Burgoyne keeps stubbing his toes on the ma deuces," she said
with a grin. She was referring to the two fifty caliber machine guns
the general's people had installed on Archangel's fore and aft
deck. "He hates them, says they get in his way."

"That Burgoyne, such a malcontent. We'll have to keel haul
him."

She laughed. "Poor David. Anyway, other than that, everything is fine. Everyone is thrilled to be working again, doing what
they were trained to do. The way things turned out..."

The general had actually considered assigning an Aegis destroyer to oceanographic duties before the perfect boat and crew became available in the form of Archangel. There was much to learn about their new ocean, considering they would have to rely on it almost exclusively for their survival. The general was a good man, and it felt right to serve under him. Peter was finally the Seal he had always wanted to be, and more. He was helping rebuild the world, and that was more important than anything he had ever done. Under Hamilton's supervision, they were getting oil wells and refineries working again out west, and even some factories. The loss of life on the West coast was just as devastating as on the East—almost total—but the damage to infrastructure was far more limited. It wasn't quite the carefree post-apocalyptic life Peter had envisioned, but knowing that they were not alone, that they could get supplies, medical help or whatever else they needed made it more than worthwhile. For the first time since he'd been on board, Archangel sailed with fuel tanks full of diesel and holds stocked to the brim with supplies. And for the first time in his life, Peter was fully committed to being part of something bigger than himself.

"Watch it!" someone shouted from the aft deck. They both turned to look.

Brad had enlisted one of the marines to help him collect water samples, and the two of them were fumbling with the robotic arm.

"That's a delicate piece of equipment!"

"Sorry doc," the young woman said.

"So," Penny said, turning back to Peter. "When is the broadcast?"

"Antarctica?" he asked, checking his watch. Another gift, courtesy of Hamilton. "Ooh, I'm glad you asked. It's only ten minutes now. I forgot all about it."

"Forgot? I can't get it out of my mind."

"Another mystery, perhaps about to be solved." He thought back to the first sight of the new shore, when he had finally accepted the fact that the old world was really dead. "Two hundred feet higher than it should be is a lot of water to account for."

"Four hundred," she said, looking away.

"What?"

"It's four hundred feet higher than it should be."

"Yeah," he agreed, looking back on what should have been the

Jersey Shore, now just more ocean all the way to Pennsylvania. "I suppose it is."

She left the deck to find Gable and try to coax him away from his data. Peter returned to the helm and watched the voltage meters for the house bank. With the diesel generator running again, they had refrigeration and laundry facilities back online, though frugality was still the rule of thumb while at sea. With nine people onboard the boat was filled to capacity. It was a small price to pay, at least for Peter. Out on the ocean it was easy to put everything out of his mind and just live life day by day, which was exactly how he liked it.

The batteries were doing well, with voltage in the green, leaving nothing for him to do but go below decks and join the others. The equipment Hamilton's people had installed in the main saloon would enable them to view the satellite feed live, so as soon as the general flipped the switch, they would all find out together. It would probably be the first time anyone laid eyes on Antarctica since the event. So many questions, so easily answered. He was aware that while Gable's hypothesis was most likely correct, it was just educated guess work. While they could not turn back time and see what actually happened, seeing ground zero—especially from space—would go a long way.

Glancing once more at his watch, Peter turned to those on deck and said, "Okay, it's time. Everyone who wants to see the satellite feed, go below."

"Aye sir," the marines said, almost in unison. Brad nodded grimly, set down his equipment and followed them through the hatch. Peter made his way to the saloon through his cabin to find the others gathered in front of the monitor, which was displaying a black screen with numbers on the bottom right corner. Gable was there too, though he kept glancing towards the corridor to his quarters. He had dark circles under his eyes and his unkempt white hair was haphazardly arranged over his big shiny forehead.

Peter found Penny and took her hand. She clamped down hard, and they both turned to look at the monitor.

"Any second now, sir," one of the marines said. "Here we go."

The screen flickered and suddenly they saw white clouds, though they were looking down at them from space. The image quality was amazing.

"Crap," Brad said. "So many damned clouds. It's hard to—" He stopped talking as his mouth dropped open. The clouds had made it difficult to make out the edges of the thing, but there was no mistaking it once their eyes had found it.

"Jesus!" Peter swore, staring at the screen. He felt Penny's hand squeeze even harder, nails digging in painfully.

It was almost perfectly round and too big for all of it to be seen on the screen at once. They were looking at one of its edges, near where the southern tip of South America used to be.

"I'm getting some data from the command post," the marine who was manning the satellite terminal said. "It's just over three thousand miles across at the widest point."

"How is that even possible?" Peter demanded, shocked. "Such an explosion! How did the Earth survive? How did any of us survive?"

"We almost didn't," Burgoyne said, his eyes distant, staring at the screen but past it.

It was a massive crater, its walls so high their shape could be made out from space. There was no water within—the rim was above sea level.

"That explains it," Penny said, her voice cracking. Peter glanced at her briefly and saw tears in her eyes. "That's almost twice the surface area of Antarctica. Some of the ice must have been blasted into space. I wonder what effect that will have on the climate…the Earth might even have rings." She turned to Gable. "Could such an explosion have shifted our orbit?"

The physicist shook his head. "Doubtful."

"The explosion that did that," Peter said. "The power of it!"

"Consider the mass of the Earth," Gable said. "It's over six sextillion metric tons. That's a six followed by twenty one zeros. As big as that crater is, it's insignificant compared to the mass of the planet."

"But it's so big!" Peter said, irrationally. His mind just could not let go of the size of the thing, and the power of the explosion that made it. What folly, to toy with such forces!

"There are bigger craters in the Solar System," Gable said calmly. "Both proportionally and otherwise. Borealis Basin on

Mars is fifty three hundred miles across, and Mars is substantially smaller than the Earth, and only ten percent of its mass. The moon, at one eightieth of the Earth's mass, has a crater fifteen hundred miles across at the South Pole-Aitken Basin." His tone was authoritative, though Peter couldn't help but feel that he was trying to convince himself, if only a little bit. Looking into Gable's eyes, he could clearly see the horror. Even though he was not responsible, it was his research that led the way to the creation of the terrible weapon that made that monster crater.

They watched for a little while longer, though there was nothing new to see. Slowly, people started drifting away, returning to duty stations or going to their quarters to be alone, to absorb. The crater didn't change anything, but knowing how close they had come to complete annihilation was unnerving. Leaving Penny with the other scientists to geek out over the crater data streaming from the general's command center, Peter went up to the deck and took the helm, sailing the boat along an ocean that suddenly seemed very different.

Chapter 34 – Leviathan

Let us not judge his seeming lapse;
His secret soul we could not see;
He smiled and left us, and perhaps
Death was his crowning victory.
— Robert William Service

He spotted Gable up towards the bow as he was getting ready to retire for the evening. The scientist was scribbling in a note-book, his wispy white hair fluttering in the wind like so many kites on short strings, struggling to break free of their tethers. As was usual of late, he looked withdrawn, distant. For a little while, during the crater viewing, Peter had seen the old Gable resurface, the confident, self assured intellectual. There was too little of that man around these days.

"Still looking for your white hole?" Peter asked as he came to stand next to the physicist.

"Black hole," Gable muttered absentmindedly.

"I don't think so, Dr. Ahab."

Gable paused, frowned in confusion, then looked up at Peter. "Excuse me?"

Peter lowered himself to the deck, sitting across from the older man, and said, "It's time you let it go."

Gable shook his head. "How can you say that? How can we not know if—"

"We know," Peter said. "We all know it on some level, and so do you."

"I know no such thing. Look, with all due respect Peter, this is not your forte. I don't tell you how to sail this boat or how to fight, so kindly don't tell me my business."

Peter smiled patiently. "I haven't, not for a long time now. But for your own sake, and that of those waiting on your findings, I think you need to face up to the fact that there is no black hole."

Gable was annoyed. "And how could you possibly know that?"

"I don't," Peter admitted. "But you do, and it shows. How long are you going to look at that data? How fine a comb are you going to use before you give up? Don't you think that if there were a black hole in the center of the Earth, you wouldn't have had to look quite so hard?"

"It's not that simple, Peter. There has never been a black hole in the center of Earth before. I might not have gotten enough data from the observatory. Maybe if we went back…"

Peter shook his head. "If we went back, you would spend the rest of your life there."

"That's absurd, I—"

"I know how you feel, doc," Peter said. "But it wasn't your fault. You don't have to punish yourself."

"My work broke the world!" Gable cried, his eyes suddenly intense, full of pain. "You have no idea—"

"You can see it that way if you want," Peter interrupted. "But that's not how I see it, and it's not how your son sees it, and I think I can safely say the same of the others. You helped invent gunpowder, but you didn't make the gun or point it at the world and pull the trigger. For that, we can only blame ourselves. Our governments, our societies, they're a reflection of our nature, and that is the culprit here, Gable, not you."

"I…" Tears formed in the old man's eyes. "I just want to be sure!"

"Do you? Or do you only want the search to give your life purpose, something to distract you from your guilt? We need you doc, and it's time you came back to us. You've spent weeks with that data. Combing, comparing, charting, plotting. Enough is enough. I want you to tell the others what you and I both know, that there is no black hole. But first, I want you to tell yourself."

Gable opened his mouth, as if to protest, but then looked down at the gel coated fiberglass of Archangel's deck, and nodded. Peter doubted he had fully convinced him, but time would take care of the rest.

He patted Gable on the back, then left him alone with his thoughts. The deck rolled gently under his feet as he walked to his cabin, eager for another evening with the woman he loved. Each such moment was a gift that so many had been denied. So much death, it was impossible to even imagine the scale of the suffering, the loss. But Gable was wrong—the world was not broken. Scarred, changed, yes, but not broken.

Peter turned back briefly, but not to look at the old physicist. He looked past the bow, at the gentle swells that faded into a distant horizon. The sun, setting behind him, painted veins of molten gold across the water's surface that glimmered beneath a red sky streaked with white and gray.

Doing what he should have done the moment of the tremor, when the first drop of Antarctic ice fell from the New York sky, Peter looked up to the heavens and said goodbye. To Jennifer, to his parents, to everyone he had ever known who had gone to rest beneath the scintillating golden waves.

"To die and part is a less evil," he said, quoting an obscure English poet. "But to part and live, there, there is the torment."

Author's Note

Thank you for reading! If you enjoyed this book, please consider leaving a review on Amazon, Goodreads and/or your various social media accounts. Independent authors need reviews and word of mouth in order to succeed. If you have any questions or want to leave a comment, look for Michael Edelson on facebook, or find the link to my facebook page on my website:

www.michaeledelson.net

If you want more but are disappointed that there isn't a sequel, check out one of my other books. Though varied in plot and genre, they will feel very familiar. If you liked this book, I'm confident that you'll like the rest as well.

My other titles include:

 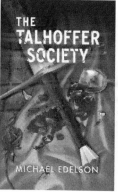 

All are available at Amazon.com and other online retailers.

Audiobook versions are available at Audible.com, Amazon and iTunes.

About the Author

Michael lives in upstate New York with his wife, two kids and too many pets. He is a firefighter with the Andes Fire Department, teaches historical fencing and, when he has the time, writes books.

www.michaeledelson.net

Made in the USA
Middletown, DE
24 March 2019